CAPTURED LIGHT

A DARK MAFIA ROMANCE

BOOK ONE IN THE KING OF ICE & STEEL TRILOGY

RAYA MORRIS EDWARDS

Captured Light
By Raya Morris Edwards

Copyright © 2021 Morris Edwards Publishing

FIRST EDITION

This book is for my husband.

He knows why.

Content Warning

Please be advised this book contains content and themes that may be upsetting to some and are not suitable for those under the age of 18.

These include content regarding disordered eating and weight. Care has been taken that ED related content is not instructional or graphic, but please be cautious if this is a trigger for you.

Please be warned that this book also contains a depiction of sexual assault, as well as discussion of rape, discussion of physical abuse, discussion of parental abuse, and discussion of spousal abuse.

There are also discussions of torture/killing, as well as a depiction of a physical fight involving gun violence and a killing. The death of pregnant woman is briefly discussed.

Care has been taken to treat these heavy subjects as respectfully as possible.

Other content includes heavy sexual themes and depictions including elements of CNC, praise and degradation and primal kink.

CHAPTER ONE

OLIVIA

SPRING

I dragged my eyes from my brother's plate to mine. His roast beef and vegetables were almost gone except for a chunk of meat drowning in a pool of gravy. The sight made my mouth water and it took everything in me to turn away. He was going to waste it because he didn't understand what it felt like to be hungry. He'd set his silverware aside and leaned forward to place his elbows on the table, conversing quietly with my father.

Focusing on my own food, I picked up my fork again and poked at the limp salad on my plate. It was a diet night, which meant my mother had the cook serve me salad instead of the meal everyone else was eating. Then, to add to the humiliation, she measured and weighed me before bed and wrote down my numbers so she could compare them when next week came. I hated it with a passion.

All to keep me thin and desirable for Lucien Esposito, my arranged fiancé. A man I was supposed to marry. A man I had never met.

A phone rang sharply, the sound splitting through the enormous dining room. My brother, Cosimo, stood up and pushed back his chair, taking his phone from his pocket as he stepped out into the hall. I kept my eyes on my plate, resentment swelling in my chest. If I had dared to bring my phone to the table, my father would have thrown it out the window and probably hit me across the face.

"Olivia."

I looked up to find my father's steel gaze boring into me. He was a terrifying underboss and an even more frightening father. From the sleek black hair speckled with gray, to the dark gray eyes, to his broad shoulders, all the way down to his polished shoes, he was an imposing figure. His soldiers fell in line before him, terrified that he might look at them the wrong way.

"Yes," I whispered.

"Speak up, I can never hear you," he said, wiping his hands on his napkin and tossing it aside.

"Learn to use your words, Olivia," my mother chimed in.

I wanted nothing more than to glare at her. My mother was the living nightmare that plagued me daily. She'd once been a great beauty, but living under my father's tyranny had aged her early. Nothing in the world was more important to my mother than looks and she transferred all her horror at aging into forcing me to become the perfect mafia princess for my betrothed.

I hated her and I wasn't ashamed of it. When I looked across the table and met her glassy, dark eyes, I felt nothing but a deep contempt. She was so desperate, so cruel, and years of living under her thumb had worn away any chance at love.

She had measured, starved, manicured, and shamed it out of me.

"Lucien wants to see you," my father said calmly, as if this wasn't enormous news.

Lucien Esposito, my fiancé, rarely made an appearance in my father's territory. But his presence loomed large over every aspect of my life. An Esposito husband was a sought after commodity for any of the young women within the outfit. They were well respected, ridiculously wealthy, and above all, the boss favored the two Esposito brothers over any of the other families.

My mother was elated when the boss, Carlo Romano, urged a match between our families, the Barones and the Espositos. It would strengthen ties and, although no one would say it out loud, force my father into a greater allegiance to Lucien, encouraging peace and solidifying generations of wealth.

At the time, Lucien had been in his late teens and I was still a baby. So my parents met with Lucien's parents and they agreed their children would wed when I was of age. Although it would take years to complete the contract, simply having the engagement in place solidified relations and put the boss's mind at ease.

It caused a stir, even for our traditionally Catholic, old money society. Even among the upper classes who often married for wealth and power, that type of archaic engagement wasn't common.

Rumor had it that Lucien wasn't thrilled by the prospect of being my husband. He rarely visited, and when he did, I was kept away from him. The last time I had laid eyes on him was a funeral for one of his soldiers and he pointedly avoided me for the ceremony and left abruptly afterward.

"Why is Lucien coming here?" I asked, forcing myself to speak up.

"He wants to talk to you. You need to become formally engaged," my father said. "It's time.

I opened my mouth to reply, but my mother cut in.

"I'll have someone come to the house to do your hair and nails. And I'll pick something out for you to wear that's suitable. Oh, and better not eat too heavily for the next few days, you don't want to bloat."

I dropped my face, a pang going through my chest. Lunch had been steamed broccoli without butter and dinner was salad with two strips of grilled chicken and no dressing. I was lightheaded and the prospect of more days like this turned my already sour stomach.

"When is he coming?" I asked.

"On Sunday night," my mother said eagerly. She jumped to her feet. "Speaking of, I have a few things to run over with the cook before she leaves tonight. Dinner needs to be perfect Sunday."

I was dying to make a snarky comment. What if dinner wasn't perfect? Did she think Lucien was going to stand up, overturn the table, cancel his engagement, and march out never to be seen again? Internally, I rolled my eyes. She probably did think that. After all, she'd spent my teenage years hammering it into my head that if I gained a pound over where I should be on her chart, Lucien would call off the wedding.

I excused myself and went up the back staircase to my bedroom. When I slipped inside and shut the door, I noticed a pillow was out of place and my heart leapt, knowing what that meant.

I locked my door behind me and went to my bed, flipping over the pillow to reveal a square package wrapped in wax paper. Stomach rumbling, I snatched it up and went into the bathroom, locking the door and sliding down against it. Then I peeled back the paper to find a sandwich—toasted pastrami on rye with a slice of Swiss cheese. It smelled like heaven.

Thank God for Mindy, our cook. Without her, I wouldn't have a single ally in this awful house.

I ate half of the sandwich slowly, wrapping up the rest and putting it in my mini fridge with my bottled water. I'd need it later. Then I went back out to my bedroom and got undressed for bed, crawling under the covers of my four poster bed.

Into my mind's eye swam the image of Lucien as I'd seen him at his soldier's funeral. He was a tall man and he'd looked larger still dressed in a crisp black suit and an overcoat. He'd kept his face turned away, deliberately ignoring me. The only thing I could see was his hand hanging at his side. Fine, square, made of angles and bronzed skin. A shiver had gone up my spine as I thought about that hand and how someday I would be his wife and he would touch me with it.

Sunday came before I knew it. I went to mass at noon with my parents and when we returned home, there was a stylist and a makeup artist from the salon. I almost rolled my eyes at the sight, but forced myself to be polite and cheerful to them. After all, it wasn't their fault that my mother was horrible.

They followed me up to my bedroom and began setting up their things. I went to my closet and took out the dress my mother had set back for me. She always bought my clothes and they were always more revealing than I liked, but I wasn't allowed to say anything against them. I'd learned that lesson early.

I put on a matching, beige set of lace panties and a bra. Over it, I slipped the cream dress and stepped to the side to look at myself on the mirror on the back of my closet door. The dress was short, coming to the middle of my thigh, with a lace and chiffon skirt and a gathered waist. The sleeves were long and sat off my shoulder, leaving the flesh just below my collarbone and up my throat completely bare. The

6

matching cream pumps completed the look and when I saw it all together, I realized my mother had done it again. Separately the dress and heels were modest enough, but together I was nothing but naked shoulders and miles of bare leg.

I sat down and let the stylist brush out my hair and straighten it until it was a curtain of dark satin. As they put the finishing touches on my makeup, I heard the doorbell ring from far below and my heart flipped in my chest.

Lucien was here.

I cocked my head, listening hard. I could make out my father's voice and then there were footsteps that I tracked to the study just off the hall. My father and Lucien were probably talking business in private before dinner while my mother harassed the cook over the menu.

When the makeup artist and stylist had left, I sat quietly in the chair by the window, afraid to move in case I spoiled my appearance. I didn't need to witness one of my mother's tantrums because my lipstick was smeared or my hair out of place. It was easier just to bend to her will than deal with the aftermath.

After almost thirty minutes of silence throughout the house, I detected my brother's tread in the hallway and then there was a tap on the door. I rose and opened it and found my brother standing awkwardly in the hall with his hands pushed in his pockets.

"Dad says he wants you to meet Lucien at the front door. He wants to walk you around the yard," he said.

"Walk me around the yard? Are we in a Jane Austen novel?" I asked.

He shrugged. "I don't know. Sorry, sis."

My brother and I weren't as close as we had been growing up, but we still cared for one another. I could tell it bothered him to watch me groomed and forced into marriage with a man I scarcely knew. But until our father's death or retirement, Cosimo didn't have a say in what happened to me any more than I did. We were both trapped.

"It's fine," I said, stepping into the hallway and shutting my door. "Let's go. I need you to help me down the stairs so I don't fall on my face and ruin my makeup. Mom would have a heart attack."

"Did mom pick out that outfit?" he asked, frowning. "If you lean over, your whole ass is going to be out. Are you sure you don't want to change?"

That rang an alarm bell in my head. My mother always dressed me like this and no one ever said anything, but something about Lucien was bringing out my brother's protective side. His mouth pressed together in a thin line and his forehead creased.

"I can't change, mom picked it out," I said. "Why?"

We started down the stairs. I clung to Cosimo's forearm as we made our way to the bottom, hoping I wouldn't topple and roll all the way down.

"Lucien gives me the creeps," he said. "You look at his eyes and it's just...nothing."

A shiver skittered up my spine and I stiffened as we got to the bottom and I saw Lucien at the end of the hall, waiting for me. He had his head lowered as he flipped through something on his phone. Cosimo sent me an apologetic look and stepped back, heading toward the study, and I knew I was on my own.

Taking a deep breath, I moved as confidently as possible down the hall toward my future husband. My heels clicked, my palms clenched, and my heart thumped in my ears. Lucien looked up from his phone, slipping it in the pocket of his dress pants, and straightened, putting his hands behind his back.

Even if there was nothing but ice in his eyes, at least he was stunningly handsome. His body was broad, but slender and tapered at the waist where his white shirt met the strip of his black belt. He had taken off his jacket and the arm it hung across was thick with muscle, visible through the fabric of his shirt.

His hair was dark brown and slicked back over his head. His face was somehow sharp and soft all at once. His square jaw was brushed with faint traces of stubble and the curve of his mouth was surprisingly soft, almost sensual. If it wasn't for the light hazel eyes, blank and cold like ice, I might have imagined his mouth could be almost tender...perhaps gentle. A shiver went through me again, but this time it wasn't out of fear.

He inclined his head stiffly as I drew near. "How are you, Olivia?"

"Good, thank you," I said. The way he moved, the way he said my name, felt incredibly formal.

Under his gaze, a chill went through my body and I was filled with the overwhelming feeling of being alone in the cold, standing on frozen ground, the world encased in ice and snow around me. The more I looked into those eyes, the more I wondered if I would ever feel warm again.

"Shall we walk?" he said.

"Yes," I said, my voice breaking.

It was spring and the air was balmy and smelled of fresh earth. Lucien was the picture of a gentleman as he opened the door for me, his hand just brushing my lower back as he ushered me through. Then he walked at my side as I lead the way around the house to the garden and unlocked the gate to let him through.

The garden was a project I'd worked on for the last few years and it had become my sole escape. It was a beautiful piece of earth with roses all along the fence and rows of soft, dark earth that overflowed with begonias, daisies, snapdragons, and anything else that suited my fancy.

This time of year, the garden was full of daffodils and tulips, their bright heads bobbing in the faint wind.

"Your garden is very beautiful," he said carefully.

"Thank you," I said. "It's mine. I grow everything here."

His brows rose as he looked around, his hands tucked in his pockets. I hadn't realized until he was standing in my little garden how large and broad he was compared to my small frame. He had to be at least six foot, three or four, but it was offset by his lithe body and graceful movements.

"So, we should probably talk," Lucien said, a little stiffly.

"About our engagement?" I looked up at him hesitantly.

"Yes," he said. "I brought your ring today and I expect you to wear it, at least whenever you leave the house."

He took a small, black box out of his pocket and handed it to me. I let it rest in my hand, something throbbing painfully in my chest. Of course it would be like this. There would be no romantic proposal, no getting down on one knee to ask for my hand, no declaration of love. Just a black box and an ice cold stare.

I blinked rapidly, determined not to tear up in front of him. He probably already thought I was weak. I opened the lid and let out a gasp at the large, oval diamond glittering on a delicate white gold band. It was beautiful and the sight struck me speechless for a long, awkward moment.

"How many carats is this?" I asked, looking up.

"Three," he said. "Why? Not enough for a Barone?"

I resisted the urge to glare at him. "No, it's just...enormous."

"But you like it?"

"I do," I said. It was true, a part of me did like the extravagance of it. "Aren't you going to put it on my finger?"

His mouth pressed together. "Why? I'm not in love with you, Olivia."

I flinched as if he'd hit me. Why did it hurt to hear him say that? I was fully aware this was an arranged marriage, a transaction more than a union, but it still felt like a kick to my stomach to hear him say it so plainly. It made me want to stamp my foot and throw the ring back at him, hit him the way his words had hit me.

Instead I clenched the box in my fist, shoving it into the pocket of my dress. "Never mind."

He scowled, clearly not happy with my reaction. A single step from his long legs ate up the distance between us and suddenly he was inches from me. His presence and heady scent filled my senses. It was enough to get me lightheaded.

Taking my wrist, he pried the box from my hand and took the ring out. I clenched my fist, but he forced my fingers apart and pushed it on. The gold scraped down over my finger, stinging my knuckle, and rested heavily against my skin.

I looked up, my heart thumping, and met his gaze. There was nothing, just a sheer wall of indifference behind the hazel irises. The thought of being alone with him in his bedroom, with nothing but his all-consuming chill sent a shiver through me. Cosimo was right, he was unnerving.

"Are you afraid of me?" he asked, sounding almost surprised.

"You didn't have to put the ring on me so roughly," I snapped.

"You have a mouth on you," he observed.

"Thank you, it's gotten me enough beatings that I'm not afraid of them anymore." I froze in surprise at the words that had unintentionally slipped out.

There was a long, tense silence. In the background I could hear birds singing in the woods behind the house and the faint whir of the sprinklers turning on in the front yard.

His brows rose slowly. "Does your father beat you, Olivia?"

The answer was yes. At least once a month either my mother or father lost their temper with me and slapped me hard enough to leave a bruise the next day. Only once had my father totally lost control and hit me hard enough to send me to the floor where he'd used the toe of his fancy shoes to paint bruises down my hips and sides. My mother was furious with him, afraid I would somehow be permanently marred and Lucien wouldn't want me anymore. But she was too afraid of my father to confront him.

The only person that had a problem with it was Cosimo and he could do nothing to help. Lucien didn't seem like the kind of man who had an apathetic bone in his body. Why did he care?

"I don't expect a lot from you as my fiancée, but I do demand honesty," Lucien said. His voice was still cold and light, like snow, but this time there was a note of gentleness.

"I don't want to talk about family matters openly," I said stiffly.

"I am your family now," he said.

I looked up and from the expression on his face I knew he wasn't the sort of man people argued with. I nodded slowly even though I was roiling with resentment inside. How dare he walk in here after years of ignoring me and expect me to treat him with an ounce of respect?

"Yes, it happens sometimes," I said. "My mother too."

His mouth thinned and he looked up at the house looming over us like an imposing shadow. I knew somewhere inside, my mother was pressed against the window, trying to guess what we were talking about.

"Is that all?" he said. "Is there anything else that is potentially dangerous to your well-being that I should know about as your husband."

"You're not my husband," I whispered.

"I will be. Answer me, Olivia."

My temper broke. I'd been bossed around my whole life, told what to do, what to wear, what to eat, who to marry and I was sick of it.

Beyond sick of it. A part of me had hoped Lucien would be different, but he was quickly proving me wrong.

"Alright, you want to know the truth?" I hissed. "My father loses his temper all the time and hits me and my mother. And she slaps me around too. I don't know why, maybe because it's the only thing she can control. But worse than that, she measures me and weighs my food and counts my calories and forces me to fit into tiny dresses I don't even want to wear."

I paused for a breath and managed to look him in the eye. There was something brewing in his gaze for the first time and it took me a moment to realize it was anger.

"Your mother does what?" he asked, his voice soft.

"She's afraid you won't want me if I gain any weight at all, so she's had me on a diet since I was fourteen. It's the most...soul draining thing to sit there and watch everyone around me eat what they want and however much they want...but I have to eat another plate of steamed vegetables. And nothing else. I'm so goddamn sick of being hungry. And that's worse than being hit."

There was a glitter in his gaze now, a dangerous kind of light that sent a chill through my body.

"I'm sick of being measured and weighed," I gasped, my throat closing and tears springing to my eyes. "I'm sick of the humiliation of it. I hate it...so much."

He reached out a hand and I flinched violently, tensing for a blow. Instead, his middle finger touched my collarbone, tracing it to the base of my throat.

"I wondered why you were so thin," he murmured. "You don't look as if you should be, you look like you should have...curves. But I can see your whole collarbone, pressing up under your skin. It's awful."

I blinked, glaring at the ground. "Thank you, I've always wanted to be awful."

"No, it's awful that you've been abused," he said.

The wave of relief at hearing someone else say those words was overwhelming. I'd known in my subconscious mind that this life, this treatment, wasn't normal, but there was no one to articulate it until now. A weight lifted from my shoulders just from a single moment of validation.

"I don't want you living here anymore," he said shortly, stepping back. "You will come live in the mansion with me."

He spun on his heel, his body like a cannonball speeding through the air toward its target. I scrambled after him as he crossed the garden and pushed the gate ajar, striding across the lawn in the direction of the house. My heart pounded in my chest and my mind whirled too fast for me to form coherent thoughts. What was he doing?

"Lucien, where are you going?" I gasped, as I caught up to him on the porch.

"I'm going to instruct your parents that you are to live with me."

"I can't live with you before we're married!"

"Strangely enough, you can do just that."

He pushed open the door and entered the house, his crisp wingtips clicking against the floor as he stepped into the front hall. I burst after him and then stopped in my tracks. What was I doing? I couldn't get in between whatever was about to go down between my father and Lucien. They were both underbosses and any altercation between them threatened their relationship as allies. This was dangerous ground and I wasn't equipped for such a precarious situation.

Lucien paused before my father's study and knocked. I lingered behind him until he turned and noticed me, holding up two fingers and beckoning me over.

"You may come in with me," he said.

The door opened and my father appeared, his eyes narrowing in confusion as they fell on us. Lucien inclined his head and reached behind him, holding out his palm to me. It took me a moment to realize he meant for me to take his hand and I did so hesitantly. It was a little rough, but warm and strangely comforting as it engulfed my fingers.

I had half expected it to be cold.

"May I speak with you, Rosario? Or rather, may we speak with you?" Lucien said smoothly.

"Of course," my father said, stepping aside.

I let Lucien lead me into the study. As I passed by my father, he fixed me with a deadly glare. He knew something was wrong and, true to his fashion, he was sure I was the instigator. I shuddered and stepped behind Lucien, unsure why I trusted him more. Perhaps because he hadn't hurt me yet.

Lucien released me and I sat in the armchair behind him, my heart beating harder than usual. My father went to sit behind his desk and crossed his arms to try to appear more imposing. Lucien, however, stood before him undaunted. Gone was any of the emotion from our conversation in the garden. Now he stood with his back straight and his legs planted apart, arms folded over his chest. Every line of his body was crisp with ice.

I leaned forward to catch a glimpse of his face and that strange shiver went through me again. He reminded me of something otherworldly from my childhood story books. I imagined for a moment that he was an ice king and winter blew in on his breath and froze everything he touched. That he would crush anything that stood in his way and grind it to a fine powdery snow beneath the heel of his wingtip.

"Olivia?"

I jumped and blushed. "Yes?"

My father scowled at me, his face a brewing storm. "Lucien just informed me that he wants you to stay at his mansion with him. Do you have anything to say about that?"

"I—I don't know," I said.

"She already agreed to it," said Lucien swiftly.

I opened my mouth to contradict him and shut it. Did I want to go with him? I wasn't sure. I scarcely knew him, but going with him did sound better than staying here. At least, judging from our brief interaction in the garden, he would allow me to eat as much as I wanted and he didn't seem inclined to hit me from what I could tell. I closed my eyes for a moment, imagining what it would be like to not live in this house.

No more going to bed hungry. No more stinging slaps when my weight increased by a pound. No more screaming and slamming doors.

"Yes," I burst out. "I want to go."

My father's nostrils flared and he leaned forward and rested his elbows on his desk. "This is highly irregular and, if I'm honest, inappropriate of you to suggest, Lucien."

Lucien stiffened. "I understand that it's not done, but you know me and you know I won't touch your daughter before the wedding."

"So why do you want her there?"

"With tensions rising on account of the Russians, I want to keep my fiancée nearby. I need to be able to ensure her safety myself. For my peace of mind, no slight to you."

My father's expression changed from anger to irritated concern. "What will people say?"

"The hell if I care, and I know deep down, neither do you," Lucien said. "Neither of us need to answer to our men and you know Romano won't give a damn if she's living with me. Just as long as I marry her."

There was a faint threat to his last words and I knew my father heard it too because his mouth tightened and he leaned back in his chair. His fingers tapped on the desk and his jaw worked.

"You're threatening our alliance over this?" he asked coolly.

"I would never," Lucien said softly.

His tone belied the exact opposite. His posture and expression were unreadable and his powerful body, though relaxed, carried a hint of a threat. He had my father dangling on a string and he knew it, but he was too careful, too intelligent, to speak those words aloud. Threats were crude and beneath him.

I swallowed, realizing he wasn't the same sort of made man as my father and brother. Men like Lucien Esposito didn't have to put their threats into words. Instead, they hung around him like smoke, etched in the relaxed lines of his body and the faint smile on his mouth.

My father killed with gore and gusto, painting his power out plainly in blood for all to see. But Lucien...surely he came in the night like a shadow, like a draft of icy wind, and slit the throats of his enemies with a gentle sigh.

My stomach turned. This man was my fiancé and he was here to take me away to a world where he was king. Where I would be his wife and let him touch me and bury himself between my thighs at night. A strange, tingling shiver went through my body. This time it was warm and a little excited. Beneath my dress, my sex gave a quick throb and I clenched my thighs together surreptitiously.

No, I wouldn't allow myself to want him.

My father lifted his head, his eyes glittering. "Fine," he said. "Take her, but once she's there, don't bring her back. And you will marry her. I don't care the state she's in when you get her to the alter, just make sure that you do it."

I gasped, unsure how to feel. Was I relieved to be leaving home or was I terrified to be going away with Lucien? Or was it both? I dug my nails into my palms and squeezed my eyes shut. I hated this, hated not having any say over my fate.

Lucien stepped back, inclining his head briefly. "I'll have someone pick her up tomorrow. And I won't be staying for dinner, it's no longer necessary."

Then he was gone, the door swinging in his wake. I sat frozen for a brief moment, my heart thudding, and then I jumped to my feet. Ignoring my father's glare, I ran down the hall after him and burst through the front door. A chilly wind had set in since we'd been inside and the sky was thick with storm clouds.

He sat in the sports car parked in the driveway and when he saw me he narrowed his eyes and turned the engine off. I scrambled across the pavement, my arms wrapping around my body to fend off the cool wind, and leaned against the side of his topless car.

"What's wrong?" he said briskly.

"Why did you do that?" I panted. "How do you know I even want to live with you anyway?"

"Given the choice between being slapped and starved and living with your fiancé, I assumed you'd choose the latter. Am I wrong?"

Ice bored into me from beneath his heavy lids. His arm rested on his steering wheel, his hand hanging. The graceful curve of his square, masculine hand caught my attention and that familiar shiver went through me. Someday soon this man would put those hands on my body and he would give me pain or pleasure. Or perhaps both.

Thunder clapped in the distance and I looked up at the side yard and saw a wall of rain advancing over the hills. Lucien stood in his seat and pulled the top of his car up and slid it into place just as the storm hit with vengeance. Large, cold droplets spattered over me, soaking me to the skin in seconds.

The passenger door opened and Lucien leaned over, beckoning me to get in the car. I hesitated, water streaming down my face, before sliding inside. The seats were buttery soft against my thighs and the leather interior smelled of cool pine. I turned and my heart flipped as I took in Lucien, so close I could feel his body heat and smell his clean scent.

I hadn't noticed before that his lashes were soft and dark around his hazel eyes. And I hadn't noticed how his throat, broad and tanned, had a vein that pulsed beneath his skin, leading my eyes down to the skin between his collarbones. A wild urge to reach out and touch it, to trace a line beneath the collar of his shirt, hit me and I looked away, hoping he couldn't guess my thoughts.

"You're soaked," he said.

"I hadn't noticed," I said.

"Cut that out," he said, his eyes fixed on the blinding rain spattering across the windshield, blocking anyone who might try to look inside the car.

"What?"

"I know you want some control, Olivia, but you have to respect me. You can't speak to me like that," he said calmly. "I expect you to be obedient and respectful when we're around others and if you have a snarky comment, save it."

"So you're telling me to be good wife who never gets to express her thoughts?" I cringed inwardly at my tone, knowing I was pushing it.

"You're being combative for no reason. I expect us to have a united front as a couple. If you have a grievance with me, take it back to our bedroom and we can resolve it there. In private."

Our bedroom. The words threw me off guard. I looked up at this man, collected and icy, and yet so powerfully masculine and undeniably attractive. My mind kept going back to the knowledge that I would have to face him on our wedding night. That he would take my virginity and we would sleep beside one another and wake up as husband and wife.

"What are you thinking?" he said.

I swallowed and looked out the window at the pounding raindrops. "Can I be honest?"

"I expect you to tell me only the truth."

"I'm wondering how it can be that we've never spoken before today and yet, in months, we'll be married. And then we're supposed to just live together and...you know."

His mouth twitched. "Are you talking about sex?"

I felt a hot flush creep up my throat and over my cheeks. "We don't love each other, so I don't understand how that sort of thing is going to work."

I could tell he was amused, but he kept his face impassive. His jaw worked as he considered what I'd said and then he gave a short sigh.

"There's nothing about sex that requires love."

The way he said it caught me off guard. There was so much detachment in his tone, bordering on glacial, but somehow completely without malice. I studied him for a long moment, my heart thumping irregularly, uncomfortable with discussing such a private thing with him.

"Are you alright?" he asked.

I dipped my head, subdued by his words. I'd never thought deeply about what our life would look like beyond our marriage and wedding night, but a small part of me had assumed that we would work towards love. But from how Lucien was talking now, it seemed like he didn't have any interest in love, or even affection.

"I'm fine, I just was thinking," I said quietly.

"You're worried about having sex with me, aren't you?" He adjusted in his seat to face me better and I looked down at his hands again and a shiver went through my body.

"A little. And it's just occurred to me that you don't want to marry me," I whispered.

"I never said I didn't want to marry you, Olivia. Why do you think so?"

"You seem to not care if we aren't in love."

His jaw twitched and he tore his eyes from me. "Love is not a necessity for a happy marriage. Trust and honesty make a far better foundation."

I scowled, turning to the window. "Why would you want sex without love?"

"Mutual pleasure," he said. "Sex is like alcohol or drugs without the hangover. You don't need love for it...in fact, you're better off without affection complicating things."

I gaped at him. I'd spent enough time reading romance novels, although I wasn't allowed to read the really salacious ones, to be horrified by his response. Was this all he was behind those icy eyes? Just a hardened made man with a penchant for mindless pleasure? A hollow feeling began in my chest and I sat up straight and reached for the door handle.

"It's pouring," he pointed out.

"I'm already soaked," I said.

"Did I offend you?"

"No," I said. "But your view of things seems horrible. You wanted honesty from me, so I'm giving it. I thought we might fall in love eventually...at least try to anyway. The way you talk...it just sounds lonely."

He sighed and closed his eyes, rubbing a hand down his face. "I'd be lying if I said I wanted this marriage. I was hoping for some choice in who I married, but this is what needs done and duty comes before anything else in our world. We both have a duty to do, so we'll get married and we'll make it work."

"That sounds thrilling." I swallowed past the lump in my throat.

He reached out, taking me by the jaw in a firm grip as he turned my face up. "Believe me, Olivia, your life will be thrilling...so long as everything goes my way."

Something about hearing him call me by my name was strangely comforting. I extracted my face from his hands and rubbed the corners of my eyes, fighting a sudden headache. I was tired from the chaos of the day and the fight had drained from me. It was time to brave the rain and make a dash for the house.

"I'm going inside," I said. "I'm already wet, I'll be fine to just run across the drive."

"Alright," he said.

I felt his eyes on me as I ran across the drive and up the stairs, my dress sticking to my body. When I turned at the door and glanced back, he had his head cocked and his lips were parted. A prickle went down my spine as I gazed back at him, my eyes meeting his, and I wondered if he desired me. Warmth pooled between my legs, and as I slipped inside, it occurred to me there might be some truth to what he said.

If we couldn't have love, at least we could have lust.

CHAPTER TWO

OLIVIA

My parents were quiet that night at dinner. The cook served ham with mashed potatoes and green beans, and when I filled my plate, my mother said nothing to stop me. Instead, she kept her eyes on her food and my father sorted through his paperwork as he ate, ignoring us. Cosimo didn't show up for dinner and I knew he was probably out at the club or with one of his women.

My parents didn't care what he did. My father actively encouraged his exploits, even taking him for a weekend when he was a teenager so he could get his first taste of the women who kept the made men entertained. I, on the other hand, hadn't received any sex education. Unless I counted a threat from my mother that if I dared to touch any of the boys at school, I would be useless to her and Lucien would cast me aside like a chewed stick of gum.

So I hadn't. I said no when boys asked me on dates and ignored their texts. I knew the future of my father's alliance with Lucien rested on my shoulders, so I closed my ears and eyes to my brother's freedom. I pretended I didn't see girls leave his room early in the morning or the pack of condoms that sat blatantly on his bathroom sink. Men had freedom to do as they pleased, but I'd been born with the fatal flaw of being a woman.

"Have you packed your things?" my mother said finally.

I hesitated, unsure what she was feeling. She didn't seem angry, in fact she seemed relieved that I was going away with Lucien. She was probably happy to be rid of me.

"Yes," I said, keeping my eyes on my plate.

"I have something for you, I'll drop it off in your room tomorrow," she said.

I nodded and asked to be excused. It was getting late and tomorrow would be a long and tiring day.

The next morning, I woke to my curtains being thrown ajar and I sat up, rubbing my eyes at the unexpected light. My mother stood there, a white paper bag in her hand. She was already dressed in a pencil dress and her hair was tied up at the nape of her neck without a strand out of place.

"Get dressed," she said. "Lucien called earlier and said he'd send someone at noon to pick you up."

I blinked, still sleepy, and obeyed. "What time is it?"

"Almost ten. You slept late." Her tone was short, but she wasn't nearly as angry as I'd expected her to be. "I brought your birth control refill and I set up for the doctor to send it to you, at Lucien's, for a while. At least until you've gotten the wedding over with. That way you won't have to worry about it until later."

I stared at her. She rarely did anything without an ulterior motive and every alarm was going off in my head. I kept quiet as she took the pink purse where she kept my birth control out of the bag and passed it to me.

"Make sure to do as Lucien says," she said. "And don't talk back to him."

Then she was gone, her perfect heels tapping down the hall until the sound died out. I went into the bathroom and took the package from the bag and frowned. The pills were larger this time and they were in different packaging. Perhaps my mother had had the doctor change my prescription without bothering to tell me. Nothing would surprise me.

I took one out and laid it on my tongue and swallowed it dry. I'd forgotten to take it for the last few days, but knowing I would be going to Lucien's mansion, I should probably start being more careful. Perhaps he would do the honorable thing and not touch me before the wedding, but it was better to be safe than sorry. He was a made man after all.

An image of Lucien's mouth, open and hot against the flesh of my throat, burst into my mind and I shivered. He was sexy, there was no denying that, even with all the passionless ice behind his eyes. Perhaps he was right, perhaps sex with him could be good. He did have a impressive body that looked incredible in his suits.

Perhaps the heat that now rose between my thighs would be enough to make our marriage good.

My two small suitcases were lined up by the door. I'd packed everything sentimental to me in a single case last night before bed. I'd cried quietly as I did, never having realized how few sentimental items I owned. There was only a few DVDs from my childhood, some jewelry my cousin had given me, and a photo of my brother and I at one of his soccer games years ago.

My brother wasn't home yet. Most likely my parents hadn't thought to tell him I was leaving and he had no idea what was going on. I sat down on the edge of my bed, my stomach hollowed out, my heart throbbing with lingering sadness.

Perhaps it wouldn't be so terrible in Lucien's house. Perhaps he would be kind, or even gentle, and I could finally live without fear.

I didn't leave my room for the rest of the morning. I didn't want to have to face my parents and pretend to be sad that I was leaving. They didn't seem to care because no one else knocked on my door or called for me to come downstairs.

Five minutes past noon, I heard the sound of a car coming up the drive. I stood and brushed my shirt off and adjusted the legs of my jeans. Then I leaned over and checked myself in the mirror, fluffing my thin bangs and twisting the longer bits that hung before my ears. The rest of my dark hair hung down my back in a curled ponytail. Then I pulled on a white sweater and padded down the hall, dragging my luggage behind me.

Neither my mother nor my father appeared as I moved down the hall. A pang went through me as I stood by the door, soaking in my last moments in my childhood home. It hadn't been a happy nineteen years. I left the house and let the door swing shut behind me as I walked down the stairs.

The car door opened and Lucien rose in a graceful movement. I paused, surprised to see him. I'd expected a valet or a bodyguard to pick me up. Instead it was the underboss himself, dressed smartly in dark dress pants and a matching shirt, an expensive watch glittering at his wrist.

"Where are your parents?" he said, frowning.

I opened my mouth and coughed to clear my throat. "I don't know."

His mouth pressed together, but he said nothing as he took my suitcases and opened the passenger door. I slid into the SUV and watched him circle the car and get in beside me. He was as relaxed and impassive as he'd been yesterday and it was impossible to tell what he was feeling.

"I thought you were sending someone to pick me up," I said.

"I prefer to handle my own business when possible."

We pulled out onto the road and I turned around to watch the house disappear into the distance. My chest was empty of anything save fluttering nerves and I was almost glad when it was gone from sight.

"Would you like anything?" he asked.

I turned, unsure what he meant. "What?"

"Would you like to stop for anything? A coffee? Lunch?" He turned his flat gaze on me for a moment before flicking it back to the road.

"Coffee would be amazing," I said.

It was strange to be asked what I wanted. Lucien pulled onto the highway and we drove for a while in silence. I dared to look over at him once and my attention was captured by a muscle working in his jaw as if he were grinding his teeth.

We stopped at a small coffee shop as soon as we reached the city. I waited in the car while Lucien walked casually inside and returned with two cups. I'd never met a made man who had the confidence to walk about like that without protection. I accepted my coffee from him, breathing in the scent of caramel and espresso. My mother never let me get sweetener in my coffee and just the smell of it had me almost melting.

I curled up in the seat, pulling my sweater closer, and sipped at the sweet foam. Lucien had black coffee, which he drank slowly. He had a way of drinking that fascinated me—a swallow and then a tensing of his jaw and tightening of his lips as he did. It was oddly sexy, watching his mouth and jaw move like that.

Tearing my eyes away, I steadfastly ignored the heat curling in my stomach. I was lucky, I suppose, that despite my marriage being arranged, at least I felt some attraction to my husband-to-be.

"There's a party tonight at the Romano's. His son just graduated and he's back in town. I'd like you to accompany me."

I sat upright. "Tonight? I don't have anything to wear."

He glanced at me. "You're a small, correct?"

"Yes," I said, unsure why I felt embarrassed.

"Then the things I picked for you should work."

"Oh...alright," I said, unsure how I felt about him choosing my clothes.

We drove in silence the rest of the way to the Esposito mansion. It was a massive, beautiful house that sat on the edge of the water on the other side of the city. I'd been here once a long time ago for a social event, but it still amazed me with its opulence like I was seeing it for the first time.

We pulled up the circular drive and Lucien parked at the bottom of the stairs. He opened my door and went around to get my suitcases as I got to my feet and stared up at the house. This was my new home.

I watched Lucien climb the stairs with my suitcases and I wondered why he hadn't sent someone else to pick me up or why he didn't have a servant carry my bags. He was a strange kind of underboss.

I caught my breath as we stepped into the entrance way, the hall stretching out before us in a dizzying array of colors. The floor beneath us was marbled cream with gold tiles and the walls were off-white with gold trim and overhead hung a series of heavy, crystal chandeliers.

"Yes, it's quite something," he said. "The man who built it was obsessed with Versailles, if you couldn't tell. Sometimes I think I should have it redone to modernize it, make it less...loud."

"It's beautiful," I said. "You should leave it how it is."

It was beautiful. A few hundred years out of date and more appropriate for royalty, but it was breathtaking. It would be a shame to change anything.

"I'm glad you like it," he said, heading toward the spiral staircase at the end of the hall.

I followed him upstairs to the second floor. There was a hallway with hardwood flooring and brass furnishings. Lucien strode all the way to the end and turned right, leading even further into this maze of a house.

Finally he stopped outside a door near the middle and pushed it ajar and stood aside. I ducked past him and stepped into a bedroom...or at least, this house's opulent version of a bedroom. The floor was a sky blue carpet and the walls were a tasteful cream and blue pattern. There was a row of windows that looked out over the water and a four poster bed with thick, velvet drapes hanging around it. The furniture was clearly antique, restored to perfection, and probably worth thousands of dollars.

"It's amazing," I whispered.

"It reminded me of your garden," he said. "And the view is quite pleasant in the morning."

He put down my suitcases and straightened his shirt, impassive and detached as ever. I walked to the center of the room, spinning around to take everything in.

"Well, I have business," he said. "I'll be back around six to pick you up. If you need anything, call the number taped to the dial phone in the bathroom. The housekeeper will pick up and she can help you with whatever you need."

"Oh...alright, thank you," I murmured.

He backed out of the door and closed it and I was left alone in my new bedroom. I went to the window and took a deep breath, a sense of peace settling over me. Whatever lay ahead, at least I was free of my parents.

In the distance, I heard a door shut and I saw Lucien's dark figure appear below, cutting across the driveway and getting back into his car. He was all business, striding with purpose; I doubted he had given me a second thought.

CHAPTER THREE

LUCIEN

I wanted to fuck her on that fifty-thousand dollar antique bed until it broke into pieces. My fingers dug into the steering wheel as I pulled out of the driveway and got up to speed. Images flashed through my mind as trees and houses sped by. The curve of her throat, the flash of her dark eyes, the way her full mouth pressed against the lid of her coffee.

Why did she have to look like that? This would be far easier if she'd been boring or unpleasant. But no, she was beautiful and she set every nerve in my body on fire and made the front of my pants uncomfortably tight.

The first moment I'd seen her up close, my throat constricted and I almost choked on my words. She was a little too thin, but her body still turned me rock hard. Full breasts, a slender waist, and a rounded ass. Her eyes were dark, bruised and beaten down.

Her mouth was full and she looked like she tasted like heaven, like ecstasy. Her nose had caught my attention, the thin bridge, the slightly curved nostrils, and the pointed tip. I wanted to run my fingers down it and trace her soft mouth. Push my fingers past her lips, feel her hot tongue curl around them as she sucked them into her mouth.

Jesus Christ, I needed to get it together.

I ran a hand over my face and drained the last, cold dregs of my coffee. I needed something stronger, but it was barely one-thirty in the afternoon and I had a strict rule against drinking during work hours.

Strict rules had protected me for the last several years. Keeping me safe from what had happened, from what Carlo Romano had done to me. My fingers found their way to my forearm, tracing the faint scars hidden beneath my tattoos. Whatever it took, I would never be so completely at another man's mercy again.

I took a left and got back on the highway, heading into the city. My only brother, Duran, was waiting for me at my office downtown. In between sleeping around, getting slapped across the cover of local tabloids, and doing shots off the tits of random women, he was a bright and talented young man.

Duran was lying on the couch in my office when I arrived, his feet up on the armrest. He wore dress pants and a white shirt, untucked and stained at the collar with a smear of bright pink. Why did he have to be so brazen about his exploits? I crossed the room and sat down, still feeling tense and frustrated from my time with Olivia.

"I met with V's assistant yesterday," Duran said, getting up and taking off his sunglasses. "He said that he'll be at the Aqua River Resort soon. I'll go there, stay for a few days and keep a low profile, and then I'll meet up with him when he shows up on Wednesday for dinner in the private lounge. He wants to see you next though, so be prepared for that."

Our plan was too dangerous to be spoken explicitly of even when we were alone. We couldn't even call our Russian consort by his real name for fear of the room being bugged. Of course, I'd gone over every inch of my office with my fingertips, but I still didn't trust Carlo Romano, the outfit's boss, not to somehow invade my privacy.

"The Aqua River Resort and Spa," I said crisply. "I own it. I'll have the manager make sure there's no undesirables around while you're there."

"Okay," Duran said, standing up and stretching. He crossed the room and opened the closet in the corner where I kept my extra clothes. I flipped open my laptop as he pulled off his shirt and buttoned on one of mine and smoothed back his hair.

"I have a girl waiting in the car," he said. "I need to head out. Anything else?"

"Who's the girl?" I asked absently.

"Don't worry, I'm not fucking around with any of the outfit girls. She's paid for and I had her sign one of your ridiculous contracts."

"Good," I said.

"Maybe you should consider getting laid," said Duran lightly. "It's been a while since you had anyone over at the house. Like a long time...years or something."

I kept my temper, looking up long enough to take a cigarette out of my desk and light it. Normally, I didn't smoke, but I was finding myself reaching for my cigarettes more and more often in the last few weeks. Stress was beginning to take a toll on me.

Duran reached out and plucked the cigarette from my mouth and put it to his lips. "Sex is healthier than cigarettes. Why don't you fuck one of the serving girls in the bathroom tonight or something? They always hire hot women to work their parties."

"Thanks, I'm not an idiot," I snapped, lighting a second cigarette.

"You're being neurotic," Duran said. He rummaged in his pocket for a moment and pulled out a condom and tossed it onto my desk. "Wrap it up and fuck someone before you drive me up the wall."

I sat back and took a drag off my cigarette and watched Duran go. He was right, it had been far too long since I'd slept with anyone. My brother would be aghast if I actually told him how long it had been since I'd had anything more than a blowjob in my car from a girl who signed a non-disclosure agreement.

I was going to wait until Olivia was legally mine and it didn't matter if she got pregnant by accident. Then I would fuck the last several years out of my system within the safe confines of my marriage. A stream of erotic images of Olivia, naked, writhing, and glimmering with sweat beneath me burst into my brain. It was going to be a long several months.

My pants were uncomfortably tight again. I dragged my mind away from the thought of fucking Olivia and threw Duran's condom into the trash. I hadn't bought condoms in years and I didn't need the temptation of having one in my pocket.

I worked for the rest of the afternoon and headed back to the mansion around five to get ready for the evening. The thought of going to the Romano's house turned my stomach with disgust. After what Carlo Romano had done to me, I didn't think I would ever be able to hear his name again without feeling sick with rage.

But for now, I had to keep my hatred hidden. I had to keep this burning anger, this desire for revenge, hidden or my life would be forfeit. And the lives of my brother and my fiancée who now waited for me in her room upstairs.

I dressed in a dark blue Italian suit and smoothed back my hair. Tonight would be a peaceful facade, but I still pushed two guns into the shoulder holsters beneath my jacket. Then I clasped my watch around my wrist and left my bedroom, heading down the hall to the Blue Room where Olivia waited. I was early, but if I had to guess, she was probably ready and waiting.

I knocked lightly on the door, but there was nothing but silence. Frowning, I turned the knob and stepped inside, but her room was empty. I stepped on the sides of my feet to the window to scan the darkening yard. It was deserted.

Had she run?

Then I heard a sound from the bathroom on the far side of the room. Of course, she was still getting ready—I was almost twenty minutes early after all. I moved across the carpet noiselessly, crossing into view of the bathroom as I did. My heart almost stopped at the sight visible through the open door.

She was on the floor, leaning against the side of the whirlpool bathtub. Her knees were cocked and her bare toes dug into the marble flooring. Her hair was done, pinned to her head with her feathery bangs over her forehead and around her ears, and her makeup glittered on her face. She wore only a black lace bra and thin stockings and her hand was working between her thighs.

I stood there, every ounce of blood in my body rushing to my cock. She reached up and grasped the side of the tub over her head, her slender fingers going white at the tips. Then, she let out a sound that would replay in my head for the rest of my life.

It was a desperate gasping cry and it burst from her mouth as if she couldn't help it, as if she were so lost in her own pleasure she didn't know she'd made a sound. Another noise escaped her lips, a kind of mewl, as she rode her orgasm out against her fingers.

If I hadn't thrown that goddamn condom away in my office, I would have walked in there and fucked her over the sink. I would have bent her over and pushed my fingers in her perfect hair and ruined it while I slammed into her pussy until her makeup ran down her face. Consequences be damned, I'd never wanted anything more in my entire life.

Fuck, I needed to leave before I did something I regretted. I stepped back noiselessly and slipped out the door, letting the knob ease into place without a sound. My blood pumped hard, pooling almost painfully in my groin. I couldn't think of anything save the sight of my fiancée on the bathroom floor with her fingers between her thighs.

I needed to get a handle on myself in the next twenty minutes or tonight was going to be a problem. Striding down the hall, I ducked into the nearest bathroom and locked the door. I needed to take care of the throbbing pressure in my cock or it was going to get hard every time I remembered seeing her touch herself and I couldn't have that happen tonight. I needed us to both be calm and collected.

I jerked off, washed up, and left the bathroom to have a cigarette on the balcony down the hall from her room. The air was cool and smelled of rain and it helped the heat around my collar dissipate.

Whatever I had expected my fiancée to be, it wasn't this. I had never imagined that after years of feeling nothing but apathy for the idea of her, all it had taken was the sight of her mouth against a cup of coffee to send me spiraling. Maybe I was just carrying far too much tension from years of celibacy.

I heard her door open behind me and I expelled a stream of smoke up into the night sky. Her heels clicked down the hall and a prickle went down my spine. God, the sound of her shoes was going to get me hard again.

Duran was right. I desperately needed to get laid.

When I turned around, it took everything I had to keep my face an expressionless mask. She'd picked the red dress from the clothes I'd left in her room. It was a silky, slippery thing that clung to her curves and showed the faint traces of her breasts above the dipped neckline. When she drew near, I caught the reflection of her naked back in the window behind her and my cock twitched in my pants.

"Are you ready?" I asked, keeping my voice cool. "You look lovely, by the way."

"I'm a little hungry," she said.

"We'll have dinner there," I said.

She blushed a little and shifted, almost as if adjusting her bra beneath her dress. The image of her on the floor of her bathroom in her black lace undergarments burst into my mind. I glanced down at her hands, at the perfectly manicured nails that had worked between her thighs just minutes ago. God, what was it about this woman?

The silver Tesla was parked at the foot of the stairs. I kept my hand on her elbow, guiding her as she walked in her towering heels across the driveway, and opened the door so she could slip into the passenger side. I took a moment before I opened the driver's side to gather my thoughts and ensure my eyes were guarded before I got in.

We sped out of the driveway and out onto the back road to the Romano's mansion. The night was beautiful and the sky was clear with a heavy spattering of stars and a crescent moon. My chest tightened as I thought about the evening ahead, of having to face Romano, of having to speak with him as though he hadn't destroyed me. Broken me into a hundred thousand pieces and left me still scrambling on the floor trying to put them back together.

I looked over at Olivia and she sighed and leaned back against the seat. Her throat was so lovely, bent back and exposed like that. It woke something primal in me, something I hadn't tapped into in a long time. My eyes skimmed lower, to the rise of her thigh beneath the silky red of her dress, and down to her exposed calf.

Her legs were crossed and her calf slid down to a slender ankle, fragile with the faint traces of veins running beneath the skin. She wore a pair of heeled sandals and her toes were delicate and manicured like her nails. For some reason, her lovely, arched feet got me hard.

That was a first.

I frowned, pressing down the gas and the engine gave a satisfying purr as the lights of the Romano house appeared in the distance.

"I need you to be comfortable being on your own if I need to leave you to speak with anyone there," I said. "Romano will want to dance with you, so be aware of that. Keep your chin up, your shoulders back, and don't shrink when any of them look at you. Understood?"

Her dark eyes darted up, running over me from beneath her feathery bangs. "Why?"

"Because it's never just a party. It's a game, it's a...chess match," he said. "And if you're going to be my wife, you need to learn how to play."

CHAPTER FOUR

OLIVIA

I frowned, unsure what he meant. "I can play chess," I said.

His eyes flicked to me and then back again as he pulled into the driveway. "Men are like rooks, we have to face our enemies straight on. But women, they are the queen, they are deadly, and they can move any way they want."

"I hardly think I'm the queen," I said.

"You will be when I'm done with you," he said.

Before I could answer, he got out of the car and circled it on his long legs. He helped me out of the car and the valet took his keys and I paused at the bottom of the stairs. I'd been to the Romano house once and it was as large and impressive as ever. When I'd visited as a child, I'd been convinced it was castle with its high, pale stone walls and dozens and dozens of glittering windows. Inside, it was even grander than the Esposito mansion, although a hundred times colder.

Lucien stayed close as we climbed the stairs and entered through the great front doors. The main hallway was carpeted in red and the ceiling overhead was hung with heavy chandeliers. The light caught on the glossy floors and the mirrors hanging on the walls in a dizzying array of color.

"Lucien."

I looked up and saw Duran, Lucien's younger brother whom I hadn't seen in several years, heading toward us. He was smaller than Lucien, but handsome with piercing, black eyes and a wicked curve to his mouth. His hand was wrapped around the wrist of a curvy redheaded girl who looked bored. If the rumors about Duran were true, she was probably being paid to be on his arm.

"Fantastic, you're here," he said. "Hey, Olivia, good seeing you. Romano wants to speak with you upstairs, Lucien, before you leave tonight."

"I assumed he would," Lucien said, adjusting his cuffs. "Who is this?"

He was staring at the redhead with a narrowed gaze that surprised me. Duran rolled his eyes and leaned close to him and whispered something. Lucien frowned slightly and replied under his breath in Italian and Duran nodded. I could speak Italian fairly well, but it was hard for me to understand unless I could hear it clearly so I wasn't sure what he'd said.

"Alright, I'll catch up with you later," Lucien said, drawing back and taking my hand.

His fingers felt large and lean in mine, the coarse pad of his thumb working absently over my knuckle. As he led me from the hall to the main area at the base of the curved staircase, I felt his thumb move from my knuckle to the enormous engagement ring on my finger. He worked it with gentle strokes and immediately the image of his hand disappearing beneath my dress burst into my mind. How would it feel for him to do the same between my legs, against my clit?

No, now wasn't the time to think about Lucien's hard, lean fingers touching my pussy. I squeezed my eyes shut for a brief moment as we drew to a halt before the bar and shook my head to clear it.

"What's wrong?" Lucien asked.

"Nothing, sorry, everything is just so...there's a lot to look at," I said.

"Romano knows how to throw a party," he said in a careful tone.

He was standing mere inches away, his elbow leaned on the cherry wood bar. I had never been this close to him before, my breasts almost grazing the front of his fine, Italian suit. He smelled of cologne, a rich, masculine scent.

When I raised my gaze up to his, I noticed for the first time that his eyes weren't truly hazel. There was a bit of blue around the iris, penetrating out with long tines, like ice spreading over dark water. The edges of his irises were green and brown mottled together and the very outer ring was a deep, deep blue. From far away, his eyes appeared to be hazel, but from close up, they were almost multicolored.

"Would you like a drink?" he asked.

I opened my mouth and then paused. "I know this is silly, but I'm not actually old enough to drink."

He hesitated and a flicker of discomfort crossed his face. "Yes, I forgot. It's alright though, no one here minds."

"I wouldn't know what to get."

"How about a Prosecco?" he murmured.

"I don't know what that is, but sure," I said.

His mouth twitched. He drew back and leaned across the bar to catch the bartender's attention.

"I'll have a cognac, neat, and a Prosecco, your choice, for the lady," he said.

The bartender handed over the glasses and Lucien led the way to the edge of the dance floor in the next room. It was a beautiful, black and white checked floor full of men and women swirling to the sounds of the orchestra. I recognized a few faces, but my parents had never had much use for taking me to social events so most of them were unfamiliar.

Lucien put his glass to his lips and made that same gesture as he swallowed. A slight grimace and then a flexing of his jaw. For some reason, I found it incredibly attractive. He glanced over and caught me staring and I looked away.

"Have you drunk before?" he asked.

"A little, not much though," I said. "I never really wanted to. And my mother didn't allow me to because it's empty calories."

He blinked. "Empty calories?"

"That's what she calls junk food or any drinks that aren't water."

He nodded slowly, but I could tell he didn't quite understand. I lifted the Prosecco to my lips and let the bubbly taste swirl over my tongue. It was good, better than I'd expected. I took another sip and enjoyed the warm, fizzing sensation as it slid down to my stomach.

"Lucien."

We turned at the same time and Lucien stepped closer to me in a fluid movement. Carlo Romano stood in the doorway, his hands behind his back. He was a tall, lean man with dark hair slicked back over his head and glittering black eyes. His nose was a little hooked and his mouth was a fine gash across his jaw. The only evidence of his age was a few bits of gray hair by his ears and a few creases across his forehead. He might have been handsome if he hadn't looked so...predatory.

"Ah, Carlo, good to see you," Lucien said, switching to Italian.

They shook hands and Lucien stepped to the side, his hand grazing my naked back as he pressed me forward. The contact of his skin against mine sent a jolt right through me and my nipples tightened.

"Olivia Barone," Romano said, taking my hand and brushing his lips across it.

My body was still tingling from Lucien's hand against my back and Romano's touch sent another jolt of electricity through me. His gaze dropped for a moment and I glanced down to find my nipples were hard and clearly visible through my bra and dress.

"You've certainly grown up, Olivia," he said.

"Thank you," I said, unsure what else to say.

He smirked and turned to Lucien, who was standing perfectly still with his eyes as impassive as ever. Nothing ruffled his feathers, not even seeing Romano look at my breasts.

"I'd like to see you after dinner, Lucien," he said "In my study."

"Of course, sir," Lucien said smoothly.

"Now," Romano said. "There is a waltz starting and I would like to dance. Lucien, may I have the pleasure of dancing with your fiancée?"

I opened my mouth to protest and then shut it. Romano was the boss, the king of the outfit, and I had no right to refuse him anything. Lucien inclined his head and stepped back and Romano took my hand.

His fingers were hard and long and they engulfed mine. I kept quiet as he led me out to the middle of the dance floor and the room fell silent. I looked over my shoulder and everyone was staring at us and whispering. I frowned and turned back to Romano, who put his hand on my lower back and pulled me closer to his body. He smelled clean, like pine.

The orchestra struck up and the room was filled with a slow waltz. As Romano began spinning me in a whirl of light and sound, I remembered what Lucien had said earlier. I straightened my back, picking my shoulders up, and tilted my chin until I was looking squarely in the boss's hard gaze.

"You are very beautiful, Olivia," he said softly.

"Thank you." I swallowed.

"Is that all you can say?" He cocked his head and I realized that he was toying with me. Or perhaps he was toying with Lucien. It was hard to tell.

"No, sir," I said softly.

I looked over my shoulder and saw Lucien standing at the corner of the room with his drink resting in his fingers. His body was relaxed, his gaze impenetrable, as he watched me in Romano's arms. As his eyes met mine, something flickered through them and a muscle twitched in his jaw.

"I heard that you're staying with Lucien now," he said.

"Yes, sir."

"How do you find the Esposito mansion? A little cold?"

I glanced up. "No, sir."

"Perhaps only when Lucien comes to your bed then. He is a man made of ice and steel," he said thoughtfully. "If you can get him to crack, you'd be the first."

I flushed. "He doesn't, sir."

"Doesn't what?" Romano frowned down at me.

"He doesn't come to my bed," I said quietly. I didn't want him to think Lucien was taking advantage of me, although I wasn't sure why I felt the need to defend him against Romano.

He studied me for a moment as the music changed, slowing down. "He has far greater self control than I would then."

The dynamic changed as I realized that Carlo Romano wanted me, despite the fact that I was already promised to Lucien. My breath quickened and I bit down on my lower lip, a wave of anxiety spreading through me. I forced my face to remain relaxed as I smiled at him and his thin mouth curved.

"Walk with me," he said. It wasn't a request.

I felt his hand on my naked back, drawing me through the crowd. I turned as he slipped through the door and saw that the place where Lucien had stood moments ago was empty. My gaze skimmed the crowd, but he was nowhere to be seen. Panic rose in my chest and it took everything I had to keep calm as Romano ushered me into the hallway.

"The night is beautiful, join me in the garden," he said in Italian.

"Yes, sir." My voice sounded husky.

We walked down the driveway to the rose garden on the other side of the front yard. The garden was edged with rose bushes and an intricate, metal fence. Romano opened the gate and ushered me through, closing it behind us with a click that set off every alarm bell in my head.

"Lucien Esposito is a very important man," Romano said carefully. "But then you come from an important family, so you're surely a match made in heaven. All thanks to me, I was the one who recommended it."

I kept quiet.

"What sort of man do you think he is?"

I paused at an archway covered in white roses. "He seems like he'll make a good husband," I said, choosing my words with care.

I wasn't sure why, but I didn't want to discuss my fiancé with his boss. It made me incredibly uncomfortable.

"He is loyal to me, is he not?" Romano asked after a moment.

So that was what he was after. Did he suspect Lucien of something? I frowned, wondering what on earth could have led him to believe Lucien might not be loyal. It was widely known that honor and duty to the outfit were the cornerstones of Lucien Esposito.

"Of course, we all are," I said swiftly.

I looked up at the mansion glittering beyond the rose garden. I was feeling incredibly helpless without Lucien, alone in the dark with a man whose power was limitless. He could take out a knife and slide it into my heart right here and there would be no one to stop him.

"Of course," said Romano, nodding. "Lucien is one of the good ones, the best really."

"He's very respectful, I have no complaints," I said.

Romano took my arm and slid it under his, the warmth of his body permeating my skin. I glanced up at him as he moved through the garden, talking absently of the party and asking after my family. I responded politely, my body loosening as I grew more comfortable in his presence.

I glanced down at his hand as he paused beside the fountain in the center of the garden. There was a faint mark on his finger where his wedding band had sat. I knew his wife had died a few years ago during a shooting in one of the outfit's restaurants. I was also aware that their marriage hadn't been a happy one and Romano had scarcely bothered to conceal his relief at his newfound freedom.

"I never realized how beautiful you are," he said. "Lucien is a very lucky man."

My throat tightened as I attempted to swallow. "Thank you, sir."

His hand came up and touched my stomach between my ribs, just below my breasts. My nipples tightened, more from the simple contact of his skin than arousal. He dropped his gaze and it lingered over my breasts for a long, thorough moment.

"You really mean to tell me that Lucien hasn't touched you?" he murmured.

"Lucien wouldn't...he hasn't," I breathed, my heart pounding.

Romano stepped closer to me and I backed up, the stone edge of the fountain pressing into my bare back. A shiver went through me as his fingers skimmed over my hip and every nerve tingled with alarm.

I shifted my thighs and realized my panties were wet, sticking to the bare folds of my sex. Was this my body's fear response? I didn't feel aroused, I felt scared. Forcing myself not to attempt to flee, I lifted my eyes to his face and found him studying me with a hungry expression. He was handsome, in his own way, not so different from Lucien. They were both made men, lethal and sexual to a degree I didn't fully understand yet.

Romano tugged my skirt up, baring my leg from the knee down. Without thinking, I dug my fingers into the fabric and ripped it from his grasp. His eyes flashed and he took a step forward, trapping me against the fountain.

"Please—please don't touch me," I whispered.

"I'm your boss, I have every right to touch you." The words came out in a hoarse rush, almost as if he growled them at me like an animal. A fresh wave of fear went through me and I wrapped my arms around my body, hoping desperately it might help deter him.

"You're wet right now, aren't you? Is that why you won't let me touch you? Or is it because you were lying and Lucien already claimed his rights with you?"

"Lucien wouldn't—"

"If you're under the impression Lucien is a good man, you're in for a disappointment, girl," Romano said. "Now, are you going to spread your legs for me or not?"

I needed to get out now. My vision started to tunnel and my mouth went horribly dry. Romano's body pressed up against mine, his hard hips pushing into my thigh, grinding his erection against me. I jerked my body and he seized both my wrists, gathering them in one hand to hold me still.

His touch slid up my inner thigh beneath my skirt and I gasped, choking back a cry of protest. Then his fingers skimmed beneath my skirt and found the scrap of lace over my hips and his body tensed against mine. He released a harsh sound, cross between a moan and a growl.

"Please," I whispered. "Don't do this!"

Why did he want me badly enough to force himself on me? Was it simply because he found me attractive or was I merely collateral in a unspoken pissing contest between Lucien and his boss?

My heart pounded so hard I could scarcely hear anything as he bent over me and his dark eyes found mine. His lips parted and I caught the flash of his white teeth in the darkness, bared in a primal expression. I wrenched my hands fruitlessly back, trying to free myself from his iron grip, but he ignored me.

His fingers curled around my panties and he tore them from me in a swift movement. I cried out, pushing back against him, at the sudden pain as they ripped away. Then his fingers pushed between my thighs and all the blood rushed to my head in a wave of panic.

Some kind of primal, survival instinct kicked in and I disengaged from my body. I was barely aware of his touch past the roaring in my ears. Sickness welled in my stomach and I pulled against his grip until he released my wrist. I clamped my free hand over my mouth as the world spun.

"So you do still have your maidenhead. That's a surprise," he said. "I'd have taken you the moment you turned eighteen."

He pulled his fingers back and brushed my dress down. The world came back into focus as I stared up at him. There was no remorse on his face; he'd probably done this to other women enough times that it didn't bother him anymore. Tears of confusion and shame filled my eyes and slipped down my chin.

"What did you do?" I whispered.

"Don't worry, I didn't break anything," he said casually. "I'll admit I'm a touch jealous of Lucien."

My throat was thick, like a lump was stuck halfway down, and I reached up and wiped the tears that slid down my cheek. He sighed and his thumb came up and ran underneath my eyes, smearing the tears across my skin.

"Your makeup is running a little," he said softly.

"I'd like to go back inside," I said, forcing my voice to steady. "I need to use the restroom."

Ducking from his grasp, I started across the rose garden, leaving my ripped panties in a heap on the dewy grass. He walked me back to the mansion without speaking and when we entered the front hallway, he took me by the upper arm.

"You'll not speak of this to anyone," he whispered, his breath hot against my ear. "If you do, swear to God, I'll make you and your fiancé pay for it."

My heart thudded in my ears as I nodded. I was desperate to get away from him, and when he finally released me, I fled down the hall to the bathroom at the far end. It was empty and I ducked inside and slammed the door and locked it.

I just needed a moment to process what had happened, what he had done. Where was Lucien and why had he let Romano go off with me?

But I knew the answer to that question already. Lucien didn't have the power to stop Romano from doing anything. If he wanted to declare our engagement void and take me as his mistress, he could do so and no one could stop him. If he wanted to keep assaulting me at parties, no one had the power to stop that from happening. Not even Lucien.

It was a long time before I felt ready to leave the bathroom.

CHAPTER FIVE

LUCIEN

Watching her with Romano made my blood pound in my ears like a jackhammer. It was everything I had to keep my composure, to keep from crushing my glass in my fist. To keep from crossing the room and wrenching her from his arms.

I narrowed my eyes as he leaned forward, his mouth close to her ear, and whispered something. And she blushed and said something back with her eyes lowered. It was too much, I wasn't going to be able to control my expression.

I strode from the dance floor and out into the hall, cutting across to the kitchen. My mind was a whirl of images, of Olivia on the floor of her bathroom, Olivia in the car beside me with her legs crossed and the arch of her foot on full display, Olivia walking down the hall in that red dress that showed off every curve in her body.

I was getting hard from the cocktail of arousal and anger flooding through me. I desperately needed a minute alone to cool down. The door at the far end of the hall opened and a slender, blond serving girl stepped out with a tray in her hand. Every nerve in my body zeroed in on her and she caught my gaze and faltered. She was pretty in her short, black dress and her legs were long and reminded me a little of Olivia's.

"Can I help you, sir," she said softly.

I knew that Romano hired women who were willing to hand out sexual favors as an extra service in between waiting tables. And I knew exactly what this girl was asking.

Taking a moment before I answered, I composed myself fully, concealing any emotion on my face. She stood quietly before me, her eyes following my every move. I hated this, hated that I was going to use her, even if she'd expected it.

"In the bathroom," I said shortly, gesturing to the one on the other end of the hall.

I took the girl by the wrist and ducked into the bathroom and locked the door. She drew back against the counter, her blond hair falling around her face as she caught her breath. I stared at her for a moment, my chest heaving.

"Get on your knees and suck me off," I said. "You offered, so go on and do it. Or was that all talk?"

I leaned back against the sink and she dropped to her knees, her fingers unfastening the front of my pants. I closed my eyes and remembered Olivia on the floor with her hand between her thighs. My cock sprang free as she tugged down my underwear and she opened her mouth, leaning forward.

Wait, I couldn't do this anymore, I was engaged. My hand shot out to cover her mouth and she jerked back in confusion. Before she could even speak, I'd tucked myself back into my pants and closed the zipper.

"Never mind," I said hoarsely.

"Did I do something?" Her brows drew together in confusion and I thought I detected a flicker of fear cross her face.

I shook my head. "No, I just got engaged and I forgot. Fucking around on my fiancé probably isn't the best way to start that relationship."

She sat back on her heels. "Well, she must be special because I've never had a made man think twice about cheating on his woman. I'm...I'm impressed."

Reaching down, I helped her to her feet. She adjusted her short, black skirt and I allowed my gaze to drift over her. Goddamn it, maybe I should have just let her suck me off. She had a beautiful body with full hips that slid up to a tapered waist and perky breasts. I shifted the front of my pants, trying to find a more comfortable position for my throbbing cock, but it was useless.

"Believe me, I'm no saint," I said, opening the door. "If you don't mind, I'll handle things from here."

She ducked from the room and I watched her ass sway as she made her way down the hall and disappeared into the kitchen. But it wasn't her body that I thought of after the door was locked and I was alone. It was Olivia's slender legs and arching ankles, her pretty, full breasts, and the little hollow at the base of her throat. The soft dip beneath her ear. God, it probably tasted amazing.

When I returned, Olivia stood at the edge of the dance floor looking miserable. Her expression caught me off guard and I wondered briefly if she'd seen me go into the bathroom with the girl. But that would have been impossible. More likely she was just feeling lonely and out of place. I cut across the hall and headed her way.

Before I could reach her, Romano appeared at my side with his son in tow. I'd never liked Aurelio Romano. Perhaps it was his obvious weakness from being raised with a silver spoon in his mouth and a father who praised his every move. Or perhaps it was the arrogant way he carried himself, looking down on every man under his father's command as if we were dirt beneath his shoes. Someday he would get what he deserved and I would be there to see it happen.

"I know we were going to discuss things later, but Aurelio wanted to talk about Sienna, so lets go and have a chat in the study before dinner," Romano said.

"Of course," I said, inclining my head.

I texted Duran on the way up the stairs and asked him to keep an eye on Olivia. As I stepped from the room, I glanced at her stiff form, her arms wrapped around her body and her face turned away. It bothered me how much her demeanor had changed in the last hour.

I followed Romano into his enormous study decorated in trophies of exotic animals and expensive paintings. Aurelio trailed in after us and shut the door, taking a seat. His father poured three glasses of brandy and sat down in the large chair behind the great, oak desk. I accepted one of the glasses and stepped back.

"You may sit," Romano said.

"I'm fine, thank you," I said.

The fact that I stood annoyed him, but he composed himself and leaned back in his chair, folding one long leg over the other. As his eyes drifted over me, a strange, satisfied expression crossed his face. Alarm bells went off in my head. Had he said something to Olivia while I was gone? I gazed at him for a long time, unwilling to be the first to break eye contact, and he looked back at me.

"I want to see Sienna," said Aurelio, breaking the tension. "She was promised to me a year ago and I've never even had a conversation with her. Now that I'm graduated, I expect we'll get engaged soon."

Sienna was my cousin, orphaned at fifteen, and left in my care. I'd sent her to an expensive, private college on the condition that she agree to marry a made man of my choosing when the time came. She'd traded her virginity, her freedom to choose her husband, and her future over for a degree in classic literature. It seemed like a raw deal to me.

Last year, Romano had approached me to set up a match between his son and Sienna. It would be good for the outfit, strengthen ties and ensure harmony between our families. The idea of seeing my ward on the arm of Carlo Romano's son turned my stomach, but I agreed to it anyway. Not because I was giving in, but because I wasn't planning to actually let them stand before the alter and speak their vows.

No, I had bigger plans for Sienna.

"She still has a summer class to finish before she graduates," I said.

"That doesn't mean she can't get engaged," Aurelio said.

I gazed at him impassively. "Where will you live with her?"

"I'm not sure yet, I might stay here for a bit," Aurelio said slowly. I could tell he hadn't thought about this until now.

"I think Lucien wants to see a more concrete plan before he hands over his cousin," Romano said lightly. "Get a ring, find somewhere nice to live in the city, and then come back and we'll talk more."

Aurelio frowned and I could tell he was more than a little annoyed. It didn't surprise me that he was champing at the bit. Sienna was beautiful, a prize not just in status, for the man who secured her hand. He probably felt insecure having her walk around campus without a ring on her finger.

"When can we expect your wedding, Lucien?" Romano said, turning back to me.

"Christmas," I said. "I think that's what Olivia said she wants."

It was a lie. For the purposes of my plan, I needed a December wedding.

"She's got you by the balls already, has she?" Aurelio said coolly.

I bit back the urge to snap at him and finally took a seat in one of the armchairs. The last thing I needed was for Romano or anyone else to believe I had a soft spot for Olivia already. It would be perceived as weakness and if things got ugly between me and the boss, she would find herself in danger. So I shrugged nonchalantly.

"Honestly, I don't care when I get married," I said. "I have a lot more important things to worry about."

"Trouble in your territory?" Romano asked, frowning slightly.

"No, we're just having some problems keeping the ports safe along the northeast river. Amadeo promised me back up last year when the Russians hit the winter shipment, but his men were attacked and now he's gun-shy. They're low on weapons."

"Duran hasn't been able to buy anything to replace them?" Romano asked, leaning forward to pull out an account book.

"He has a meeting later this week," I said. "He has thirty AR's coming, but we need more."

"Why isn't Barone offering his soldiers? He'll be your father-in-law by the time our winter shipment hits and he should be willing to help you."

"We're not on the best of terms, but I can try and get him to talk to me."

Romano tented his fingers and stared at me critically. "What did you do?"

"Apparently he didn't like that I asked for his daughter to live with me before the wedding. I think he feels I disrespected him."

"Is that all?"

"We were on fine terms before then."

"I'll have a word with him," Romano sighed.

"What was it you wanted to speak with me about earlier?" I asked.

"This, actually. I need to know how you plan to secure the northeast shipping ports before the winter. I need that product and I can't give you leeway like last time if you lose it."

"I promise, I'll keep it secure."

Romano leafed through his book and made a note in the bottom corner. "Amadeo's wife passed last month, which is likely why he's not been as responsive. I'm not sure why, but he was enamored of her, so I gave him a little breathing room, for a few weeks anyway. But that time is over. I'll speak with him after I talk to Barone."

"I do need his answer soon," I said.

"We need to do something about the fucking Russians before the winter," Romano said, his face darkening. "Either they back off or we end up fighting. Something has to give soon. Put pressure on Duran for more weapons—as many as he can get right now. Is this a money problem?"

"Supply chain issue," I said.

"Well, whatever it is, fix it."

"Yes, sir."

"You may go," Romano said, sitting back and waving a hand dismissively.

I loathed being treated like nothing more than a common soldier, but I concealed my emotions and rose smoothly. Aurelio glowered at me as I crossed the room and opened the door.

"Oh, and one more thing," Romano said. "Better keep an eye on Olivia. She's a lovely young woman and you never know what could happen."

Was he threatening her? I stared at him for a long moment before deciding his words didn't merit a response. Silence was safer. Inclining my head, I stepped outside and shut the door firmly behind me. From inside, I heard Aurelio laugh and anger sparked in my chest.

Someday they would both pay for their arrogance.

Back in the main room, I located Olivia by the bar. I checked my phone, but Duran had never answered my text, which meant he was probably somewhere fucking that redheaded girl. Composing myself, despite my rapidly draining store of patience, I crossed the room and put my hand on Olivia's back.

She jumped a little and turned, blinking up at me. I frowned, taking her chin in my fingers to study her face. Her dark eyes were a little bleary.

"How much did you drink?"

She lifted the glass of golden champagne, the enormous ring on her finger catching the light. "Just two glasses."

"That's a lot for someone of your size," I said, gently prying her fingers off the glass. "Perhaps we'd better take you home before dinner."

She stared after the glass as I handed it back to the bartender. I slipped my arm around her body and ushered her gently toward the door. On the way out, I pulled aside one of the serving girls and told her to let Romano know that Olivia was feeling sick and I was bringing her home.

She allowed me to help her into the Tesla and buckle her seat belt. Kneeling, I lifted her upper eyelid to check if her pupils were dilated and she pulled back, frowning.

"What are you doing?"

"Are you feeling tipsy? Or more than that?"

She sighed, looking a little better as she settled into her seat. "I'm just tired and a bit buzzed. I feel better now that I'm outside and I got some fresh air."

I studied her until she grew uncomfortable and looked away, her fingers twisting in her lap. Her eyes were a little puffy and red, but I wasn't sure if that was from drinking or something else.

"Can you stop looking at me? I'm fine, really," she said quietly.

I nodded and circled the car, settling into the driver's seat. She was quiet on the way home and when I pulled up to the house, the light fell across her face. She was asleep, her chest rising and falling peacefully. I carried her up the stairs and laid her fully clothed onto the bed.

God, she was beautiful. I was fucked if I thought I wasn't going to fall for this woman.

CHAPTER SIX

OLIVIA

WINTER

Months passed in the Esposito mansion without anything eventful happening. Lucien was polite and distant with me. We ate dinner together, fulfilled our social duties as a couple, but when the night came, he walked me to my door and left me there with only an absent caress across my back or hand. When I came downstairs for breakfast, he was always gone and he never returned to the mansion for lunch.

A few weeks after my arrival, Duran surprised everyone by meeting a young woman at one of Lucien's resorts and marrying her after just six months. Lucien was astounded, confiding in me that he never imagined anyone could convince his wild brother to settle down.

It didn't confuse me; Iris was easy to like and we became friends almost instantly. She was a little reserved, intelligent, and kinder to me than I was used to. I was flattered and surprised when she asked me to be her bridesmaid. A few weeks later, I decided to ask her to be mine. Knowing that I had at least one person in my wedding that I liked made the whole prospect less bleak.

Iris made living at the Esposito mansion bearable. We shopped, worked in the garden, and cooked together. It was with a pang of sadness that I stood at Lucien's side and waved goodbye as they embarked on their month-long honeymoon in Cairo, Egypt.

Then it was just Lucien and I and it would remain so for the next five weeks. Lucien spent even more time at his office. Apparently there was a delivery of something coming in via the river that required his constant attention. His work must have paid off around mid-November, because he came home visibly relaxed and we had dinner in his study that night. Before I went to bed, he tapped me under the chin and brushed a bit of my hair back. That little bit of affection was enough to keep me going for a while.

It was pathetic, but isolation did strange things to my head.

A week before the wedding, I stood in my room while the seamstress pinned my dress. Outside, it was already snowing lightly over the water and a light dusting of white stuck to the frozen ground. We would have a winter wedding, at Lucien's insistence, although I'd expressed to him that I wanted a spring, outdoor wedding. But Lucien said that wouldn't be suitable for an underboss and I knew it wasn't any use arguing with him.

I looked up at my reflection. The dress I'd chosen was beautiful and perfect for a winter wedding. The bodice clung to my breasts, traces of cleavage showing above the V neckline. The skirt was heavy satin that draped around me in an elegant swirl and the long sleeves were gauze with lace patterns like snowflakes over my skin.

I was beautiful and I wondered briefly if Lucien would think so when he saw me walk up the aisle. Or would he be coolly indifferent as he always was?

There was a soft knock at the door and I jumped. The seamstress looked up questioningly and I stepped down from the stool and crossed the room, cocking my head to the door to listen.

"Who is it?" I called.

"Lucien."

Since the night of the party, he'd hadn't come to my room unless he was dropping me off for the night. I frowned, my stomach fluttering with nerves. Was something wrong?

"I'm in my wedding dress, I can't come out," I said. "Is everything alright?"

"Yes, I just forgot to tell you that your mother called the house phone," he said. "And we'll have dinner early tonight."

"What did she want?" I asked, frowning.

I had purposely ignored my family. I didn't want to see my mother before the wedding. I didn't think I could handle being reminded of the pain of not having a doting and supportive mother readying me for the most important day of my life. Watching Iris's wonderful mother spoil her the weeks leading up to her wedding had been enough to keep me up at night in tears several nights in a row.

"She wanted to see you before the wedding," he said.

"Did you talk to her?" I asked, surprised.

"I was passing by so I answered the phone," he said. "I told her you would call her back."

I hadn't talked with my family since leaving the house, except for texting briefly with Cosimo a few times a month. I sighed and squeezed my eyes shut. "I'll text her."

"Do whatever you feel is best. I'm just the messenger," he said. "Just bear in mind that I'd rather not have discord at our wedding."

He was playing a game, he was always playing a game. I'd been to enough parties and dinners with him at this point to know that everything was a game of chess to Lucien Esposito. He showed up to a room full of lethal made men and their equally deadly wives and swept through them like a breath of icy air, freezing them in their tracks. And somehow, he dominated the men's conversation and charmed their women until they gazed up at him like he made the sun rise and set.

I hated the parties and dinners. Not because it was tiring to smile and pretend to make conversation with people I barely knew. No, it was because wherever I went, Carlo Romano's sharp gaze followed my every move like a wolf hunting its prey. Luckily, Lucien hadn't left me alone after that first night so I felt safe, but just seeing him turned my stomach.

The memory of his violating touch kept me up at night sometimes with bubbling anger in my gut. He had taken a piece of my innocence that night in the garden and now I had to live with that secret forever. It felt treasonous to even form the thought, but deep inside I wished he was dead. I wished Lucien would take the knife he kept in his desk in the study and tear it across his throat.

I stood in my wedding dress, listening as Lucien's footsteps died away and I was left leaning against the door with a hollow sensation in my chest. That night at dinner, we made casual conversation over roast chicken and vegetables. It was such a confusing thing to sit here with him, so much awkwardness and space between us, knowing that within a week he would be my husband.

Within a week, he would claim his rights.

I was too anxious to eat so I spent most of dinner cutting my food into little pieces. After a while, there was a knock on the front door and Lucien stood abruptly, gesturing for me to rise. I set down my glass and pushed back my chair and he took my elbow and pulled me from the room.

"Are you expecting company?" I asked.

"Yes, but I don't want you around for it," he said, his jaw tense. "It's outfit business and not safe for you to know about."

He pushed me into the hall and pointed in the direction of my door. A wave of humiliation washed over me and I bit my tongue and fought the urge to snap at him. Flip him off for treating me like a child. Instead, I released a huff and rolled my eyes before pivoting on my heel and marching down the hall.

"Olivia," he snapped.

I paused, turning. "What?"

"Don't fucking roll your eyes at me again." His icy gaze bit into me and a shiver of something that felt a lot like arousal went through my body.

"Okay," I said quickly, not wanting to rouse his anger.

"Please respond to me with a little more respect than that," he said coolly. "Yes, sir, will do."

I swallowed. "Yes, sir."

"Good, now go up to your room, please."

He turned and was gone, the crisp sound of his shoes on the polished floors echoing behind him. I stood in the hall for a moment and grappled with the sudden ache between my legs and then I ducked into my bedroom and went to change into my nightgown.

As I left the bathroom, I heard Lucien say something through the floor and someone responded to him in a Russian accent. I frowned, getting down on my knees to press my ear to the heating vent. Yes, it was definitely a Russian accent. How was that possible? The outfit had never been friendly with the Bratva, but over the last six months, tensions had risen to dangerously high levels. Why on earth would Lucien have a Russian in his house? And why was he so insistent that he conceal it from me?

I couldn't hear what they were saying and my curiosity was overwhelming. It would be incredibly stupid to leave my room, but I couldn't just sit here. I opened the door quietly and stepped back into the hall. The floors creaked in the middle so I kept to the edges as I made my way to the top of the spiral staircase.

They were in the living room. I could hear the gentle rise and fall of their voices as I began ascending the stairs in my bare feet. My heart pounded in my chest and my palms were slick with sweat. This was a stupid thing to do and every nerve in my body screamed for me to turn around. Begging me not to provoke Lucien's wrath.

The lace on the edge of my nightgown tickled the middle of my thigh with every step. I probably should have put a dressing gown on because my nightgown was little more than a silk slip. It would make Lucien even angrier if he caught me sneaking around half naked than it would if I was properly clothed.

Just as I stepped onto the landing, the living room door opened and Lucien walked out. His eyes fell on me and he froze, his mouth pressing together in a hard line. My heart hammered against my ribs and I let out an involuntary squeak and stepped back, tripping over the corner of the stairs and sprawled onto the floor. The sound reverberated through the house and Lucien's jaw twitched beneath his expressionless eyes.

"What is it?"

It was the Russian man. I heard his footsteps and then he appeared at Lucien's elbow, a glass balanced in his fingers. He was broad, a little larger than Lucien, and he wore a fine, tweed vest, a white shirt, and trousers. His face was all angles, high cheekbones, a straight nose that jutted out over a thin mouth. His hair was a dusky brown and his lashes and brows were so light I could barely make them out. The eyes that fell on me were a striking shade of bright blue and they glittered with amusement.

"Who is this?" he said.

"Believe it or not, that is my fiancée," Lucien said, sighing.

I got to my feet and back up against the railing. "I'm sorry, I came down for some water. I'll go back."

"Olivia Barone, isn't it?" the Russian said.

He stepped gracefully from the doorway and held out his hand, palm up. I hesitated and then laid my fingers in his and he brushed his lips across them.

"Viktor Anatole, godfather of the Bratva," he said. "A pleasure to meet you."

What was the head of the Russian mafia doing in Lucien's house? I glanced at my husband and a quick shiver went up my spine. It seemed there was more to him than I'd realized.

"A pleasure to meet you," I echoed nervously.

"You are a lovely woman."

"Thank you, sir."

If it had come from anyone else, I would have felt uncomfortable. But Viktor had a strong, almost paternal demeanor that put me at ease. I blushed and couldn't keep my face from breaking into a small smile.

"Olivia, go upstairs now."

Lucien's voice was quiet, almost deadly. I backed up, my throat going dry, and nodded. Without looking back, I scrambled up the stairs and fled down the hall to my room.

Once there, I curled up beneath the thick coverlet and lay with my heart pounding in my ears. Would Lucien finally snap and release some of the anger I just knew was brewing behind his expressionless face? I closed my eyes, dreading whatever would happen when morning came and listened to the distant rumble of voices below me.

I woke at some point in the night to the faint smell of cigarette smoke. Heart pounding, I sat up and looked around. The bathroom light was on, falling across the floor and illuminating the room in a dusky glow. Directly opposite the bed was the chair from the desk and in the chair sat Lucien.

My stomach flipped and I bit down hard on my tongue. He still wore his dark dress shirt and pants, but they were disheveled and a bit of his hair fell over his forehead. There was a lit cigarette hanging from his fingers, the tip glowing cherry red in the dim light. I could make out his eyes, hard and icy cold, beneath lowered brows.

"Curiosity will kill the pussy cat, Olivia," he drawled, his voice a little slurred. "Or whatever the saying goes."

Something about hearing the word pussy come out of Lucien's heartless face roused a dull ache despite the hammering of my heart. I sat up a little further and leaned forward on my knees to peer through the darkness at him. He blinked slowly and his jaw worked.

"Have you been thinking about it?" he said.

He was drunk. A ripple of shock went through me at the realization. Letting go of control was so unlike him that it hadn't occurred to me it was possible for him to get drunk.

"You've been drinking," I whispered, drawing back against the headboard.

"You are correct." He pointed at me with the cigarette before looking up at the ceiling and putting it to his lips. His throat was bared to me, broad with a rivulet of sweat running down to the space between his collarbones.

"You should probably go back to your room," I whispered. Seeing him like this frightened me.

"No," he said. "And I asked you a question. Have you been thinking about our wedding night?"

My throat went dry. "Yes."

He cocked his head. "What do you think about?"

"The same things I was before. I wonder how we're supposed to have sex when we barely know each other."

He laughed, a short, humorless sound. "Sex is fucking easy. Fucking is easy. It's everything else that's goddamn hard."

I kept silent, unsure how to answer him. He got to his feet and moved with a slow, silent tread to the end of the bed. He put the cigarette to his mouth, breathed in slowly, and rested a hand on the corner post. I could make out a sliver of skin between the buttons of his shirt.

"Do you know what happened with the Romano girl?" he said, his voice thick with something I didn't recognize. It sounded almost like pain.

I did. Everyone did. But he wanted to tell me, to spill the words out to someone, so I kept quiet.

"Carlo Romano was so convinced I'd fucked his daughter...she was a lying whore and she'd gotten knocked up by one of his soldiers. He didn't want to believe it was by just a common soldier and she lied and told him the baby was mine. That bastard kept me in a cell, naked, helpless. He tortured me, cut me, burned me. There was one night when he flayed bits of skin from my back."

My stomach roiled. "I'm sorry, Lucien."

He sighed like he'd heard it all before. "He wanted me to marry her and she was obsessed with me...I think she thought lying that I was the father was the best way to entrap me. I said I wouldn't until I saw a paternity test and Romano was livid. He was cutting the skin off me, piece by piece, and he made his daughter watch. So she broke and admitted the baby wasn't mine. And Carlo fucking Romano wanted things to just go back to the way they were, as if he hadn't just spent three weeks torturing me, starving me, treating me worse than an animal."

There was a note of despair in his voice. He raised his eyes to mine and they were like falling through cold water, sinking slowly into an abyss that threatened to suffocate me.

He pointed at me with the two fingers that held his cigarette. "And don't think I don't see the way Romano looks at you. Like he wants to bend you over and fuck you like you're his paid whore."

I gasped, heat surging through my body. "He wouldn't dare."

"He wouldn't. But I will."

The silence that followed his words was deafening. My body was on fire, my mind inundated with images of Lucien taking me from behind, his broad, slender body driving into me without mercy. My breasts were hot and sensitive, rubbing against the inside of my nightgown. There was a needy pulse between my legs and, as we sat there looking at one another through the dark, I felt something wet slip down my thigh.

"Swear to God, I can smell how wet you are," he said. "But that's probably just the whiskey talking."

Never in the last seven months of knowing my fiancé had I imagined that he was capable of saying anything like this. It was a whole new side to him that held me totally enraptured, ready to do anything just to hear him speak to me like that again.

He put the cigarette back to his perfect mouth and held the smoke in his lungs. "I saw you," he said, the smoke drifting out as he spoke.

"You—you saw me?" I dug my fingers into the pillow. Was he talking about the night Romano had touched me in the garden?

"Do you masturbate, Olivia?"

My mouth dropped open as I stared at him, too shocked to speak. There was nothing on his face to suggest he was uncomfortable with such a direct question. His eyes bored into me, waiting for an answer.

I floundered. "No," I lied.

"Really?" The corner of his mouth jerked up.

"I don't," I whispered, mortified.

He tapped his fingers against the post, leaning back to look up at the ceiling as he expelled another lungful of smoke. Drunk Lucien was far more expressive, far less guarded. Although those eyes were still made of solid, icy rock.

"The night you got here, I came looking for you early," he said, his voice thick with something. Perhaps it was desire. "And I didn't find you in your room, so I stepped inside and there you were. On the bathroom floor, touching yourself. You had stockings on...I watched you come all over your fingers. Goddamn, I don't think I've been that hard before. Ever."

Absolute mortification rose in me and I dug my fingers into the sheets and drew myself back against the headboard. I remembered that night, how confused and aroused I'd been from sitting beside him in the car. How I had slid down onto the floor and stroked my clit as I imagined him pushing his lean fingers into my pussy. How his hard eyes had swam into my mind as pleasure spiked through my body.

"How dare you," I whispered.

"It's my home," he said. "I can say and do exactly as I please."

He loomed over me, dark, disheveled, and drunk. There was no doubt in my mind that he would do just that and there was nothing I could do to stop him. I swallowed, my throat dry as his eyes bored into me with a flat stare. Did they ever light up or flicker with any kind of expression at all? Or would I lie beneath him on our wedding night and let him drive into me as he looked at me from behind a wall of icy cold?

"I want to see you do it again," he said huskily. "Lie back and spread your legs."

I shook my head quickly, pressing my thighs together. "No, I don't think I should."

"I'm your husband and you answer to me."

"No, you're not."

"I'm as good as. Now, do you want to be a good girl and do as I say?"

A bolt of arousal went through me and my pussy throbbed. My breath was coming in short gasps as I slid onto my back and pulled the sheet up to my waist. He considered me for a moment and I was sure he would rip the sheet away and force me to bare myself to him. But he only brought the cigarette back up to his mouth and expelled the smoke in a steady stream. Sweat glittered on his forehead and throat and his gaze glinted in the darkness. He was the devil, wrapped up in ice and wreathed in smoke, and he was going to make me burn from shame and pleasure and everything in between.

"Please let me keep the sheet on," I whispered.

"No, I don't think so."

He pulled it from me in a smooth gesture, leaving my legs naked, my pussy barely covered by the hem of my nightgown. Then he stepped back, going to the desk and putting out his cigarette. He moved back to me, rolling his sleeves up slowly to reveal his forearms. They were marked in dark tattoos, slashes of ink across his golden skin.

"Please," I whispered. "I don't know if we should do this."

"Do what? I'm just enjoying watching you do what you're too ashamed to admit you enjoy," he said.

"I didn't ask for any of this. For you or our wedding."

He put his knee on the bed and bent over, his hands pressing down on either side of my thighs. "Neither of us did. But it was always going to end like this. You and me, in this bed together because someone more powerful than either of us willed it."

What was he trying to say? That he didn't desire me? My gaze drifted down to the front of his pants and there was a telltale ridge beneath the fabric.

"But...you want me," I whispered.

"I do. A lot of things don't make sense. This is one of those things."

He lifted the fabric of my gown, his eyes fixed on me, and spat onto my clit. My hips jerked at the contact of wetness and he moved away, turning his back to me as he went to the desk to light another cigarette. His saliva made an achingly slow trail down my sex.

"Be a good girl and touch yourself for me," he ordered.

He came back to the bed, his fingers unfastening the front of his shirt. For a moment I thought he was stripping, but then I saw the sweat glittering over his ridged chest. He was riled and warm with desire and drink. I let my eyes glide over the sliver of torso visible through his open shirt, at the tattoos that decorated his skin.

"Touch yourself the way you did in the bathroom that night."

My fingers trembled as I slid them down my body and spread his saliva over my clit. A pulsing ache went through my pussy, clenching my core, and wetness leaked down onto the sheets. His eyes fixed on my fingers as I worked and his mouth was parted, the cigarette hovering just inches from his lips. He was transfixed and knowing I was the reason made my head spin.

I slid my other hand down and used the tip of my finger to draw back the hood of my clit. His mouth moved slightly and his tongue flicked out and ran over his bottom lip. My other finger swirled over the sensitive nub and my hips arched as pleasure flooded through me. I was already on the edge, swollen and wet from his eyes on me. I changed my rhythm, circling the edges of my inner folds, putting off my orgasm.

He knew I was teasing him and he didn't like it. "Finish yourself," he ordered.

Locking eyes with him, I slid the pad of my index over my clit and came hard. Our gazes remained locked as pleasure rippled through me and I bit my lip, but a sharp, gasping cry burst from me. My body stiffened again and again, clenching as my release worked through my hips and thighs.

"You come fast," he said. "For a woman."

I exhaled, shaking and confused if he meant to insult me with his words or praise me. My emotions roiled and for some reason I was crying, hot tears slipping through my lashes and wetting my hair.

"He touched me," I whispered.

Lucien froze. "What did you say?"

Everything that had been knotted up in me for the last several months came rushing out like an uncontrollable flood. I had to confess what had happened or it would eat away at me slowly every time I laid eyes on him.

"The first night I was here, at the Romano's house," I whispered, my voice shaky. "I danced with Romano and he took me out to the garden and he—he did things I didn't want. Then he said he would hurt us both if I told you."

"What did he do?" Lucien's voice was quiet, deadly. All of the arousal was gone from his face and body, leaving him as cold as ever.

"He asked me about you, if you were faithful to him and I said yes. And then he wanted to know if you had had sex with me yet and I said no, but he didn't believe me. He pushed me against a stone fountain in the garden and tore my panties off...and put his fingers...you know.

Then he said that he was surprised you hadn't taken my virginity yet and that he would have taken it the minute I turned eighteen."

"Fuck," Lucien said quietly.

"I was too scared to tell you," I whispered. I took a shuddering breath and tried to compose myself. "He told me not too, that he would hurt us both if I did."

His jaw worked a little.

"Sometimes I think I could have stopped it," I said miserably. "But he was really strong."

"I'm going to kill him," Lucien said casually.

I gasped, sitting up and drawing the sheet around my lap. "You can't say things like that, Lucien."

He took a drag from his cigarette, totally composed again. "No, I'm going to kill him and Viktor Anatole is going to help me. You met him last night. He's the Pakhan for the Bratva, the Russian godfather. We've collaborated since the tension began to rise, faking conflict between us to throw Romano off our trail. He'll give me the firepower I need if things go wrong. We will kill Carlo Romano and his son."

I gaped at him. "And then what?"

"And then I will be king," he said. "And you will be queen."

So that was what his talk of chess, of me being queen, had been about. Now that I thought about it, he'd made a good many cryptic remarks alluding to his plans, but they hadn't made any sense at the time.

"How long have you been planning this?" I whispered.

He considered my question for a moment. "Since the moment Romano threw me into that cell and tortured me like I was nothing more than a rabid dog. He is unfit to be boss."

"Why would Viktor Anatole do this for you? It's probably a trap," I said, fear making me frantic.

"He's doing it in exchange for peace, for redrawn territory. And I'll give him a bride and seal it by making him family," Lucien said.

"A bride?" I whispered.

"He and my cousin, Sienna, will marry once Romano is dead."

I had met Sienna a few times before and she was a sweet, headstrong woman a few years older than I. Lucien couldn't be so cruel as to send her away to wed the godfather of the Russian mafia, a man old enough to be her father.

"You would force Sienna to marry him?"

He blinked and I thought I saw a ghost of irritation cross his face. "She made a deal with me. I allowed her to get her degree and now I get to marry her to whomever I choose."

"That's barbaric!"

"It's the reality of our world," Lucien said. "We're both making the same sacrifice. Now, I'm sure I don't have to swear you to secrecy about this. If you tell, it won't just be me who's killed. It'll be all of us. You, Duran, Iris, likely even Sienna."

I shook my head. "I swear, I won't tell anyone."

He regarded me for a long moment. Then he stepped back and put the cigarette to his mouth and ran both hands over his hair, slicking it down. He paced from one side of the room to the other, finally stopping to linger by the desk where he'd left a glass of amber liquid. He downed it in a single gulp and turned back and beckoned to me.

"Come here, Olivia." His voice was a little hoarse.

My stomach fluttered, but this time it wasn't from fear. I slid from the bed and padded barefoot across the room to where he stood. It hadn't hit me before now how tall he was, how broad his body was towering over mine. Something about his crisp shirts and suits made him seem tamed, almost contained, but now that he was disheveled and his naked torso hovered at eye level, his presence was almost stifling.

"I will kill Romano, not just for what he did to me, but for daring to touch you," Lucien said flatly. "I'll slit his throat for hurting you."

My nipples hardened and my heart began thumping wildly. I had no doubt he would do just that. It felt strange, but it also felt good, to have someone in my corner at last.

"And I won't let you out of my sight around Romano," he said. "I wish I could say you don't have to see him again, but I don't have that power yet. Now, you need rest and I need to get sober. Goodnight."

Then he was gone, the sound of his shoes echoing down the hall after him. I stood in the middle of the room with my heart pounding from the roller coaster that had been the last hour. It was going to take a while for me to fully register what he'd just told me, to understand the gravity of what Lucien had planned.

CHAPTER SEVEN

LUCIEN

The morning after I went to Olivia's room, I woke with my mouth dry and my stomach roiling. As I pushed a finger to the back of my throat and vomited up the rest of the whiskey in me, the memories of last night came flooding back. My mind was a confusing mess, inundated with images of her on her back, her legs spread, her fingers playing in the valley between her thighs.

Fuck. None of that should have happened.

I leaned back against the bathroom wall and ran a hand over my face, rubbing my burning eyes. It was just days before my wedding and I was horrifically hungover and Duran was texting me asking if anyone was going to pick him up from the airport because he'd forgotten to have his car dropped off. Steeling myself, I got to my feet and turned the shower on and stepped beneath the ice cold spray.

It didn't matter that I'd told her about my plan to kill Romano. I was using our honeymoon as a cover for a secret trip to Moscow to fine-tune my plans with Viktor, so she would find out soon anyway. But the news that Romano had touched her sent a whirl of rage and guilt through me. While I'd been in the bathroom with a girl I didn't even know, Olivia had been outside at the mercy of that man.

I was going to enjoy every second of killing him.

Despite my anger, images of Olivia last night kept flashing through my brain. My dick hardened despite the cold spray running over my body. That place between her thighs, that sweet thing that was always in the back of my mind, was everything I'd imagined. Her bare pussy a soft shade of light brown with delicate folds and a clit I couldn't stop imagining between my teeth.

And her legs. The way they stiffened when she came, her lower back lifting a little off the bed. For some reason, I couldn't stop thinking about how her slender feet arched as that gasping cry ripped from her mouth. I'd never had an interest in any woman's feet. Legs, yes, but feet had always seemed so decidedly not erotic to me. Until Olivia.

I closed my eyes. Into my mind swam a mental image of her splayed out on the countertop before the bathroom mirror with her ankles up on my shoulders. Beautifully delicate ankles with blue veins pulsing beneath the skin, sliding down to elegant arches, her perfectly manicured toes curling as I moved in and out of her tight pussy.

What the hell was wrong with me?

My phone rang loudly and I sighed, leaning my head against the shower wall. My cock was so hard it hurt and the incessant sound of my phone split my throbbing head like a knife. I needed to get it together and handle my responsibilities like I wasn't still hungover and borderline drunk.

The next few days were filled with wedding preparations. Duran took me to the tailor for last minute alterations to my suit and then we went down to one of our clubs for a drink. I'd insisted that I didn't want a bachelor party, but several of the other men from the outfit showed up. At least Duran had the restraint not to hire strippers, although I suspected that had more to do with Iris forbidding it than anything else.

It was a late evening of drinking. After my third glass, I had the bartender bring me out water because I wasn't going to be hungover on my wedding day. I needed to be fully sober, collected, and ready to face not only my boss, but every underboss in the outfit.

And I wanted to be in a fit state to bed my wife on our wedding night.

The next day, at eleven in the morning, I stood at the front of the cathedral with Duran at my side. The pews of the church were packed with members of the outfit, hundreds of eyes all fixed on me. Olivia's family sat in the front on the left side, her mother's eyes glazed with excitement. Disgust rose in me at the sight; she wasn't excited for her daughter, she was eager for her new social standing.

I kept my shoulders back, my spine straight, my face impassive, and my eyes guarded. Today was a day to show strength, to show unity, because soon enough I would raze the Romano family to the ground. Then I would be their boss, their king.

But, until then, I was a dutiful underboss obediently wedding the woman his boss had picked for him.

The music changed and Iris walked up and took her place opposite Duran. Then the doors opened and the tempo picked up and there was Olivia on her father's arm. I was too transfixed by the sight of her to even notice the detestable man who led her up the aisle, the man who had vented his temper on her for years. I would deal with him when the time came.

The woman on his arm, my wife, drew my attention and kept it. She wore a white gown that draped around her legs and trailed behind her as she walked. The torso of her dress clung to her like a second skin, the sleeves going down to her wrists, and the neckline forming a sharp V down between her breasts. Her cleavage was extraordinary and it took all I had in me to drag my eyes away before I embarrassed myself.

Her father didn't embrace or kiss her when he handed her over. In fact, he seemed incredibly relieved to be rid of her as he shook my hand and went back to his seat. His behavior didn't surprise me anymore; it was clear to me that my wife's family regarded her as little more than chattel to be traded for social status.

I looked down at Olivia and for the first time it hit me how frightened she was. Her slender fingers wrapped around her bouquet of roses were pale and her mouth trembled a little as she looked up at me. A part of me wanted to reassure her, but I couldn't show that kind of weakness in front of the outfit. Instead I held out my palm and she let Iris take her bouquet and placed her clammy hand in mine as we turned to the altar.

I scarcely remembered the wedding mass or our vows. But when it came time for us to kiss, time slowed a little as we faced each other. Other than brief touches here and there, we'd remained completely separated. And we'd barely spoken since I'd gotten drunk and forced her to touch herself in front of me.

God, I was a monster.

All eyes were on us, waiting for me to make a move. I slid my fingers around the back of her neck and bent low, my mouth brushing hers and I waited for her to respond. She stayed completely still, her cold mouth a hair's breadth away from mine. I kissed her swiftly, her lips soft against mine, and drew back to face the congregation.

There was a round of applause and the wedding bells struck up as I swept her down the aisle. I had no wish to stand around outside the doors to greet the guests, but it was tradition, so we didn't have a choice. I kept her close to me, my hand on her waist, as Romano approached to congratulate us. To my relief, Iris stayed on her other side the entire time, buffering her against the swell of guests.

It took at least an hour for us to greet everyone, with the exception of Olivia's parents, who kept their distance after I sent her mother a cold glare. Then I took her by the hand as the bells rang out for the last time, and led her down the steps to the limousine. Olivia gave a quiet sigh when the doors shut, a little color returning to her face. She seemed more relaxed now that we were alone.

"You didn't kiss me in the church," I said.

She gave a little sigh. "I'm sorry. I've been so anxious, I can barely remember the ceremony. I guess I just froze up."

I dropped my gaze to her mouth, a little swollen from how hard she was biting it. Yes, I had technically kissed her, but I hadn't gotten a chance to taste my wife the way I wanted to. Leaning forward, I took her by the elbow and drew her close. She looked up at me, her dark eyes wide, and her breasts rose and fell over her neckline as she breathed hard.

I kissed her, parting her lips just enough to swipe my tongue through and taste her mouth. It was everything I could do to keep from moaning. My wife tasted like nothing I'd ever experienced, like sweet champagne and lust all mixed together. I put my hand on her throat to steady her head as I drove my tongue between her lips, needing another taste of her. Fuck, she was exquisite.

I pushed her dress up to her knee and my fingers found her calf, smooth as silk. She gave a moan as I traced the inside of her knee and I felt the sound reverberate in her throat beneath my hand. When she drew back for a breath, I bent her head to the side and kissed up the impossibly soft skin of her neck to the little valley below her ear.

My brain had one track and it was moving fast. I pulled her onto my lap, my cock twitching as her thighs clenched on either side of my legs. It would be so easy to just open the front of my pants and pull aside her panties and sink into her wet heat. I could tell she wanted this, that she wouldn't refuse me. But no, she deserved to lose her virginity properly, not in the back of a limousine on the way to her wedding reception where everyone would know what we'd done.

We paused, both breathing heavily, the air thick with desire between us. God, I wanted her so badly it was a tangible ache. Her dark eyes glittered with trepidation and her breath caught as she gazed up at me. If she kept looking at me like that, I was going to have the driver take us home and skip the reception altogether.

"You want me," she said. She'd said this before and each time it seemed to surprise her.

"I do," I said.

She hesitated. "Sometimes it's hard to tell. You're very...stoic. Maybe a little cold."

"Not the first time I've heard that," I said.

"It just surprises me when you want me," she whispered.

"You're beautiful. Any man would be a fool not to want you." I picked up her hand and slid it between us, pressing her palm against the hard ridge beneath the front of my pants. Her eyes widened and a pink blush crept up her throat and stained her cheeks. She looked beautiful like this, her hand on my hard cock and her face flushed with arousal and embarrassment.

"I can take it out if that's not enough proof," I said.

"Lucien!" she gasped.

The limousine slowed to a halt and I leaned over and pulled the curtain aside. Our families and the rest of the outfit waited by the hotel entrance. Sighing, I turned back to my new wife and brushed the strands of her bangs from her face.

"They're waiting for us," she said softly.

I nodded, lifting her from my lap so she could check her hair and makeup in the fold down mirror. There was something oddly erotic about watching her lean forward, her focus on her reflection. Her middle finger reached up and dabbed a bit of gloss onto her lower lip and then she pressed her lips together to spread it. She had a beautiful, full mouth and I found myself imagining her going down on her knees before me, her fingers unfastening the front of my pants.

Pull it together, Lucien.

"Are you ready?" I asked.

She nodded and I opened the door, taking her hand, and we stepped out onto the strip of white carpet waiting for us. I hated this, all the formality, and I could tell my nervous wife wasn't pleased about it either. The crowd broke into applause again. They were eager to eat, drink, and dance all night, far away from their problems for a little while. After all, life in the outfit was fragile and we had to enjoy the time we had.

At the head table, I kept my hand on my wife's thigh. She was quieter than usual and her pale hands worried at her food, cutting her chicken into smaller and smaller pieces. She did that a lot, picked apart her meal until it was a mess across her plate. I wasn't sure why and I hadn't bothered to ask her because the subject of meals sent her into spirals of anxiety.

She reached out and picked up her champagne flute and drained it. The waiter moved up to the table to refill it, but I put my hand over the glass and shook my head.

"No, thank you," I said firmly.

"I wanted more," Olivia said.

"If you eat some of the food that you've been mutilating, you may have more."

She sighed and shoved a spoonful of sweet potatoes into her mouth, chewed wearily, and swallowed. Unswayed, I sipped my beer and watched as she trudged through half of her plate of food, her eyes downcast. She kept glancing up and then down again as though she expected me to snatch her plate away. I looked over and caught a fleeting disapproving look on her mother's face from across the room and it clicked into place.

"She said something to you, didn't she?"

Olivia nodded. "On the way in. She grabbed my hip and said I'd gained weight."

I studied her body for a moment. Her mother was right, Olivia had gained about a half-size, but that was a net positive in my book. Her waist was still slender, but her breasts had filled out a little and her ass and hips were firm and rounded. The hollows around her collarbones had finally filled in. The way her leg had felt when I'd pushed my hand beneath her dress in the car had conjured a series of images of thrusting into her hard enough to make her hips and thighs quiver. I shook my head quickly and looked back down at my plate.

"You needed to gain weight. Your mother is a bitch who unfortunately crawled out of hell to be here today, but that doesn't mean she gets to talk to you that way," I said coldly.

Olivia gasped, her mouth falling open, and then she started laughing hard. Her shoulders shook and her silverware clinked on her plate. A few of the nearby tables turned to stare. I squeezed her thigh briefly and she got the message, taking a gasping breath, and composing herself.

"I'm sorry, I just wasn't expecting that," she whispered.

I looked up and the wedding planner was gesturing at us and pointing to the dance floor. It took me a moment to understand what she was trying to tell me, and then it clicked. It was time for our first dance. Olivia looked up at me as I pushed back my chair and took her hand. Taking their cue, everyone stood and gathered around as I led her out to the center of the floor.

She was frozen in place, her face paler than ever. It was dawning on me that my wife had stage fright.

"Can you waltz?" I asked quietly.

She nodded. "I took four years of dance. My mother said I had to learn."

I held up three fingers to the band and they nodded and the wedding planner lowered the lights. For a moment it was just us and the breath between our bodies and then the band struck up a Viennese waltz.

She was a little wooden at first, but then she leaned into me as she warmed up. As the music swirled on, her body became pliant in my arms and she allowed me to guide her through the movements. There was a moment when I lifted her in the air as I turned and I saw her face and it almost broke my shell wide open. Something about the way her dark eyes glittered and her face flushed had me right on the edge.

The music ended and there was a round of applause, but there were more whispers than anything else. I led her off the dance floor and back to our table with my hand on her lower back. The last thing I wanted was for Romano to try to claim the next dance with her. She didn't need that kind of stress on her wedding day.

"You can dance," she said breathlessly.

"My mother taught me. It was one of her required hallmarks of a gentleman that she insisted Duran and I learn," I said. "That and how to use the correct fork, dress properly, and speak French."

"No, you can really dance. Like...really dance." Her dark eyes were still glazed with excitement. "I don't think any of my instructors ever danced with me like that."

"I certainly hope they didn't." I kept my face impassive.

She ran her tongue over her lower lip and I caught a hint of desire in her eyes, but she dropped her lids and concealed it. "Wait, so you can speak French too?"

"I can. Why?"

She took a sip from her champagne. "Is there anything you can't do?"

"Apparently, I can't get my wife to feel comfortable at her wedding reception," I said.

She looked guilty, which wasn't my intention, and dipped her head. "I'm sorry, I'm just not used to being the center of attention. It makes me anxious."

"Well, let's just get through the rest of this reception as quickly as we can then," I said lightly.

The evening wore on and drink flowed until the men were loosening their collars and their women were falling asleep in their chairs. Then came the expected, but not welcome, jovial calls for me to do my duty and bed my wife. Olivia and I sat at the head table as I sipped my cognac and she turned bright pink at the offending cries. I'd known this would happen, but I'd forgotten to warn her how crude people could be at the end of a night of drinking.

"We should go," I murmured in her ear. "It's just upstairs."

"We're not going back to the mansion?" she asked.

"This is one of the outfit's hotels and they've kept the bridal suite reserved for us. It's only customary and polite we stay here."

Our guests had gathered by the door, urging us to our feet. I led my wife past them, my hand firm on her lower back. Her eyes were downcast and a mortified blush stained her cheeks and throat. As we paused at the door and I raised a hand in farewell, I caught Romano's gaze from where he stood by the bar. There was a glitter of raw jealousy in his eyes.

CHAPTER EIGHT

OLIVIA

The bridal suite was beautiful. The living area was set with ivory couches, a marble coffee table, and a baby grand in the corner by the windows draped in silk curtains. Lucien slid the lock down and took my hand, his palm rough and dry beneath my cold fingers, and led me toward the bedroom.

The bedroom matched the living area in elegance and opulence. Heart hammering, I hovered near the door as Lucien went to the dresser on the far side and began taking off his watch and jacket. He'd worn all black for the wedding—black shirt, tie, vest, and jacket, and it suited him. My first impression of him when I saw him at the front of the church was of steel and ice.

"Would you like to shower?" he asked.

I nodded. "I might need help getting out of this dress," I said quietly.

He took off his vest and crossed over to where I stood, taking my upper arm and turning me around to face away from him. His fingers brushed the bare skin between my shoulder blades as he unfastened the clasp at the top and slid the zipper down to the small of my back. A tingling shiver went through me. For a moment, I thought he might brush the fine hairs from my neck and kiss it, but then he stepped away.

He hadn't cracked and shown any emotion this whole time, not even when I'd walked up the aisle. When he'd taken my breath away with that completely unexpected dance, I'd thought I'd caught a flicker of something behind his eyes, but then he drew the shutters closed once more.

I went into the bathroom and slipped out of the gown and laid it over the chair in the corner. Then I stepped in the shower and washed with shaking, anxious hands and dried off. There was a vial of creamy lotion on the sink and I spent a long time rubbing it into my skin, making sure every inch of my body was soft.

Iris had packed me a bag that she said was for the wedding night, but I hadn't opened it yet. I unzipped it and found a silk slip in pure white with a lace thong to match. Underneath it was a little glass vial of honeysuckle perfume and a bottle of lubricant. Surprised, I picked it up and found a note taped to the back.

Use this even if you don't think you need it the first time around. And remember to relax and tell him what feels good for you. You deserve for it to be good! X

There was a winking face drawn at the bottom and I smiled, grateful for her words. I hoped she was right, that I did deserve for sex with Lucien to feel good. Setting aside the box, I slipped on the silky lingerie and brushed out my hair. Then, butterflies in my stomach, I stepped out into the bedroom.

My husband sat on the end of the bed looking at his phone. He lifted his head and his eyes fell on me, roving over my body, but his face remained impassive. I knew him well enough at this point not to hope for a big reaction, but I'd hoped for something more. Trying to ignore my disappointment, I padded softly on my bare feet around the side of the bed and sat down by the pillow.

"I'll shower and be out in a moment," he said, getting to his feet.

He didn't look at me when he got up, but I glanced over my shoulder as he pulled the door shut and a rush of triumph rose in my chest. He might be able to conceal his emotions behind those icy eyes, but he couldn't hide the hardness straining beneath the front of his pants.

I'd half expected him to take his time in the shower, but he washed quickly. I lay on my side, studying the wallpaper, and listened to him move about in the bathroom. When he came out, I sat up and my breath caught a little at the sight of him.

He wore only a pair of black lounge pants. His hair was wet, glossy black, and hanging over his forehead. There were tattoos all over his torso, a few marred by the faint scars across his chest and shoulders. I'd expected him to be more scarred, but most of the ink on his skin was intact in the front at least.

He was well muscled, but it was in an elegant way where everything blended together nicely. There was dark hair across his chest and down his stomach where the V of muscle disappeared beneath his pants.

My core gave a throb as I got to my feet slowly and crossed to him. He held still as I drew near and inspected his tattoos. The large one on his upper stomach roused my curiosity the most. It was a black and white traditional of a dead sparrow hung by its feet with a noose. Above it was a pair of skeleton wings spread over his pectorals and when I leaned closer I could make out tiny roses blossoming over the bones. His arms were a blend of writing and similar images. There was a strong theme of death and flowers.

"Find what you're looking for?" he asked.

"I was just curious," I whispered.

I looked up at him, barely reaching his shoulder now that I was barefoot. His eyes fixed on mine and a shiver went through me as they drew me in. Even as my husband, our warm flesh just inches apart, he was still locked behind an impenetrable wall.

"How would you like to do this?" he asked.

I swallowed past the dryness in my throat. "I don't know. I—I was hoping you could...sort of guide things. I assume you've done this before."

His mouth twitched. "I have. But, admittedly, it has been a long time since I've had actual sex."

"Oh," I said, surprised. "Well, you're still more experienced than I am."

"What would make you feel the most comfortable?"

I thought about it for a moment, grateful for his consideration. I'd half expected him to push me down on the bed and have his way with me, never mind if it hurt. He was an underboss with a reputation for being a lethal killer after all.

My eyes dropped down to the front of his pants. "I—I know this might be a little strange, but I'd like to see it first. I just don't want to go in blind."

His mouth twitched again and I was beginning to understand that that was his version of a smile. I kept my eyes lowered, too mortified to meet his gaze, and watched as his lean fingers found the tie of his pants.

"You can look, you can touch," he said. "I certainly don't mind."

His fingers slowly untied the drawstring on his pants and he loosened the waist. My heart thumped in my chest, sending a flush up my throat, and I clenched my hands behind my back. In a fit of courage, I glanced up at him, but he was completely unperturbed. Baring himself to me didn't seem to phase him one bit.

He pulled down the front of his pants and there he was in front of me, all hard like the rest of his body. The dark hair over his groin was trimmed and there was a tattoo of a skull with flowers blooming from the empty eye sockets just above his penis. He was thick around and longer than I'd expected. There was a vein running up the side of his length to the ridge encircling the tip.

"Oh," I said quietly.

"Disappointed?" he said.

I shook my head. "It's larger than I thought it would be. I don't know...I'm not sure that's going to fit honestly."

He laughed and I looked up at him, startled. It was a short, hoarse sound, but it was definitely a laugh. It didn't reach his eyes though, they remained as impassive as ever.

"I'm sure we can get it to fit," he said. "I noticed in the bathroom that Iris gave you a bottle of lube, so we can use that to make sure it doesn't hurt."

"I think it's going to hurt," I said thoughtfully. "Iris said it hurt a lot for her the first time."

"That's because Duran is an impatient motherfucker," he said.

"Okay," I said slowly. "May I touch it?"

He nodded and I reached out and traced the tip of my finger down the hot length of his cock to the rounded head. It was much softer than I'd expected and I ran my fingertips over him, enjoying the sensation. When I touched the underside, the whole length of him twitched and I pulled my hand back, startled.

"It's alright," he said. "It's just more sensitive there."

He pulled the waistband of his pants over his cock and reached up to run a finger under my chin and turn my face to his. I kept still as he bent and his mouth touched mine softly, easing my lips apart, his hot tongue swiping over mine. When he pulled back, his chest was rising and falling rapidly.

He backed me up slowly until we were against the bed and then he lifted me and set me down on the edge. He took a seat opposite me, leaning forward to brush my hair back from my throat, and ran soft kisses down the side of my neck.

"You got to see something of mine, now I'd like to see something of yours," he murmured.

"You want to see my...my pussy?" I said.

"I meant your breasts," he said. "I'll get to your pussy in a moment."

I nodded and he drew back and unhooked the straps of my nightgown and eased them from my shoulders. The white silk fell away to reveal my breasts, my nipples hard and flushed with arousal. I didn't get a chance to see the expression on his face because he pushed me onto my back and laid his broad body across my legs, pinning me to the bed.

Between us, I could see the hard ridge of his cock beneath his pants. He bent and his tongue flicked out, catching the pale brown of my nipple. A shock of pleasure went through me, curling down my belly and into my core. His mouth worked my sensitive nipples in soft strokes, sucking them gently onto his tongue. I closed my eyes, releasing a sigh as heat spread through my body, wetness pooling in my sex.

"Does that feel good?" he asked, lifting his head.

I nodded. "Very."

He eased my silk slip down my body until I was clad only in my lace thong. As his fingers skimmed down my body, he released a low moan. My pussy throbbed at the sound, a sensation of desperate emptiness blossoming between my legs. Despite my anxiety, I felt the desperate need for him to fill me, to thrust his hard cock into my pussy until I was satisfied.

Faster than I knew what was happening, he pulled me to the end of the bed and knelt before me, his face just inches from my sex. His hard palms cupped my calves, raising them up until I fell back, propping myself up on my elbows.

"You have fucking exquisite legs," he said.

"Thank you," I whispered.

His cold eyes flicked up at me and I thought I saw something in them. A flicker of warmth maybe? Or was it desire? The rest of his body betrayed his need in the sharp rise and fall of his chest and the flush at the base of his throat.

He skimmed my legs with his fingers, exploring every curve of my thighs right up to the lace barrier across my pussy. Then he moved back down, his mouth pressing against the soft skin of my calves again and again. Then it was on my ankles, kissing and flicking with his tongue. I jumped a little as he bit the sensitive skin on the top of my foot.

"I've never in my life been turned on by a woman's feet," he said, without a hint of embarrassment. "But the first night we went out and I saw yours in those heeled sandals, it made me rock hard. Especially whatever you do to your nails."

"It's French tips," I said huskily.

"Well, whatever the hell it is, it's doing a number on my dick," he said. "I've been having fantasies of fucking you on your back with your ankles on my shoulders...and goddamn, it gets me going."

His admission sent a flood of wetness to my pussy. Somehow this icy, gorgeous man wanted me and he wanted me badly. The realization increased my arousal tenfold and I let myself slide back with a whimper, the ceiling swimming overhead.

CHAPTER NINE

LUCIEN

She fell back against the bed and her back arced just a little, her hips working against the air, desperate for friction. A quiet sound escaped her lips, a breathy moan, and she closed her eyes. I slid my fingers beneath the lace thong that barely covered her pussy and peeled it from her hips, letting it fall to the ground. My breath quickened and my dick throbbed as my eyes fell on her sex, the light brown folds that looked as soft as silk.

I gently pressed her legs apart, but she stiffened.

"What's wrong?" I asked, doing my best to be patient with her.

"Nothing, I'm sorry," she whispered. "I just got nervous."

I kissed the side of her knee and down her calf as I parted her thighs. Her delicate folds were wet with arousal and her clit was swollen. For a moment, I just stared at her, dumbfounded by the sight of her lovely pussy. Then the overwhelming need to taste her flooded me and I bent my head and ran my tongue from her entrance to her clit.

Fuck, she tasted good. Sweet and a little tangy, like expensive champagne.

Her hips jerked and she released a cry. I pushed her up onto the pillows and settled between her thighs, slipping my right arm up her body to play with her nipples. I'd waited a long time, watching her slender body move about my house, wandering what it would be like to bury my face between her lovely thighs. I was going to savor this moment.

I ate her slowly, listening to her body to find her most sensitive points. She wasn't very vocal so it was difficult to tell what felt good, but I was able to pick up small things like the quickening of her breath or the slight clench of her thighs against my head. Her body seemed to respond best to quick, short strokes against her clit, but at least twenty minutes passed of that and she still hadn't climaxed.

I lifted my head. "Am I doing something wrong?"

She released a shaky breath. "I don't know. I'm right on the edge, I just can't get it to happen."

"You touch yourself at least every day, don't you?" I asked.

Pink stained her cheeks. "Yes," she mumbled.

"It's nothing to be ashamed of. But I think you've conditioned yourself to come like that and it's probably going to take some work to get your body used to finishing on my tongue."

"Oh," she said, sounding a little surprised. "I didn't know."

I ran my tongue over the entrance of her pussy, swallowing her wetness, and got to my feet to remove my pants. She watched me with wide eyes as I retrieved the lube from the bathroom and returned to the bed.

"I'd like to fuck you for a minute and then I want to try something," I said. "I'll be as gentle as possible and if you hurt, tell me."

She tensed as I knelt between her legs and began working lube over her pussy, dipping into her tight channel. She clenched, her slick entrance pulsing once around me, and my cock throbbed. I circled her clit with my thumb and her eyelids fluttered and her lips parted. She was so responsive, she just needed time to let her body relax and get comfortable with my touch.

I set aside the lube and slid atop her, our faces just inches apart. Her slender legs wrapped around my waist in a trusting gesture that almost made me lose control. Her ankles brushed the sides of my thigh, soft and delicate. Digging my fingers into the sheets beside her head, I took a moment to calm down. I wasn't going to embarrass myself on my wedding night.

She gasped as I guided my cock to her entrance and slipped the tip inside her wet heat. My God, she was tight. I gritted my teeth against every muscle in my body that wanted to thrust into her, to take her hard and ride my orgasm out against her body. No, I wanted this to be good for her, I wanted to experience her pleasure, to feel it intimately as she came around me.

"Are you alright?" I asked.

She nodded, her eyes glassy with desire and nerves. I rotated my hips a little as I worked myself inside her until I was fully sheathed, her slick walls contracting around me. She dug her nails into my ribs, making me wince, and I bent and kissed her mouth. Her tongue curled out and caught my upper lip and I almost came. The sensory overload of being buried in her wet heat with her tongue on my mouth was almost too much.

"Does it hurt?" I breathed.

She shook her head.

I pulled halfway out and thrust back in and she gave a hoarse cry and her body jerked.

"Ouch," she whispered, her brows drawing together.

I reached between us and my fingers came away smeared with blood and lube.

"I think that was the worst part," I said. "Are you alright for me to keep fucking you?"

"I think so, it just hurt for a moment, but it just feels...strange now. Like pressure, like there's no space left."

I kissed the side of her throat and thrust back into her. This was heaven, being buried in her slick, clenched pussy with her scent staining every part of me. Her body was warm beneath me and I lost myself in her, fucking until her breasts heaved with pleasure instead of pain.

Gathering her in my arms, I flipped onto my back. She stilled against me and then sat up slowly until she was upright, straddling me with my cock buried between her thighs. I took her hips between my palms and rocked her gently and her eyes widened at the sensation. God, she was beautiful above me like this, her full breasts heaving and her lips parted.

"You feel big," she whispered. "It's different at this angle, I can feel you all the way up."

"Yes, feel me inside you," I breathed, shifting my hips to rub against her G-spot. "Now reach your fingers down and find your clit and touch yourself."

She looked hesitant, but she obeyed, sliding her hand down. Her stomach tensed as her fingers began working gently between her thighs. Her eyelids fluttered and her pussy clenched around my cock.

"It's good," she said breathlessly.

"God, you feel perfect. Can you ride me while you touch your clit?"

She moved her hips experimentally, finding a slow rhythm atop me, and began stroking her clit. Her fingers dug into my hip as she steadied herself against me. My cock was throbbing, harder now than I could ever remember it being. There was something so deeply erotic about watching her chase her pleasure, her hips working hard against mine, her lower lip caught between her teeth.

After a few minutes, she gave a sharp gasp and her movements grew unsteady as a tremor moved through her body. I took hold of her thighs to keep her upright and her grasp fumbled against my arm, pulling my hand free so she could weave her fingers between mine. The gesture made me pause for half of a second. Did I feel more than just lust for my wife?

I didn't have time to contemplate my emotions because my wife was orgasming on my cock and every rational thought left my mind. I seized her hips, lifting her up an inch and hammered into her, forgetting that she was still tender. Her pussy contracted around me hard, the hot wetness clenching around my length, gripping me with each pulse.

She came down from her high slowly as I fucked up into her, pleasure rising in my hips. Her back arced, her pussy slick around me as I thrust deep. As her orgasm wound down, she made a quiet sound, a defeated whimper, and I came hard, emptying myself into her tight, wet heat.

"Jesus Christ...fuck," I swore.

She was shaking a little as I lifted her from my body and laid her on the bed beside me. She rolled onto her side, her hair falling across her face, and lay still as she caught her breath.

I lifted her thigh to part her legs and she didn't protest as I inspected her pussy. She was slippery with lube, a little bloody, and my cum was seeping out onto her inner thigh. A rush of satisfaction filled me at the sight. She was mine now.

I bent and kissed her forehead. "You took that so well."

"Thank you for not hurting me," she whispered. "At least, not very much."

I gathered her against me, knowing she needed warmth and comfort after what we'd done. She seemed a little stunned and overwhelmed. She must have been exhausted because it took about five minutes for her body to fall slack and her breathing evened. I closed my eyes, releasing a sigh, and followed her soon after.

CHAPTER TEN

OLIVIA

I woke before Lucien did and slipped from the bed to shower. The muscles between my thighs ached as I sat down on the toilet. Turning on the shower, I stepped beneath the warm spray and let it pound down on my back and wash away the sticky wetness from the night before. The evidence of what he'd done to me that was now seeping down my thighs.

A shiver went through me. Last night had been exhausting and overwhelming, but it had been far and away better than anything I'd imagined. I'd thought he would have his way with me and then roll over and fall asleep. But no, he'd given me pleasure that shook my body to the core and then he'd held me as I slept. Was there warmth somewhere below all of the ice and steel that was Lucien Esposito? Or had he given me an orgasm only as a point of pride?

But even better than the pleasure was the relief. My virginity, this thing I'd carried around with me, that my mother had used to shame and manipulate me for years, was gone. My whole body felt lighter.

I washed the blood and semen from my thighs and scrubbed my hair with cherry blossom shampoo. As I wrapped myself in a towel, the door opened and Lucien walked in looking sleepy. His hair was rumpled and there were faint smears of blood on his cock. He didn't say anything, just stood by the toilet and, to my mortification, relieved himself. I kept my eyes stoically on my reflection as I rubbed cream into my face and neck.

He moved to the sink and kissed my neck as he bent past me to pick up his toothbrush. "Good morning." His voice was deliciously husky.

"Good morning," I said.

I reached for my pink bag and took the bottle of birth control out and unscrewed the cap. Lucien glanced over and frowned, setting his toothbrush aside.

"What is that?" he said.

"Birth control," I said, frowning.

"It doesn't look like it," he said, taking the bottle from me. He studied the label and then dumped a pill out into his hand. "Who gave you this?"

"My mother set up for the doctor to send it to me when I moved in with you," I said. "Can I have it back?"

He shook his head. "I don't know what the fuck this is, but it's not birth control. I know what the various kinds of pills look like and this isn't one of them. Also, it's in a generic bottle."

"I did notice the packaging changed," I said nervously. "Do you think it's something...dangerous?"

His face was dark and all traces of sleepiness were gone from him. "Your mother has no reason to kill you. But the security of our marriage benefits her and your family."

"What does that mean?' I asked, confused.

"I would bet money these are fake," he said.

I stared down at the pill in his hand and everything clicked into place. He was right, the pills didn't look like any birth control I'd taken before. And my mother had spent her life ensuring I would wed Lucien and she would surely do anything to make sure it stayed that way. To make sure there was no chance Lucien would go back on his word.

I swallowed a dry lump in my throat. "That means...last night—"

"It means I fucked you without contraception," he said, every emotion gone from him. He was as cold and distant as he'd been at our first meeting.

Turning on his heel, he left the room and I heard him unzipping his suitcase. I stood by the sink with my stomach flopping, feeling incredibly foolish. How could I have taken fake birth control for almost a year and never realized it? A surge of hatred toward my mother rose in my chest, choking me and turning my stomach. What she'd done was violating.

"Olivia," he called from somewhere outside the bedroom.

I slipped on the silk nightgown from the bedroom floor and padded out into the living area. Lucien stood in his boxers in the kitchen with a glass of water in his hand.

"Come here and take this," he ordered.

I drew near and he held out his palm with a small white pill in it. I glanced up at him, looking for some reassurance, but his eyes were as blank as ever.

"What is that?" I whispered.

"Morning-after pill. Take it," he said, without room for argument.

I accepted the glass of water and swallowed the pill and only when it was gone did his shoulders relax a little. He bent forward and kissed my mouth briefly and headed toward the bedroom. I followed him, hovering in the bathroom door to watch him strip naked and turn the shower on. He had a strong, attractive body and it seemed like he knew it because he moved just as confidently naked as when he was clothed.

"Will everything be alright now?" I asked hesitantly.

He stepped beneath the open shower and let the water run over his head. "We caught it early on, so it should be fine. I sent for real birth control for you so we'll have it for most of the honeymoon and in the meantime I'll use a condom. Don't worry about it, I have it handled."

The honeymoon. In all the anticipation of the wedding, it hadn't occurred to me to ask about it. It was customary in the outfit for the bride's family to handle the ceremony and reception and the groom to make all the honeymoon arrangements. The subject of where we were going had never been brought up to me as it wasn't deemed my responsibility.

"Where are we going?" I asked.

"I'll tell you when we get there."

I frowned. "Why can't I know now?"

He glanced over at me. "Take off your nightgown and get in the shower with me."

His commanding tone sent a pleasant shiver through my body and I obeyed, letting the fabric fall from my body. He pulled me against his chest, the hard muscles of his torso slippery and warm. Then his mouth brushed over the side of my neck and hovered by my ear.

"Always assume any building belonging to the outfit is bugged," he whispered. "We're going to Moscow, to Viktor's mansion."

I glanced up, looking around the room. "Bugged?"

"Better to be paranoid than dead."

"Oh," I said, barely audible through the spray of water. "So we're staying in Viktor's house for our honeymoon? Isn't that a little awkward?"

"It's bigger than my house. We'll have plenty of space to do as we please. And when we're not busy, Viktor and I will have time to work on our plan to put Romano under the ground. For everything he did to me and everything he did to you."

I stilled in his arms. Sometimes I forgot who he was, that he was an underboss and a practiced killer. He'd been so attentive last night, so reassuring...almost tender. But as I looked up into that cold, blank stare, I believed him fully capable of killing anyone he pleased.

When we stepped outside the hotel, Lucien's Tesla was already parked in the driveway with our bags in the trunk. The wedding guests were either gone or still sleeping off the night before so we were undisturbed as we left the hotel and drove off toward the airport.

The drive was only twenty minutes, but it felt like forever. Lucien was quiet, leaning back in his seat with his hand hanging over the steering wheel. I'd wondered why he never had his driver take us places, but now that I knew him better, it made sense. Lucien wasn't a man who gave up control. He drove himself, and wherever he went, there was a pair of pistols in his shoulder holsters, tucked beneath his fine suit.

Just as we pulled up to a landing strip where a private plane sat waiting for us, Lucien reached over and squeezed my thigh. The gesture sent a shock of electricity through me and my nipples tightened. It was possessive, just like the hand on the small of my back as he helped me into the plane a few moments later.

I was a little flushed from his touch when I sat down and put my seatbelt on, but Lucien didn't seem to notice. His phone had just rung and he was pacing back and forth talking quietly in another language. I leaned a little closer and realized he was speaking French rapidly, throwing a few English words in here and there when his grasp of the language failed him. He was far more expressive when he spoke French, although his face remained blank. His hands moved more and he gave a shrug here and there that I hadn't seen when he spoke English or Italian.

He hung up the phone and sat down beside me, loosening his tie. A smattering of hair was visible beneath his collar and I had to drag my eyes from it.

"Duran?" I asked softly.

He nodded. "How did you know?"

"You said your mother taught you both to speak French," I said. "I don't know anyone else who does."

"It's proved useful," he said.

The stewardess brought out a tray loaded with eggs, toast, espresso, and a single mimosa in a crystal glass. I tasted the mimosa and looked over at Lucien who was tearing bacon apart with his fingers between sips of his espresso. The cup looked ridiculously tiny in his large hands.

"You don't want a drink?" I asked.

He glanced up. "I need to be alert. You don't have to be, I'll make sure you're taken care of until we arrive."

I obeyed, settling back in my seat. The constant tightness in my chest that had plagued me for the last six months was gone. I was wedded and bedded and free of my family at last. Perhaps it was my newfound freedom, but my mind didn't rebel at the idea of eating so I filled my stomach with eggs and toast. Perhaps I was finally beginning to realize I was rid of my parents once and for all.

The mimosa made me incredibly sleepy and the last thing I remembered was Lucien adjusting my seat so I could lie down. Then warm darkness enveloped me and I slept.

CHAPTER ELEVEN

LUCIEN

I felt a little guilty about giving her a sleeping pill, but it was the easiest way to make sure she stayed ignorant. And ignorance meant safety. Viktor had only shared the location of his house with me and made me sign a binding contract that I wouldn't disclose it to anyone else. So I put a pill in her mimosa and she slept hard for the next ten hours.

Viktor had sent a car with darkened windows and an eerily silent driver to pick us up at the airport. I found a thick blanket in the backseat and wrapped it around my wife, keeping her close on the drive. The Anatole House rose in the distance as we drove through the dark, snowy, Russian landscape. It was situated at the edge of town, surrounded by a large, manicured lawn and garden and acres of woodland.

I stretched out in the back seat and laid my wife on her back beside me, letting her head rest on my thigh so I could adjust the blanket around her shoulders. Her mouth twitched and she moaned softly in her sleep. Heat stirring in my groin, I watched her breasts rise and fall in gentle movements, my mind awash with images from our wedding night.

The car slowed and I heard the scraping of iron gates drawing back and felt the road change as we pulled up a driveway. Then we came to a halt and the driver came around the side of the car and opened our door, a shock of frozen air hitting my face.

I was aware of the size and opulence of the Anatole house, but seeing it in person gave me pause. It was truly enormous, towering high above like an ivory palace, like something built for a Victorian king. At least four stories high, it had hundreds of windows and two rows of balconies carved with ivory railings. The front entrance was made up of three large glass doors that were hung with silver wreaths. I'd been so wrapped up in my wedding and my consuming desire to kill Romano, I'd forgotten next week was Christmas.

I'd never liked holidays. Usually my father got drunk early in the day and left the house to fuck his mistress while my mother forced a smile and pretended everything was alright. Dinner would be tense, my mother sitting stiffly at one end of the table, probably hoping my father wouldn't hit her in a drunken rage after Duran and I were sleeping.

I wouldn't allow that to happen in my home. I might not be wildly in love with her, but Olivia would never know fear or sadness the way my mother had. No, she deserved more than that. I would give her everything, make her a queen over the outfit. And our children would love us, not fear us the way Duran and I had feared our father.

"Mr. Anatole is waiting to welcome you," the driver said.

I stepped from the car with Olivia in my arms, still wrapped in the blanket. The snow crunched under my feet and my breath hung in the air, the cold so intense it seized my lungs. The lights were on inside, golden and warm, and as I drew near, a housekeeper opened the door and dipped her head as we stepped into the front hallway.

"Lucien."

Viktor stood at the far end of the hall in a dark gray suit with a glass of brandy in one hand. He moved softly down the long hall, a Bratva king in his glittering castle, and halted before me. His brows moved in a hint of concern as he leaned forward to see who it was I held, wrapped in a blanket, in my arms.

"Your wife is sleeping?"

"I gave her something so she wouldn't see where we were going," I said.

"Probably best," Viktor said. "My housekeeper has your room ready. You may bring her upstairs and then, if you would like, join me for a glass of something in the living room."

I nodded. "Thank you."

The housekeeper led me upstairs, pushing our bags in a cart. The house was enormous, even larger than mine, and the amount of rooms and doors we passed as we made our way to the second floor was dizzying. We stopped at the far end of the hall and the housekeeper pushed open the door to the last bedroom and stepped aside.

"*Komnata Zvezdnogo sveta*," she said softly. "The room of starlight. Mr. Anatole has had it cleaned and prepared for you. He thinks you will enjoy it because of the beautiful view of the garden. And of the sky. You will see when it is the day."

"Thank you," I said, carrying Olivia's limp body over the threshold.

When the housekeeper had unloaded our bags and left us alone, I laid Olivia on the bed and took a moment to look around. There was a lamp on low and it cast a pale light over the vast room. The carpet was deep blue and so thick my shoes sank into it almost an inch and the walls were a pure white. Overhead, the ceiling was a half-dome, with heavy, dark wood beams. It was the far wall, as long as the hallway in my house, that made me understand why this was called the Starlight Room. The entire length was glass and below us stretched the shadowy garden and above us was a sea of stars so thick and bright they seemed unreal.

This was a strange and beautiful world. Not the kind of world brutal men like Viktor and I had any right to occupy. I looked down and saw my wife laid out on the bed, her face relaxed in sleep. This was the perfect place for her—safe, beautiful, and almost magical.

I undressed her gently, tucking her naked beneath the thick comforter, and left the room.

It was strange walking through the dark house. The hallway that cut through the first floor was lined with paintings, all probably worth hundreds of thousands of dollars. The floor was a deep blue rug over polished, dark oak that caught the faint light of the chandeliers hanging overhead. The house was different than what I was used to—there was an older, more cultured feel to it that I liked.

I found Viktor in the enormous living room. A fire burned in the vast fireplace below a large painting of the Russian countryside and several mounted deer heads. There were three couches in a square and to my right was a full bar, the polished wood and dozens of glasses glittering in the low light. Viktor leaned against the bar, his brandy rested in his palm.

"What will you have?" he asked as I drew near.

"Irish whiskey," I said.

"No vodka? This is Russia," said Viktor, pouring my glass and passing it to me.

"I'm here for three weeks. I'll have plenty of time for vodka," I said.

"An Italian and a Russian walk into a bar," Viktor said.

"And what?"

He considered me, his face thoughtful. "Kill the king, I suppose."

I clinked my glass against his. "I'll drink to it."

"No, let's drink to peace," he said. "To a bond between family. After all, I'll wed your cousin before next year is out."

"To family then," I said.

Viktor was a strange man and I always struggled not to let my guard down too much around him. He was only ten years my senior, but there was something paternal about his angular face and sharp eyes. Perhaps it was the way he filled every room with his calm, controlled energy.

He valued politeness, tradition, and culture more than anyone I knew. Yes, I had seen him slit a man's throat without a muscle moving in his face, and yes, he was a brutal godfather and a trained killer, but he was also charming and, without meaning to, I trusted him.

"How is your wife?" he said.

"She's alright, I just gave her a mild sleeping pill," I said.

Viktor moved to sit on the couch before the fire, crossing his legs neatly. I sat opposite him, the heat from the fireplace seeping into my bones and chasing the cold away. I'd expected Russia to be cold, but not like the brutally icy chill that had enveloped me the moment I'd stepped from the car.

"You know Romano best," Viktor said. "Tell, me what's your plan?"

"We spend the next three weeks planning everything out carefully while I'm here. Then during the Romano's New Year's Eve party, one of my men will break into the security system, shut it down, and that allows me to get Romano away from the party and kill him. You and your men will surround the house to provide firepower should we need it."

"And then what? Your men rally around you?"

"Once the boss and his son are dead, I'm next in line," I said.

"And they will respect you after killing your own godfather?"

"Romano isn't well liked," I said, remembering what Olivia had told me, what he'd done to her in the garden. "He's cruel to the men, terrorizes the women. I'm not the only man he's tortured. There will be no love lost between him and his men. And if it comes down to it, we'll use force."

Viktor considered me for a long moment. "He did more than just torture you, didn't he?"

I took a sip of my drink, gazing into the fire. "He touched her."

"Well, that can't stand," Viktor said quietly.

"No, it can't."

There was a long silence where the only sound was the crackling from the fireplace. Then Viktor released a sigh and changed the subject abruptly. We talked of nothing and everything for the next hour and then I excused myself and returned to the Starlight Room. Viktor realized I was eager to get back to my wife and he let me go without complaint.

She was awake when I returned, sitting up in bed with her arms wrapped around her torso. When she saw me, a wave of relief passed over her face and her hands fell away, revealing her breasts. My eyes gravitated to them at once and she blushed, tugging the blankets up.

Without speaking, I stripped and slid beneath the covers and gathered her body against me. My dick hardened as her perfect ass rubbed up against it and a bolt of desire went through me. Suddenly, I was wide awake and painfully aware of her warm body against mine and the sweet, flowery scent of her hair.

"How did I sleep through the whole trip?" she whispered.

"I gave you a mild sedative. I'm sorry, but Viktor insisted you not know the location of his house," I said.

I'd expected her to get angry, but instead she just sighed. "Oh," she said softly. "I guess that makes sense."

I rolled her over on her back. "Are you alright?"

She nodded, but there were tears in her eyes. I wiped them away and brushed her hair back. It bothered me more than it had any right to that she was upset.

"What's wrong?"

She hiccuped. "I don't know, I just woke up and I was alone. This room is so beautiful, it felt like maybe I'd died and it frightened me. And it also just feels so...big and lonely here. I don't know."

I considered her for a long moment. "I think perhaps you're just overwhelmed. Maybe a hot bath and then try to go back to sleep?"

She nodded weakly and I rose and went to the bathroom. There was an enormous clawfoot tub in the corner and I filled it with hot water and found some towels in the cupboard. She appeared in the doorway, naked and small, her face pale and her arms wrapped around her body.

"Get in," I said.

She leaned over the sink to grab her makeup bag and take out a hair tie and my eyes fell on her body. There was a single muscle in her thigh that tensed and then another in her calf and her delicate feet arched as she stood on her toes. Her ass jutted out, round and perfectly soft. My dick hardened again and I found myself stepping up behind her and letting my fingers trail down to her hip.

She stilled. "You're hard," she said softly.

"Very," I breathed.

I knew what she wanted even if she wasn't saying it out loud, I felt it in the way she pushed out her ass, her soft pussy brushing against my dick. Stepping back, I pulled the bag of toiletries from the cupboard and took out a condom and laid it on the sink.

A flush rose in her face, chasing away the paleness, and spread across her throat and breasts. I ran my palm up her spine, tracing her warm skin, and slid it around to her front. She bit her lower lip and a soft sound escaped her mouth, a swift intake of breath, as I pinched her nipple between my fingers.

Seeing Olivia bent over the sink, her dark eyes fixed on mine in our reflection made my cock pulse. With my other hand, I traced her folds and found them wet, so soft and slippery with her slick heat. Impulsively, I plunged my middle and index fingers into her and her pussy clenched around them as she whimpered.

I flipped my fingers and caressed her experimentally until I found her G-spot and she gasped, her hips jerking. If I didn't put a condom on and fuck this woman I was going to go insane. But I forced myself to hold back because the sight of her stiffened spine and her wide eyes glittering with desire as she watched me thrust my fingers into her was extraordinary.

"Touch yourself," I ordered.

She braced herself on the heel of one hand and her other hand slid between her thighs. I pulled my fingers from her with a wet sound. Tearing my eyes from the sight of her working her clit, I ripped open the condom and rolled it down my length. Then, taking her hips between my fingers, digging my grip into the softness of her body, I slid into her until I was sheathed to the hilt.

Fuck, she was hot and wet and impossibly tight around my cock. I rode her with light strokes for a few moments, allowing her to loosen until she could take all of me without wincing.

"Keeping touching yourself," I said, my voice coming out hoarse. "I want you to be a good girl and come around my cock."

She obeyed, clinging to the edge of the sink as I thrust into her from behind and she rubbed her clit with those slender, little fingers. She was such a good girl, so obedient when I fucked her. That had surprised me because she had a mouth on her when she wasn't on her back with her legs open.

I leaned forward, covering her body with mine, and braced my hands on either side of her. "Come for me," I breathed in her ear.

Her body jerked beneath me and she moaned, her fingers working faster. I felt her pussy tighten around me, pulse once, then twice, and then she exploded. That gasping cry burst from her lips and she squeezed her eyes shut.

"Fuck, that's it, that's my girl," I whispered, right on the edge of my own orgasm. "Now look me in the eyes when you come on my cock."

Her eyes snapped open and fixed on mine, dark and desperate. "Oh my God," she breathed.

Slipping my hand up to wrap around the base of her throat, I held her against my body and fucked her hard from behind. The bathroom filled with her quiet moans and whimpering cries and the slick noise of our bodies meeting. She was so wet I could feel it dripping down my balls.

The way her body responded to me, yielding to me until she was pliant in my hands, tipped me over the edge. I came hard, filling the condom as I rode out the aftershocks of my pleasure, buried deep in her hot pussy. For a long moment, we remained as we were, bent over the sink, slick and panting for breath. Then I straightened and pulled from her, standing back to survey her wet, swollen pussy. The sight filled me with primal satisfaction.

"I'm not so cold anymore," she said huskily.

I removed the condom and tied it, tossing it in the garbage bin. "Get in the tub. It'll help you sleep."

She sat down on the edge of the tub and let her legs sink into the steaming water. "Will you take a bath with me?" she asked quietly. I could tell it made her nervous to ask.

I considered her for a moment. She didn't trust me yet, but she didn't really have any reason to. I'd given her the bare minimum by not hurting her more than necessary on our wedding night. And given who I was, she had every right to be wary of me. But a small, unfamiliar part of me wanted her to look up with nothing but trust in those dark eyes.

I shook my head. I was going soft for this woman and it bothered me. I needed all of my focus on killing Romano right now, but ever since she'd come to live with me, I'd caught myself fantasizing about her multiple times a day.

"Alright," I said reluctantly.

I slipped beneath the swirling, hot water and she crawled onto my lap and turned so her back was flush against my chest. My dick hardened again, pushing against the small of her back. Her breasts poked through the surface of the water, her nipples hard, inviting me to slide my hands up and caress them.

"When will you kill Romano?" she asked softly.

"Soon," I said. She didn't need to know the gritty details. It was better if she didn't.

"And then what?"

I slid my palm beneath her forearm and lifted her hand, inspecting the rings on her finger. The diamond glittered in the low light. "And then I will be the boss and you will be the boss's wife. And the outfit will be better for it."

"What about the women in the outfit?" she asked. "Will things get better for them too?"

I considered this for a moment. "Honestly, it's not the boss that dictates the treatment of women. It's about money and keeping power centralized. Upper class women's marriages are often used to build relationships as Sienna will between Viktor and I. How they're treated tends to be up to the man they're wedded to. It's not something I can really fix."

"I hate being a woman sometimes," she said softly. "It's not fair. You're lucky to be born a man."

"Yes, I've always thought that," I said. "My father raped my mother, hit her, fucked other women as often as he liked. He had it out for her specifically and I never knew why. There are no protections for women in those situations because that would involve bringing outside law enforcement into organized crime and that could never happen."

She turned halfway, her mouth ajar. "He raped her?"

"Does that surprise you? In all honesty, I'm sure some of my men have probably forced themselves on their wives at some point. At least the older men...the younger ones seem to understand consent a little better."

She turned to face me, her arms wrapped around her legs. There was a long silence as she chewed on her lip. "That's horrible."

"My mother used to scream when he did it," I said, bracing myself against the stirring memories. "Then the longer they were married, the less she screamed. I think what he did to her just broke her after a while."

"What about Duran? Surely he doesn't do that to Iris?" Her eyes were wide, horrified.

I shook my head. "No, Iris has him by the balls. He's head over heels for her, but he wouldn't do that anyway."

She went quiet for a moment, her eyes lowered. "I'm sorry about your parents. It sounds worse than what I went through."

"It's over. My mother is dead and, thank God, my father is too."

Her dark eyes fixed on me, but she didn't say anything. I pulled her near once more and gently worked soap through her silky hair. Her body relaxed against mine and her eyes began closing, her lashes fluttering dark against her cheek. I lifted her from the tub and she stood by the sink while I dried her with one of the plush towels. Her gaze followed my every move as I toweled off my body and then I led her back to the bedroom.

The sky was the deepest black and the stars stretched endlessly over the snowy fields, barely visible in the night. I rolled on another condom and pulled her beneath the thick comforter and slid into her slick heat. A sigh escaped her lips as I fucked her lazily, my face buried in the warmth of her throat. Everything about her was perfect, the softness of her body, the faint flowery scent that hung around her, and her quiet sounds as I thrust into her pussy. It had been far too long since I'd had a woman in my bed.

Despite having slept all day, Olivia was already sleeping when I got back from throwing the condom away in the bathroom. I slid into bed beside her, gathering her against my body to keep her warm, and fell into deep oblivion.

CHAPTER TWELVE

OLIVIA

Lucien was already awake and getting dressed when I opened my eyes. But it wasn't my half-naked husband that drew my gaze, it was the absolutely breathtaking view out the floor-to-ceiling windows. Awed, I rose and padded naked, goosebumps rising on my skin, across the room to the window and touched my fingertips to the icy glass. It was so cold it sent a shiver through me.

Below me stretched a garden, cleared for the winter and frozen beneath a layer of sparkling white. And beyond it stretched miles and miles of trees and snow covered hills. It was something right out of a fairy tale and I almost laughed aloud, a thrill going through my body at the sight.

"Do you like it?"

I turned and Lucien stood behind me, his eyes washed out in the light from the window. I remembered the day when he'd told my father he was taking me away, how I'd thought he looked like something from one of my childhood storybooks. And he did now more than ever. He was as brutally cold and beautiful as the landscape stretching out below us. Perhaps Lucien would have thrived far better in a world like this than the gray confines of the city back home.

"Get dressed," he said. "We're having breakfast with Viktor before he leaves for a few days."

I went to the closet and found my clothes hung up on one side with Lucien's on the opposite end. Except someone, definitely Lucien, had purchased me an entirely new wardrobe of warmer clothes. I selected a pair of thick, dark gray leggings and a soft woolen sweater and pulled on a pair of leather boots that zipped to my knee. Then I went to the bathroom and applied my makeup and braided my hair, wrapping it around my head and fluffing my thin bangs.

Lucien didn't say anything when I came out of the bathroom, but I felt his eyes on me. He wore a dark suit that fit his slender, broad body beautifully. As he moved to strap his watch around his wrist, I noticed that he wore a thigh holster on his right leg. It struck me as odd because he usually hid his weapons out of sight.

"Why do you have that?" I asked, pointing.

"When in Rome," he said. "Viktor's men don't conceal their guns and neither does he. I wouldn't want them to think I was trying to be secretive. I think they consider it good manners to have them out in the open."

He took my hand and we stepped from the room and out into the hall. I was quiet as he led me through the house, dumbfounded by the sheer size and beauty of everything. It felt like we'd fallen through a rabbit hole and landed in a dark, wintry fairy tale, like something from the Russian ballet.

We turned a corner and found ourselves in a smaller room with a long table and an enormous fireplace crackling loudly and bathing the room in a warm glow. Viktor sat at the far side of the table in a tweed suit, a pair of glasses resting on his nose as he read a book. When he noticed us enter the room, he looked up and removed the glasses and laid aside the book.

"Good morning," he said. "How are you finding the house, Olivia?"

Lucien pulled out a chair for me and I sat down. "Everything is very nice. I didn't expect it to be so big."

Beside me, the corner of Lucien's mouth twitched, but he kept quiet as he poured our coffee.

"The house belonged to my great-grandfather," Viktor said. "He was a prominent man in Russia, a fascinating character."

"Did he build the house?" Lucien asked.

"He did. All except for the heated pool room attached to the back of the house. You're welcome to go for a swim, any part of the house is open to you."

"Thank you," Lucien said.

We ate an unfamiliar breakfast of thick, cheesy pancakes lathered in berry syrup, hearty porridge, and sandwiches of thin sliced meat on a dark, rye bread. Everything was good and I was starving from not having eaten the day before so I focused on eating. The niggling voice in the back of my head was quiet again this morning and I was able to eat without feeling a rush of anxiety.

Lucien and Viktor talked as we ate, switching to French when they clearly didn't want me to understand what they were saying. I was going to have to learn French at some point if my husband was going to use it this often. It struck me as rude and I was beginning to get annoyed when Viktor finally pushed back his chair and stood.

"I have a box at the opera in the city," he said. "Lucien, you aught to take your wife this weekend."

"Would you like to go, Olivia?"

I turned and found Lucien's passive gaze fixed on me. I'd never been to a play, much less an opera, and the concept was daunting. My mother had seen fit to make sure I had some skills, like dance and piano, but she hadn't bothered to give me any further experience with music or art. Was I the sort of person who went to the opera? Would I fit in among the people in their best clothes sitting at their balconies, surrounded by red, velvet drapes?

"Yes, I think so," I said.

"The opera is an experience," Viktor said. "Now, if you'll excuse me, my driver will be here soon and business waits for me at the office."

He left us with a polite nod and Lucien leaned back in his chair, running a hand over his face. He looked a little tired after yesterday. I'd slept hard despite having spent the day unconscious, but he hadn't gone to bed until sometime after midnight. When he'd finished thrusting lazily into me, I was already half-asleep.

"Would you like to go for a swim after breakfast?" he asked.

"I don't have a swimsuit," I said. "I didn't think I'd need one."

"I'd rather have you naked." His gaze bored into me, dragging down to the swell of my breasts beneath my sweater. My breath quickened and a curl of warmth rose between my thighs.

We finished eating breakfast and Lucien took my hand and we took a tour of the house. I lost track of the endless rooms, all lavishly decorated and spacious. When we got to the pool room, Lucien closed the door and turned to me, his hands skimming up beneath my sweater. The front of his pants was tight already, the hard outline of his cock visible.

The pool room was painted dark blue and the walls were made almost entirely out of large windows that looked out into the back garden. It was lucky, I thought as my husband stripped my clothes from me, that the snowy fields were deserted because we were completely exposed.

Lucien turned me around and pressed my body against his chest, his hands skimming up my naked stomach to my breasts. His fingertips were rough and his palms hard, but the way he touched me was impossibly gentle. Heat pulsed in my pussy and when I shifted my thighs I felt wetness between them.

"Get in," he said hoarsely.

I slid into the steaming water and turned to find him stripping naked. His body was beautiful in the morning light. He'd never seemed like the type to have tattoos, but now that I could see him more clearly, the ink on his torso made sense. Beneath the tattoos, I could just make out the faint lines of scars. He'd gotten inked to cover up the marks Romano had left on his body.

He sank into the water and took me by the waist and backed me against the wall. A gasp tore from my mouth as he lifted me in his arms. The hard length of his cock nudged between my thighs and he closed his eyes and released a low moan. His hips worked his hot length over my pussy and his hand teased my breast and nipple, pinching it between his fingers. Shivers of pleasure moved through me and, to my surprise, the faintest hint of an orgasm began between my thighs.

"Do that," I breathed.

"Do what?"

I wrapped my arm around his neck, his face just inches from mine. "Rub my clit with the tip."

He complied, holding his cock at the base for better control. I gasped and pressed my forehead against his shoulder as pleasure built up fast in my hips. He let go of his cock and slipped his fingers inside me beneath the warm water and worked my clit with his thumb. My hips bucked hard. God, he was going to make me come.

"You want to be a good, little slut for me and come on my fingers?" he murmured into my hair.

I was taken aback for a moment, less by his choice of words and more by how my body responded to them. My sex ached around his fingers and I whimpered, digging my nails into his back. He swore softly and his thumb dragged over my clit, building my orgasm with alarming speed.

"Who do you belong to?" he asked quietly.

I hesitated, a flush creeping up my throat. "What do you mean?"

"I mean, who do you belong to?" he said, his voice hard.

"You." My admittance both embarrassed and aroused me.

"Good girl."

He flicked his fingers, finding my G-spot and working it hard. I gasped, crying out softly, and came hard, my pussy clenching around his fingers. He swore under his breath and pressed me against the wall, the heel of his hand rubbing against my clit.

"Be a good girl and ride my hand," he purred.

My God, if he kept talking like that, I was going to come again. I obeyed, clinging to the side of the pool as I worked my hips, grinding my clit against his hand and thrusting onto his fingers. The sensations burning through my body were almost too much to bear and a quiet wail burst from my lips as my back arched.

His mouth was on my breasts, sucking hard on my nipples, his teeth grazing over the sensitive skin. Heart pounding, I came down from my high slowly, flushed with heat and arousal.

"You called me a slut," I admonished.

He slipped his fingers from my body. "You enjoyed it. I think we both did."

"Maybe," I said, looking down at the rippling surface of the pool.

"Admit it if you like something, Olivia," he said. "Between the two of us and the things I want to do to you, there isn't enough room for shame in our bed."

I stared at him, unsure how to answer because he was right. My nipples hardened and into my mind flashed an image of him driving into me, his slender body merciless, as he whispered those things against my throat.

Before I could respond, he dove beneath the water and swam to the other side of the room before emerging. For a moment, I forgot how to breathe as he rose from the pool and ran his hands over his face to clear the water. His body glittered with water droplets and steam rose from his skin. Against the backdrop of wilderness and cold, he looked like something from another world.

I leaned back and let my legs float in the water. As I watched him, a thought popped into my mind that, for some reason, had never occurred to me before now. How old was Lucien? I knew he'd been a teenager when I was born, but how big was the gap between our ages?

I looked down and saw him moving toward me beneath the water. He surfaced just inches from me, bending his head and nipping at my breasts as he stood.

"Swim with me," he ordered.

"Can I ask you a question instead?"

He cocked his head and then nodded. "Go ahead."

"How old are you?"

His mouth twitched as his gaze bored into me. "It's a little late for that to matter. You're already my wife."

"I just want to know," I insisted. I had a right to know my husband's age.

"I'm thirty-six," he said.

"You're...what?" I gasped.

He raised a brow. "Thank you, that's very flattering."

I floundered, trying to walk back my reaction. "No, I just thought you were younger than that. I mean—you just look much younger so I thought you were like thirty. I'm sorry, I didn't mean to be rude or anything."

"Duran is thirty. My mother had trouble getting pregnant again so there's a six year age gap between us," he said.

"That's a lot, I'm surprised you're so close," I said.

He stared out the window, floating in front of me with his lean hands on the edge of the pool. "It saved him from a lot of horror. He hated our father, but he didn't have to live through the half of it. He never had to listen to our mother get abused, our father had gotten more discreet about the things he did by the time Duran came along."

"You really hated him," I said softly.

"He was an evil man."

I put my hand on his chest, enjoying the sensation of warm skin and the tickle of hair against my palm. Lucien watched me for a long moment, not speaking. The sensual line of his mouth was soft, lips parted with a sliver of teeth visible. His dark lashes fell as my hand trailed across his chest, dragging through the water as I traced the lines of his abdomen.

"You and Duran really loved your mother," I said quietly. "She must have been lovely."

"She was," he said, his face still emotionless. "But it's selfish of me to talk about her when you never knew what it was like to have a mother like that."

I dipped my head, a lump in my throat. "Is it bad that sometimes I wish she was dead? And my father too."

"No," he said. "What did you father do to you?"

I blinked hard and focused outside on the glittering snow, on the pines rustling in the icy wind. "He hit me a fair bit, but that wasn't the worst. It was this one time...this one time where he just snapped and I thought he was going to kill me."

Lucien's eyes narrowed a minute amount. "What did he do?"

My shoulders gave an involuntary shiver and Lucien's hand slid up my waist, warm and comforting. "I was fifteen and I had just come back from spending the day with my cousin. She'd put her wallet in my purse while we were shopping and accidentally left it in there. My mother would always make me empty my pockets and purse to make sure I wasn't doing anything forbidden. Both my parents lived in fear I would have sex and you wouldn't want to marry me anymore. I guess my father really needs the alliance and my mother wants the status of being related to your family."

"The alliance is important," he said. "But your parents took things too far. Then what happened?"

A sick feeling rose in my stomach and I swallowed it back down. "My mother found my cousin's wallet and there was a condom in the side pocket. She freaked out, I mean, freaked out. She pushed me against the wall so I couldn't move and she was slapping my face so hard I couldn't breathe. Then she dragged me to my father's study and he was even angrier than she was. He shoved my mother into the hall and locked the door." I paused, my voice shaking.

"Are you alright?"

"Yes, I'm sorry."

"You don't need to apologize."

"My father dragged me by the hair and hit my face...I don't know, maybe a dozen times. My teeth hurt so badly. I remember trying to hold my tongue out of the way so I wouldn't bite it off. Then...then he shoved me down on my side on the floor. He was yelling something about how I was a whore, how I would have to get checked. Then he started just...I don't know...just kicking me in the ribs and hips. I don't remember much, but eventually I threw up and fainted."

Lucien's eyes were fixed on me and for the first time, I saw something real in them. A glitter of lethal rage.

"Two weeks later, after my bruises healed a little, they took me to one of the outfit's doctors," I said. I could still almost smell the disinfectant from the doctor's office. "He did a cervical exam on me. It was...humiliating."

Lucien's jaw worked, a flickering movement beneath his skin. "What Romano did to you...it was made worse because of all of this?"

"There's just a lot of fear and bad memories that I associated with my virginity. It was such an important thing to everyone around me," I said slowly. "I felt like I was carrying around this thing made of delicate glass, and if I broke it, my life was over. But when Romano touched me it felt like...more like he was fetishizing it."

"He probably was," Lucien said coldly.

I hesitated, looking up at his stoic expression. I still didn't trust him fully, but he'd listened this far and he hadn't reacted with anger toward me. In fact, quite the opposite.

"When you took my virginity on our wedding night," I whispered, dropping my gaze. "It...it was such a relief. I'd been saved for you for so long and I just wanted it done."

He ran a finger under my chin in a thoughtful gesture. "Your parents really fucked you up, Olivia."

"Yes," I agreed, sighing. "Didn't you feel anything like that on our wedding night? No relief?"

"I felt relief that you came and that you enjoyed yourself. But no, that's not what I felt when I fucked you."

"What did you feel? What were you thinking."

He lifted himself, dripping, from the pool and stood steaming and naked above me. Then he reached down and pulled me up beside him. I straightened, cold air making goosebumps rise on my skin, and wrapped my arms around my body.

"It felt like being buried in your tight, wet cunt. And I don't think I had any coherent thoughts in my head."

I gasped and the corner of his mouth twitched. He retrieved two towels from the cupboard in the corner and I dried off, my cheeks still pink from what he'd said. As I dressed, I couldn't keep my eyes from straying to him. There was something incredibly attractive about watching him put his suit back on, his hair still wet from the pool.

"I want to fuck you," he said, rolling his sleeves up. He hung his jacket over his forearm. "Come with me."

My heart pounded and my pussy soaked the thin strip of underwear between my thighs as I obeyed. I wanted this and I wanted it rough, the way his voice and his hard eyes promised it would be. A deep, primal part of me wanted him to press me down, bend me over and make me helpless, to tear my clothes from my body and stake his claim.

We paused at the bedroom door and he turned me around to face him. Then his hard body was on mine, pushing me back against the door. His hand fumbled behind me, turning the knob and pushing me into the bedroom. My heart hammered as his fingers skimmed up, pushing beneath my sweater and tearing it over my head. He gave a low groan at the sight of my bra and knelt before me, pulling down my leggings. Teeth grazed my thigh, sinking into the soft flesh, and I jumped.

I arched into him, euphoric with the high of his desire. He gave a quiet growl and released me to shrug out of his vest and unfasten the buttons of his shirt. Then his hands were on me, spinning me to face away as he pinned my arms back against his body. I panted and wetness slid down my thigh as my clit gave a frustrated throb. Despite my earlier orgasms, I was desperate for another.

He pushed me to the window, taking my wrists and planting my hands on the sill. Chilly air radiated from the glass and my nipples tightened. God, I needed this, needed him to fuck me bent over like this. An ache rippled through me and my eyes rolled back as he wound his fist into my hair and pulled my head back. His teeth grazed my throat and in the distance, through the roaring in my ears, I heard him unfasten his pants.

His thick, hard cock pushed into me and I cried out at the mixture of pleasure and pain. My pussy throbbed around him, tensing and drawing him in further, and he swore under his breath. He adjusted himself behind me, pressing me closer to the glass until my breasts just touched the window. The icy cold sent a shock of arousal through my body. He began fucking me, slowly at first, and then with increasing force. With each thrust, my nipples grazed the cold glass and set my body tingling.

Wetness slipped down my thighs and the sounds of our bodies meeting filled the room. He fucked me like this for what felt like forever before his hand snaked around my hips and found my clit. It took two strokes across the sensitive nub before my orgasm hit me and my legs collapsed, my body falling against the window.

He growled and pulled me to his chest, riding me hard through my orgasm. I gasped and cried out at each throb of pleasure and he responded with whispered praise, his mouth pressed beneath my ear.

"Take it in that sweet, little cunt," he breathed. "Fuck, you feel so good, you're doing so well."

He picked me up and carried me to the bed, throwing me unceremoniously onto my back. His body loomed over mine as he slipped between my legs and pushed back into me. A moan escaped my lips and I arched against him, still riding out the aftershocks of my orgasm. Every thrust sent ripples of pleasure through my body as his cock caressed the deepest parts of me.

His length hardened until his strokes were almost painful. He lifted me roughly and flipped me onto my hands and knees, driving his cock so deep it felt like I might split in half. I whimpered, my legs shaking, and bit hard on my lip. My inner walls were so sensitive I wasn't sure if I could take it for much longer.

Then he pulled from me and hot wetness spattered across the middle of my back. I dropped my head, biting hard on my lip. Why did it turn me on so much to have him spill his cum onto me? He let out a low groan followed by a release of breath and I heard his zipper hiss as he tucked himself back into his pants.

"Fuck," he murmured.

I slid onto my belly on the bed and listened as he went to the bathroom. Then a warm, wet washcloth slid over my skin, wiping me clean. There was something tender about his hands as he cleaned me up and it stirred warmth in my chest. He was a guarded man, but sometimes when we were together, his shell softened and bits of his humanity shone through.

CHAPTER THIRTEEN

LUCIEN

I stood over the table in the dining room, the floor plan of the house laid out in front of me. Viktor sat on the edge of the table beside me, one hand in his lap and the other holding a cigarette. It was almost the weekend and the Russian godfather had returned from business in Moscow earlier that day. We'd been up for a few hours past midnight, drinking vodka, smoking, and going over the plan for Carlo Romano's murder.

"So if things go wrong, you want me to drop my men in through the third story window here," Viktor said, pointing. "And somehow they're supposed to get all the way over here within minutes? Seems implausible."

"No, I meant we have them grapple up the western side," I said, turning the map. "They enter through the western corner, cross only one room as far as I can tell, and they'll be in the north side."

"And then?"

"And then Romano and I will be in the study, which is less than thirty paces down the hall," I said. "Duran will be here. The control room is connected to a back staircase from the kitchen. All Duran has to do is pretend he's trying to fuck one of the serving girls and they won't look twice at him disappearing with someone in the stairwell."

"Does he usually fuck the serving girls?" Viktor asked.

"Before he met his wife, yes. That's what they're for. Romano pays girls who are willing to serve drinks and open their legs." I took a sip of my vodka, not bothering to add that in my younger days, I had utilized the services of these women even more than Duran.

Viktor's brows rose. "Your godfather pays for whores?"

I nodded.

"Not the way I do things here," he said. "I wouldn't encourage that at my house. My men are as...wild as yours on their own time, but I don't sanction that sort of thing in my home."

"Do your men not want to fuck at parties?"

"I pay escorts to work my parties, but they don't have to please the men if they don't want to. They are more like companions, something beautiful to look at, and if they desire it, to be touched. But they're not whores and I wouldn't allow them to be treated as such."

"Perhaps I'll take that into consideration as something to change when I step into power," I said. "Although I don't particularly care if my men want to fuck whores, as long as they're responsible and don't cause any issues I have to deal with."

Viktor's eyes lingered over the map. "When I took over after my elder brother died, I transformed the way we lived, changed the culture. I believe you and I can bring our worlds into a better future, together, so that our sons may benefit."

My son. The notion was foreign, but not unpleasant. A mental image of Olivia, her stomach swollen with my child, floated through my brain. I'd spent the last several years terrified by the possibility of accidentally getting a woman pregnant, but I didn't have to feel that way any longer. An unexpected desire to see my wife like that rose in me and I blinked, shaking my head. It was too soon, she needed time to settle in before having to deal with a pregnancy.

"I hope our alliance continues beyond our generation. It could be incredibly beneficial," I said.

"Speaking of our alliance," Viktor said. "As soon as Romano is dead, I would like Sienna released to my care so I can bring her to Russia."

"I already planned on sending her after New Year's Eve," I said. "And I would like to send my wife and my sister-in-law here if things go badly and I'm killed."

Viktor took a slow drag of his cigarette and considered me for a moment. "If you die, Duran will also die. What am I to do with two Italian widows?"

I hated the thought of anyone else touching Olivia, but I had to make sure my wife was taken care of if Romano killed me.

"Surely you have soldiers who would marry them," I said almost bitterly.

"Most of my soldiers want Russian women. It is possible they could be higher ranking mistresses."

Rage flared in my chest at the thought, but I kept control of myself. "Not my wife."

"But your sister-in-law?"

"Please, just do this for me. If we die, my only request is that you care for my wife and my brother's wife."

Viktor relented, dipping his head. "I'll see that it's done."

"Thank you," I said quietly.

There was a long silence and I began gathering up the blueprints and stacking them. Viktor took a sip of his vodka, his eyes lingering on the fire. There was an expression of longing on his face and it occurred to me suddenly that the renowned Russian godfather was lonely.

"You never married?" I asked.

His gaze flicked to mine and back down again. "No. I never married the woman I loved. She was my father's mistress, it would have been a scandal. Her name was Yulia and she was not much older than I was...nineteen, I think. We had a secret love affair. My father was losing interest in her and he stopped sleeping with her so when he...when he found out she was pregnant, he knew she was cheating with someone. He found out I was the father."

I kept silent, pretty sure I knew where the story was going. Viktor took another long drag from his cigarette and put it out in the ashtray on the table.

"He snapped her neck," he said, his voice a little husky. "She was three months pregnant with my child."

"Your father sounds like he was an asshole," I said.

Viktor's mouth twitched into a sad smile. "To put it lightly. I would have killed him, but a month after it happened, he was shot and killed by an assassin. They never found out who did it, but if I had to guess it was one of you Italians."

"It's quite possible," I said carefully.

"It was the best fucking thing the Italians ever did for me," Viktor said. He shook his head as if to clear it and sat in one of the armchairs, crossing his legs. "Tell me about Sienna?"

I loitered near the fireplace, a newly lit cigarette in my fingers. "Her parents died in a train crash, of all things, and I gained custody of her. She grew up at a Catholic school for girls."

"What is her disposition?"

I considered the question, hesitant to answer truthfully. I knew it was best to be honest and upfront with him so there were no surprises later.

"She's headstrong," I said. "Very willful. She wanted to go to college for a degree in English literature, I wanted to marry her off as soon as she was of age. There were a good many fights in the Esposito house while she was there and she spent a lot of time locked in her room."

"But she is in college now, no?"

I sighed. "We made a deal eventually. But I signed a contract with her that in exchange for her entering, untouched, into a marriage with a man of my choosing, I would allow her to attend college. She's intelligent and she knows when to accept when she's been beaten and make the best of it."

"How old is she?"

"Twenty-three."

"Does she know of me yet?"

"No, she thinks she's engaged to Aurelio Romano," I said. "I'll have to kill him when I kill his father."

"It would be stupid not to," Viktor said, nodding. "If you're going to keep your place, you can't have anyone challenging you."

There was a quiet sound out in the hall and we both froze. I drew my gun and Viktor stood slowly, his hand going to his pistol. Stepping silently on the sides of my feet, I slid against the door and turned the knob, letting it fall ajar. The space of hall directly ahead was deserted, but as we waited, there was a quiet sniffle from somewhere to my left. I released a sigh and slipped my gun back in its holster.

I stepped into the hall and found my wife standing with her arms wrapped around her body. Her face was pale and her cheeks were wet with tears. She wore only her thin, silk slip that came down to the middle of her thigh and she was shivering.

"My God, what are you doing?" I asked.

Her chin shook. "I'm sorry, I just had the worst nightmare and...I needed you."

It took everything I had not to melt in front of her. She looked so small and afraid, shivering half-naked in the dark hallway. I stepped back through the door to find Victor watching me with concern.

"Olivia had a nightmare," I said. "I need to take her back to bed."

"Go on, we can continue this meeting tomorrow."

I dipped my head and returned to where my wife stood swaying in the hall, her lower lip trembling. I considered her for a moment and then I lifted her in my arms and carried her down the hall. Her body went stiff at first, but then it softened against me and her arm wrapped around my neck. Her cheek rested trustingly against my shoulder and a glimmer of warmth sparked in my chest.

Back in our bedroom, I laid her on the bed. She leaned against the headboard and wrapped her arms around her knees. Her lashes fell as she gazed down at the comforter, her fingers worrying together in the sheets.

"I'm sorry I took you away from your meeting," she whispered.

I shrugged out of my clothes and sat on the edge of the bed in my boxers. She looked pathetic, wilted and afraid. It was unlike her. Even when frightened, Olivia had fire and fight in her small body. I sighed and ran my palm up her leg, gently rubbing her smooth skin until she relaxed a little.

"What was your nightmare?" I asked quietly.

She gave a shuddering breath and looked toward the window. The sky was cloudy tonight and the only light outside came from the lamps along the driveway.

"I dreamed I was back in my family's house. That I was hungry and my father was beating me," she said. "I think talking about it earlier stirred things up in my mind."

I studied her face for a long moment. "You can't be afraid of them anymore, Olivia," I said firmly.

She turned quickly, frowning. "What?"

I slid into bed beside her and held out my arms, coaxing her to lay against me. She stared at me, still scowling, and then she relented and allowed me to pull her body against mine. Her ass pushed up against my hips and I forced myself not to think about grinding my dick into her.

"The first time I took a life that wasn't just an ordinary soldier, I realized that if I was going to make bold moves within the outfit, I had to be unbreakable. If you're going to strike, you hit your target on the first try. That means you need impeccable control, you need to know where your head is at all times, you need to master your fear. And you can never let them see you flinch or back down."

She lay still, not speaking for a long time.

"As my wife, everything you do will be analyzed for weakness," I said. "Show them your neck and they will cut it."

"I thought you would protect me," she whispered.

"Do you want to hide behind me? Or do you want to stand beside me?"

"Beside you," she said slowly. "I've just spent all of my life at the mercy of someone else. I don't know how to be free and not afraid."

I flipped her on the back and braced myself halfway over her body. Her thin bangs had fallen back and her lovely face was fully exposed. The soft curve of her mouth was open just enough to see the pink tip of her tongue. Bending, I pressed my lips gently against hers, coaxing them apart so I could get a taste of this woman. She made a soft noise in her throat and from the corner of my eye I saw her fingers tighten in the sheets.

I drew back, flicking my tongue over my bottom lip to gather the remnants of her taste. "You need to learn to shield yourself as I have."

"I don't know how to do that. I can't bury my emotions the way you do," she whispered.

"You don't have to bury them. Withhold them—not everyone deserves to see you raw. In fact, I'd argue only I have the right to witness your fear, your indiscretions, your weakness. Give that to me. Give everyone else a version of yourself they can't break."

"I don't know what that version is."

I pressed a kiss between her breasts. "You have a lovely throat and shoulders. It was first thing I noticed about you, other than your legs. Your mother, as much of a bitch as she is, did right with the clothes she picked for you."

"Really?" She sounded uncertain.

"Tomorrow for the opera, you will wear a black dress that clings to your body," I murmured. I gathered her nipple in my mouth and sucked hard until her hips jerked and I released it. "You will walk in on my arm, knowing you are a queen. You will keep your head high and your shoulders back. All of the men will see you, glittering with jewels, and they will want to fuck you. And their women will see you go by and wish they were you."

Her mouth parted in surprise. I rarely talked to her like this and it was throwing us both off guard.

"I've seen you like that before and you're a natural," I said. "You are better than all of them. And I am the only person you need to get on your knees for ever again. Do you understand me?"

She nodded, her eyes glittering with desire.

"The only person who gets to see your weakness and fear is your husband," I said, my gaze boring into her. "In many ways, those things are more intimate than your body."

She nodded slowly and I kissed her mouth again, trailing my lips down her throat. A little gasp burst from her as I curled my tongue around her nipple and lapped at it gently, eliciting a little moan from her. I slid my palm up her ribs, enjoying the feel of her breath growing faster beneath my hand. There was nothing more pleasurable than the sensation of her silky body beneath my fingers and tongue.

I rolled onto my back and picked her up by the waist and lifted her up to set her over my face. She gasped, grabbing at the headboard to steady herself.

"What are you doing?" she breathed.

"I'm eating you out," I said. "But first, hold yourself up a little. I'm going to lick your clit until you drip into my mouth."

Her inner thighs shook, a barely perceptible movement, and her pussy clenched overhead. There was nothing in my vision but the silky smoothness of her inner thighs on either side of my head and her pale brown sex. She shifted her hips and I caught a glimpse of wetness, glittering along her inner folds.

Digging my fingers into her thighs, I tilted her so I could lick her clit without touching the rest of her pussy. I was going to tease her until she dripped her sweet arousal into my mouth and only then would she get to come. The thought made my throbbing cock twitch, the pressure almost painful. Hopefully I could hold out that long.

She whimpered as I softened my tongue and ran it, wet and hot, over her clit. I lapped over her, barely grazing her most sensitive point as I teased her swollen flesh. Every time I drew back, I glanced at her pussy to check the wetness gathering there. She looked so beautiful, so edible, it took everything I had not to swipe my tongue over her entrance and gather her arousal in my mouth.

"Please," she whispered. "Don't tease me. Lick my pussy, just once."

I ignored her, taking her clit into my mouth and working it. She liked it when I flicked her in long, quick strokes. As soon as I fell into the rhythm, her thighs tightened and began shaking just a little more. My dick throbbed and I fought the urge to reach down and rub it. No, I wanted to focus on her, on tasting her all over my tongue.

"Fuck," she whispered. "I think I might come."

It would be the first time she'd come from my tongue. Excitement rose in me and it took all I had to keep up the same pace, flicking her bundle of nerves as she trembled in my hands.

I could tell she was on the edge, but she remained there, unable to get over. She needed more, needed something else. I slid my hand over her backside, dipping just a little into the wetness between her thighs, and found her asshole with the tip of my finger. She jerked at the contact, but I kept her steady with a hand to her lower belly.

I circled her slowly as I flicked her clit. I wouldn't go in—perhaps someday soon, but now wasn't the time. She responded beautifully to my touch as I caressed her asshole with the tip of my finger. A little moan escaped her lips and she flushed, pink staining her throat and cheeks. I pulled back from her little bundle of nerves and there it was between her thighs, a glitter of wetness ready to slip down her thigh.

Shifting down, I continued touching her, keeping my eyes on her soaked entrance. A gasp came from above and she shook, her pussy clenching. The movement sent a tremor through her and I caught her wetness on my tongue as it fell. Sweet and tangy. Feral need flooded me and I pressed my face up into her, lapping at her pussy, cleaning the arousal from her folds.

"Sit on my face," I ordered, pulling back.

She looked down, her nipples hard and her eyes burning. "What? On your face?"

"Sit on my face," I repeated.

"You want me to put my weight on your face?" she stammered.

"Yes, sit on it, grind into my mouth. I want you to come on my face."

I pulled her down onto me and she relaxed slowly. Then there was only the sweet slickness of her pussy and the heady scent of her building orgasm against my mouth. Her wetness slid down my chin and I felt it trail down the side of my neck. Fuck, this was heaven. I found her clit and began flicking it the way she liked, my finger tracing her asshole with gentle strokes.

She began panting again and her thighs shook hard on either side of my head. My dick throbbed, but I barely felt it through the sheer ecstasy of having her all over my face and mouth. Then her pussy gave a quick throb and she gasped and cried out as her body shuddered.

Fuck, she was coming on my tongue for the first time. I grabbed her hips and held her steady as she came apart, whimpering and shaking through her pleasure. She rode her orgasm out against my mouth, every pulse and throb of her tender flesh acute. Her wetness slipped down my throat, coating my tongue with her familiar taste.

"Oh my God," she whispered.

I lifted her off me. "Get on your knees," I ordered.

She hesitated for a moment and then she slid off the bed and onto her knees. I rose and stood over her, wrapping my hand through her dark, tousled hair. Her mouth was swollen from how she'd bitten it as she came and her dark eyes were wide as she watched me.

"Be a good girl and close your eyes," I said.

She obeyed and I took my cock in my hand and palmed it. I was hot and twitching with needy desire and all it took was a few quick strokes before pleasure hit me hard. It surged through me and a harsh sound rose in my throat as my cum hit her face in long ropes. She flinched and then, in a movement that almost killed me, she opened her mouth to let me finish onto her pink tongue.

As I came down from my high, I'd never had such mixed feelings after sex than I did now. Back when I was still sleeping around, I'd done this exact thing to countless women. But as my wife opened her eyes slowly, my cum dripping down her chin to her breasts, I felt a twinge of regret. Perhaps I shouldn't have done that—it seemed like something I would have done to a woman I cared nothing for. And, despite my best efforts not to admit it, I cared for Olivia. Now that my post-orgasm clarity had returned, it felt a little demeaning, despite how much it had turned me on. I ran a hand over my face and released a sigh.

"What's wrong?"

I considered telling her for a moment, but decided against it. Going from fucking any woman I pleased to several years of celibacy to having almost unfettered access to my wife was confusing to say the least. But telling her all this required revealing how promiscuous I'd been as a young man and that wasn't something I wanted to get into right now.

"Nothing. Are you alright?" I asked.

She nodded and I knelt down, taking some tissues from the bedside table and wiping her face. Her dark eyes fixed on me as I cleaned her off and went to the bathroom to turn on the shower. She came in a few minutes later and joined me beneath the hot spray.

"Thank you for that," she said quietly.

"For finishing on your face?"

"No, for giving me an orgasm. I was starting to think I couldn't finish without using my fingers."

I brushed a wet strand of hair from her eyes and kissed her mouth. She still tasted a little bit like me, but it didn't bother me. A small part of me liked knowing she had my cum on her tongue and down her throat. Soon I would get her on her knees and show her how to use her mouth on my cock.

The next day, I stood at the bottom of the stairs waiting for her so we could leave for the opera. I was getting antsy. She'd been in the bathroom for a while, running the shower, then the hairdryer, and then filling the room with perfume until it seeped under the door. I hadn't realized until living with a woman how much effort it took to look perfectly groomed.

I heard her heels on the floor and she appeared at the top of the stairs. Blood rushed to my groin as I stared, unable to formulate words. She wore a black dress that fit her like a second skin, just as I had requested. The long sleeves were made of lace and the skirt was silk and clung to her all the way to her feet. It was the bodice that drew my attention. Her breasts were covered only by two square panels of fabric that must have been held up with wire or her tits would have spilled out. As it was, I could see the entire inner and upper cleavage of both breasts.

She hesitated, biting her lip nervously. "Do you like it?"

"I—of course I do," I said, struggling to keep my face impassive. There was no hiding the erection in my pants though. "But I'm not sure I'm comfortable with you wearing that out."

She frowned, disappointment crossing her face. "But I like it."

"I thought you didn't like showing your body. You seem to hate that your mother put you in revealing clothes," I pointed out.

She squirmed a little. "I know, I've just been wearing clothes like this so long I don't feel beautiful in anything else. And I got to choose this, so it's different."

"It's very beautiful, you're very beautiful," I said carefully. "Come here, baby."

It was first time I'd used any term of endearment with her and it felt good. Very good. If she was surprised, she didn't show it. She lifted her skirt a little to descend the stairs, revealing a slender pair of black pumps, the arch of her feet rising up into her delicate ankles. My dick throbbed as she stopped in front of me, her dark eyes searching my face, begging me to relent.

Fuck, she had me wrapped around her little finger.

"I'll make you a deal," I said.

"What?" She cocked her head, her long, glossy ponytail twitching. She'd done something to her hair so that her bangs were slicked back into her high ponytail and her hair was straightened until it shimmered in the low light.

I pulled her closer to me, my mouth just brushing her ear. "Suck me off at the opera, in the private box, and I'll allow you to wear the dress."

Her eyes widened and her pupils dilated with arousal. Her hips shifted in that subtle movement that meant she was pressing her thighs together.

"I've never done that before," she whispered.

"I'll show you."

"Then yes, it's a deal," she said, holding out her hand.

I looked down at her hand and fought the urge to smile as I shook it. Her nails were manicured and painted dark red and she wore her enormous ring. She was a beautiful wet dream and she was mine, not just for tonight, but for every night ever after.

Goddamn, I needed to win, I needed to kill Romano. I had too much to live for now to fail.

I helped her into her coat and pulled on mine. Viktor had had them waiting for us as a welcome gift, one I was very grateful for because I hadn't packed anything that held up against the Russian cold. Olivia's coat was made of creamy wool and lined heavily with fur, complimenting her dark hair beautifully. I had to tear my eyes from her as I helped her into the car and slid into the heated seat beside her.

"I could live here," she said quietly.

I turned, surprised. "Really?"

"Yes," she said, sighing. "I love the summer, love gardening, but I love how beautiful everything is here. I just feel like everything in the city back home is just gray and boring and modern."

"Yes, I suppose that's true," I said. "Perhaps when everything is over, we'll come back and visit. I imagine I'll have business here occasionally."

"But as long as you have your duties with the outfit, you'll never have the freedom to go where you please," she intoned.

"True."

"Won't you have more freedom when you're...you know?" she said. She glanced up through the glass at the driver, unsure if she could speak plainly about my plan to kill Romano.

"You get less freedom with power, not more."

"Then why do it?" she asked.

I leaned my forehead against the cold glass for a moment, the lights of Moscow glittering in the distance. "I have to. Sometimes you know you need to do something, even if it isn't what you want," I said. "I was born to change the outfit, of that I have no doubt."

She studied me for a moment, her face unreadable. "You are an ambitious man. It scares me sometimes."

"Why?"

She hesitated and then released a sigh. "Because I worry it'll never be enough for you. The more I know you, the more I realize you aren't the kind of man who is ever satisfied."

I had nothing to say to this. She was right. Growing up under my father's thumb and watching helplessly as he beat and abused my mother had made me determined to never answer to anyone. I would never be helpless again.

"I will be satisfied when I am done," I said shortly.

"It's because of your father," she said, as if she could read my mind.

I nodded reluctantly.

She was quiet for a moment and I glanced over as we entered the city. The lights glittered off her face, catching the sheen of makeup on her mouth and eyelids.

"How did he die?" she asked quietly.

Her question caught me off guard. I knew the grisly truth, but I was loathe to tell my beautiful, innocent wife. It was bad enough I had revealed the morbid details of my upbringing to her. I shrugged, deciding to stick with the reported details.

"He was killed by an assassin," I said. "We never found out why or who it was."

She studied me, her intelligent, dark gaze digging into mine. "Is that true?"

"I never looked into it," I said. "I was just glad to have him gone."

She opened her mouth, her brows drawn together, and then she shut it. I could tell by the way she worked her jaw that she was annoyed. Her reaction stirred a little irritation in me. She was acting like she had the right to know personal information about my family.

We kept silent as the driver pulled up to the curb before the Bolshoi Theater and came around to open the doors for us. I stepped out, instinctively glancing over the street and pressing my arm to my side to feel the hard metal of my gun. There were only throngs of men and women dressed in finery moving into the theater, chatting and laughing as they went. It felt safe, definitely safer than the city did back home.

I helped my wife from the car, sliding my arm around her to keep her close to my body as we entered the building. An attendant took our coat and led us to our private box near the front on the right side.

As I had suspected, eyes followed her as she went. She'd taken my advice seriously and she floated at my side, her spine straight and her shoulders back. The double string of diamonds at her throat caught the light, drawing every eye to the firm swell of her breasts. Men looked and then looked again and women gazed at her with jealous admiration.

I slid my arm around her waist again, pressing the swell of her hip against my thigh. They could look with thinly veiled desire, but tonight when her dress and jewels came off, I would be the man buried between her thighs.

The boxes were separated by a wall and draped halfway in front with a curtain for privacy. Olivia was quiet, her eyes wide as she took in the opulent room, the ornate ceiling and the red velvet seats. As she took her seat at my side, I found myself glad for the curtain and the darkness of the room. I shouldn't have let her wear that dress, but it was too late to do anything about it now. Even as the orchestra struck up, I still found my eyes drifting through the shadows to the curve of her bare throat and the outline of her breasts.

"What is this performance?" she whispered.

"It's called *Prince Igor*," I said. "I thought you might like it because it has ballet sequences. Viktor recommended it as his favorite. Here's the libretto."

There was just enough light for her to read over the short synopsis of the opera. I forced myself to look ahead instead of watching her as she bent over the paper. When she was done, she folded it primly in her fingers and turned her attention to the stage.

The opera had been cut down to two acts, which was a relief because, according to Viktor, the unabridged version was four hours long. I didn't have the patience to sit for that long with Olivia beside me in that dress. As much as I appreciated the artistic talent of the performers and the beauty of the music, I appreciated my wife's tits a lot more. It took everything I had to keep my hands to myself so she could enjoy the show.

When the curtain rose for the intermission, Olivia sat back with a sigh, blinking in the sudden light.

"Are you enjoying yourself?" I asked.

She nodded. "I've never been to an opera or a real ballet. It's so...different from watching it on a screen. It's beautiful and it feels so real."

Her eyes glittered as she looked up at me and something warm and foreign welled in my chest. I bent quickly and kissed her, tasting the sweetness of her mouth mingled with her lipstick. As my tongue swiped over hers, she gave a quick sigh, her shoulders drawing up.

"What's wrong?" I asked, drawing back.

She shook her head. "Everything is just so different than it was a year ago, you know?"

I cocked my head and studied her until she looked down. "Are you happy?"

She nodded. "I think so. I would be more...never mind."

I leaned on the seat, turning to face her better. She was blushing and for some reason my blood ran faster and my dick hardened at the sight.

"What were you going to say?"

She hesitated. "I—I was just going to say that things are perfect. It would just be better if we...if we weren't arranged. If we were in love."

I considered her for a long moment. What did she feel for me? Over the last week, I'd noticed she had softened toward me. I could see it in her eyes every night when she looked up at me as I fucked her and when I drew back from kissing her mouth. And I had softened to the point of this strange warmth rising in my chest, threatening to crack through the years of numbing apathy.

The lights flicked and I looked away.

"You should use the restroom if you need to," I said, rising. "That's ten minutes until the lights go down again."

She frowned as I led her out into the hall. I wasn't comfortable leaving her for long, but luckily the men's restroom was just across the hall from the women's. Even in Moscow, far from the outfit, I didn't feel safe from Romano.

When she returned, I could tell she had freshened her makeup. As I led her back to our box, the faint scent of sweetness and flowers teased my nose and sent my mind spinning. The lights dimmed and the curtain drew up revealing a stage full of dancers who sprang to life as the orchestra started. Olivia leaned forward, enraptured at the sight, her fingers digging into the railing.

I brushed my lips over her ear. "When this dance is over, I want you on your knees," I whispered.

She kept her gaze straight ahead, but her breathing hitched. The dancers swirled and vaulted, their white-clad bodies like spots of light across the darkened stage. The tension in my groin increased as I watched the tiny pulse in her throat. How tender, how delicate it would feel beneath my fingers. I would trace it while her mouth entertained my cock. Fuck, I needed relief and this goddamn ballet sequence felt like it was hours long.

As the music reached a crescendo and began winding down, Olivia tore her attention from the stage and turned to me. Her fingers slid up my arm and I turned, her mouth meeting mine with sudden heat. She was intoxicating, her taste like liquid fire to my veins.

I pulled back. "Get on your knees and give me some goddamn relief," I breathed. "You've been teasing me all night and I can't take it anymore."

"I haven't been teasing you." Her brows drew together as she searched my face.

"You wore that dress knowing what it does to me."

She flushed and dipped her head. I leaned back, spreading my knees wide enough for her to fit between them, and pointed at the floor. She obeyed this time, removing her shoes quietly and kneeling between my legs. In the dim light, I could just make out her lines of her face and the glitter of her eyes.

"Open my pants," I whispered, keeping my tone gentle.

Her slender fingers began working the button of my pants, unfastening it and drawing down my zipper. My cock strained against the fabric of my boxers and when she drew it aside, her mouth parted as she gazed down at my erection. Her soft, slender hand wrapped around my cock, grasping it experimentally.

"That's good, baby," I breathed. "Now bend your head and take it in your mouth."

She hesitated, her eyes searching my face in the dark. I ran my knuckles gently up her throat and cupped her chin, drawing her lips closer to my cock. She opened her mouth and took the tip between her lips. I bit my tongue hard, forcing myself not to thrust forward. Her mouth was hot and gloriously wet as she slid me further inside. I tensed my jaw, breathing hard, and released a quiet groan. My God, she felt so good.

"You're doing so well," I said, keeping my voice low and gentle. "Now suck gently. You can hold it, yes, just like that. Fuck, you're perfect."

She drew me into her mouth, her tongue moving against the sensitive underside of my cock. My thighs tensed and I dug my free hand into the railing behind her head. I was already on the brink, trying not to finish just from the sight of her on her knees with her mouth on me. From this angle, I could see her barely covered breasts and her naked shoulders. Her dark head bobbed, her long, silky ponytail shimmering.

"Move your mouth up and down slowly while you suck," I whispered through gritted teeth. "Oh my God, you're such a good girl."

She obeyed and I bit back a gasp. Every time she slid her soft mouth back over me, she took a little more of my length. After a few minutes of this, she let my cock slide from her lips and wrapped her hand around the base. Her tongue slipped from between her red mouth and she licked me from top to bottom.

Fuck, I needed to get inside her mouth or I was going to make a mess of both of our clothes.

"I need to finish. Can you take it?"

She nodded, taking my cock back into her mouth. She sucked a little harder, drawing me to the back of her throat. A little moan vibrated around the tip of my cock and my orgasm hit, pleasure making my legs twitch as it washed through my body. She slowed, but kept sucking as I filled her mouth with my cum, and then she drew back a little, letting my cock slip from her mouth.

"Be good and swallow my cum, baby," I whispered, running my thumb over her chin.

She complied, her throat bobbing. There was a little bit on her lower lip and I swiped it off with my finger, pushing it between her lips. She sucked it off, her dark eyes fixed on mine. Dear God, she was a wet dream, an erotic fantasy come to life. Before I could pull my finger from her lips, she bit me gently in a tender gesture.

"Good girl, baby, you did such a good job," I said, helping her to her feet.

She sat back down in her seat and I knelt before her to help with her shoes. Her little foot rested in my palm, so delicate. I bent and kissed the underside, just beneath the arch, dragging my mouth up over her ankle. Her breath hitched, but her dress was too tight to lift her skirt any further than her knees.

I slipped my hand between her thighs and found the skimpy fabric of her thong and pulled aside the soaked lace. Her pussy was hot and slippery as I delved my fingers between her folds. Her eyes followed my hand as I pulled it from her skirt and licked her wet arousal from my fingers.

Jesus Christ, she was so sweet.

CHAPTER FOURTEEN

OLIVIA

I felt eyes drag over me as we left the theater at the end of the performance. The red curtains and gilded walls swirled around us as I walked at his side, his taste still on my tongue. His hand was on my lower back, guiding me and keeping me against his body. I'd never had so many men look at me before, their eyes flicking to my breasts and lingering there as we passed. I saw the way the women looked at Lucien and I caught the envious glances they cast my way.

He cast an impeccable figure in his gray suit, the fabric fitting his body like a glove. His dark hair was slicked back neatly over his head and his wrist was laden with one of his expensive watches. When he helped me back into the car, his coat and jacket shifted and I saw the flash of his gun. For some reason, seeing the weapons on his broad body sent a bolt of arousal through me.

We rode back to Viktor's mansion in silence. Across from me, Lucien sat with his legs spread and his hands rested on his thighs. His eyes barely left me the entire time and the air was thick with tension. Having him in my mouth had already soaked my panties, but having him look at me like this, like he wanted to devour me, had me throbbing with need.

I was painfully empty between my thighs.

We moved up the stairs, still not speaking, and Lucien locked our bedroom door behind us. There was a long silence and then my husband slipped his coat from his shoulders and moved toward me, his fingers stripping his tie, cuff links, shoes, and shirt.

Then those lean, hard hands were on me, tearing the beautiful dress down the middle. I gasped, too stunned to speak. Even if I'd had time to protest, I wouldn't have dared. There was darkness in those normally placid eyes and it both aroused and frightened me.

He stripped the shreds from my body and pushed me down on the bed, flipping me to my stomach. I heard his pants hit the floor and then his hard, warm body was on mine, pressing me down into the mattress. His hand pushed between my thighs, parting them. His arm slid beneath my lower belly to lift my hips.

He penetrated me with a single thrust, filling me with his heavy length. A cry burst from my lips and he covered my mouth, his fingers blocking the sounds as he drew back and slammed back into me. This wasn't about pleasure, this was fulfilling some primal need within him.

I whimpered against his hand as he pounded into my swollen pussy, his breath coming in short, hoarse pants.

He pulled his hand away from my face, wrapping my ponytail around his fist, and dragged my head back.

"Who do you belong to?" he asked through gritted teeth.

He slammed back into me and I cried out.

"Answer me."

"You," I breathed.

"Whose pussy is this, Olivia?"

"It's yours."

His free hand pushed beneath me and found my clit, stroking my arousal over the sensitive nerves. I had been wet all night from his touch, from the icy drag of his eyes over my body, and especially from having his cock in my mouth. He swirled his fingers over my clit once, then twice, and I came with a sharp cry. My inner walls contracted hard, drawing him deeper into my body, and he swore under his breath.

"Come for me." His voice was low and urgent. "Oh, fuck, come on my cock, baby, just like that."

My orgasm hit its crescendo and he slammed into me one final time. Warmth blossomed deep inside as he came in my pussy for the first time since our wedding night. He groaned, pressing me down, holding me steady as he rode out the aftershocks of his orgasm. I bit down on the bed covers and a tremor of arousal went through my body.

There was a heavy moment of silence and then he released a shuddering breath and pulled from me.

"Are you alright?" he asked.

I got to my hands and knees, my legs feeling like water. He lay on his back beside me, his cock still halfway erect. There was still a trace of vulnerability in his gaze, a touch of warmth to drive away the endless cold. He held out his arm and I went to him, curling into the heat of his body.

"Open your legs," he said huskily.

He always looked at my pussy after sex, even when he used a condom. Now that it had been a while since I'd started birth control, he was free to finish inside me again. The sight of his cum spilling onto the inside of my thigh made his mouth part and his eyes glitter. He inspected me with a satisfied expression on his face and then he slid his fingertip through my folds.

"Did you like the opera?" he said.

I nodded. Every pass of his finger sent a jolt of electricity through my hips.

"You need finished again," he observed.

I bit my mouth, a little ashamed by my arousal. He gathered my wetness and his cum and began stroking it over my clit, curling his tongue around my nipple. I was already on the edge, so aroused by how he'd held me down while he came, pinning me like an animal. My orgasm burst to the surface and I gasped, keeping our gazes locked. For a moment, I spun into nothing, into cold, into desolation.

It would never change. I would see flashes of life and light in him as I had tonight. But he would always be a man made of ice and steel and it had nothing to do with the color of his eyes. Perhaps that was the story he told himself, but I knew better. He'd been broken by cruelty, entrapped in world that had stolen his innocence long before its time, and I would never be able to change that. I could only love him through it.

My God, I loved him.

The realization sent a shock through me that squeezed my lungs until I let out a sharp gasp. I rolled over and pressed my face against his side. He gathered me in his arms and we lay in silence for a long time before I fell asleep, wrapped in his heat and drenched in longing.

The next two weeks passed quickly. Lucien was absent most of the time, but he came to me at night and we fucked until the early morning. He enjoyed oral and wanted to go down on me every time we had sex, but I still struggled to orgasm from it. I did, however, find that when I was riding his cock, I could come more than once with my finger on my clit. We spent hours testing the limits of the antique bed, hoping that the creaking of the springs couldn't be heard downstairs.

But I still didn't have the courage to tell my husband how I felt.

Occasionally, Lucien wouldn't come to bed and I knew he was up late working on his plan to kill Romano. He was always in the study with Viktor and his right hand man, Leonid. He was a large, blond man with a smooth face and bright blue eyes. He spoke a little English and no Italian, but he always behaved respectfully toward me, even though we couldn't actually converse.

They spent long hours meeting in the study and studying blueprints and maps. It was grisly, this whole process of planning an assassination, when I stood back and thought about it, but on the surface, they made it seem so ordinary. As though they were planning a work event. They were all so analytical, breaking everything down to the smallest steps and the tiniest details. Despite how much I hated Romano, it bothered me a little.

That was why they were the men in charge, I supposed. But I didn't like that part of Lucien, the power hungry, calculating man I knew he was inside, so I stayed away and let them work.

We left Russia four days before the end of the year. The week leading up to our planned departure felt slow and sad. I trailed around the house, anxiety growing in my chest. During dinner, I found myself falling back into old habits. I worried my food, cutting it to shreds, pushing it around my plate. I was hungry, but the prospect of returning to the States and facing everything we had left behind weighed on my chest like a ton of bricks and I had no appetite.

We left Viktor's mansion during the night in a car with blacked out windows. I slept through most of the ride, although this time I wasn't drugged, and woke as we pulled up to the private plane. Lucien guided me aboard and he held me on his lap for a long time, his hard arm circled around my body, and his cheek rested against the top of my head. Neither of us spoke.

It was late when we arrived at the Esposito mansion. It hadn't occurred to me until we were climbing up the spiral staircase that we were heading to Lucien's room. Duran and Iris were already in bed and the house was completely quiet. The only illumination came from the moonlight reflecting off the snow outside.

Lucien's room was along the hall that ran the other direction from my old room. He carried two of our bags in one hand, insisting as usual to do things for himself instead of leaving it for the servants, and held my hand with the other. His fingers felt rough and comforting in mine, the palms warm around my cold hand.

We arrived at what was clearly the master suite. Unlike the other rooms, this one had double doors with gold embellishment over the painted wood. Lucien unlocked it and ushered me through, flipping the deadbolt behind him. Then he turned on the light and I was in his room, the place where my elusive husband had slept alone for the last several years. It felt incredibly intimate.

The floor was made of polished dark wood and the walls were a soft cream. The enormous bed was made up in white with several thick pillows and a fur throw across the end. Across from the bed was a pair of couches with a circular marble table adorned with a vase of a dozen white roses. The four enormous windows looked out over the woods and the side garden.

I was expecting something dark and dispirit, befitting a bachelor, but this was warm and clean. Lucien crossed the room and set the bags down by the closet door and began taking his coat off. I released a sigh and sat down on the edge of the bed to remove my shoes.

"Do you like it?" he asked.

I nodded. "It isn't what I expected, but I do love it."

"I had it renovated while we were gone," he said, removing his vest and unfastening his shirt. Each button he undid revealed a little more of his broad, tattooed chest. "I thought you might like something a little more appropriate for a woman."

Warmth blossomed in my chest. "Thank you."

"You'll be here more than I am," he said, shrugging. "I know you probably know this already, but I'm usually very busy. And when I become boss, I'll be busier still. You'll likely not see me most days until later in the evening."

I hesitated. "Perhaps we could talk more about it?"

He stepped out of his pants and crossed to me in his boxers. "I don't know what there is to talk about."

"Perhaps we could compromise?" I looked up at him towering over me.

"I have my work and my duty to the outfit," he said.

"I know. I just—"

"Let's continue this discussion tomorrow," he said. "I'm tired and I want to fuck my wife before we sleep."

He stripped me and we fell into the bed, sinking into the plush comforter. I sighed, almost contented in what we had. Yes, I did love him, and no, I didn't know if he would ever truly return that feeling. But this was good, this felt warm and safe, like something that could last.

He pushed my legs open and sheathed himself. For a moment, an expression of pure bliss and satisfaction crossed his face, shattering the ice, and then it was gone.

"It's good to be back," he murmured.

I heartily disagreed, but I kept quiet, tracing the tattoo on his chest. The hanged bird rippled as he drove into me in lazy strokes. He fucked me in silence for a while, seeming to understand that I wasn't in the mood to do anything more than lie beneath him. When he finished, he kissed my mouth and rolled from my body to lie beside me in our bed.

"You're not happy to be home," he said quietly.

Tears threatened to spill over. I blinked rapidly and looked up at the ceiling. "Russia felt like a new world. Here...there's just bad memories and uncertainty. I hate it."

He gathered me against his body, pressing his chest to my back. "I will kill Romano and I'll build you a world you want to live in. It will be beautiful, just like Russia, like Viktor's mansion."

"That's what you do, isn't it?" I murmured. "You just reshape the world in the image you want."

"Yes. I do."

"Is that what you did with your father?"

Ever since our car ride to the opera, I'd had the question in the back of my mind, but it wasn't fully formed. Now, the words rolled from my tongue in a burst of recklessness. He had lied to me in the car, I could tell, and I didn't like it. Lucien was so meticulous, so calculated, there was no way he hadn't looked into who had killed his father. He knew what had happened, but he was protecting someone.

"What does that mean, Olivia?" His voice was stiff.

I flipped over to face him. He was propped up on his elbow, his eyes fixed on me.

"You lied," I said quietly. "When I asked you what happened to your father, you lied. It's like, you didn't like what happened, so you're just trying to force a narrative that you agree with."

He gazed at me, his face frozen. There was nothing, no expression, no darkening or lightening of his countenance.

"I'm not afraid of you," I whispered.

He cleared his throat. "Why the fuck do you think you deserve an answer when it comes to my family?"

His words stung. We lay in silence for a long time and then his breathing changed and he was asleep. Feeling deeply hurt and confused by his reaction, I closed my eyes and forced myself to at least pretend to get some rest.

The next morning when I woke, I blinked through sticky eyes and saw Lucien standing before the mirror adjusting his tie. I lay in bed, not moving, and watched him fasten his cufflinks. Then he smoothed his hair back and turned to face me, cocking his head. I scowled a little and balled myself up, pushing the blanket up to my chin.

"You need to get up," he said. "Iris is throwing a customary party to welcome us home tonight. It's tradition for newly married underbosses. Why don't you help her put it together?"

"I don't know how to put together a party," I said quietly.

"You're about to learn."

He stepped up to the edge of the bed and pulled back the covers and his eyes fell on my naked body. His gaze perused me for a long moment and the tips of his fingers grazed over my hips. Then he slipped his hand between my thighs and drove his index and middle finger into my pussy. An ache of pleasure and pain went through me and I bit my lip, determined not to let him see my arousal.

"There are some parts of my life I will never be able to share with you," he said. "I ask that you respect that and don't ask about them."

He flicked my G-spot hard and his thumb circled my clit until pleasure began building. I gasped and arced my lower back, an orgasm rising quickly to the surface. At the last minute, he pulled his fingers from my pussy and stood back.

"What was that?" I cried out in frustration.

He traced my stomach with his wet fingers, trailing my arousal across my skin. "I'll fuck you tonight. In the meantime, be a good girl and do as I say."

I managed to bite back the angry retort on the tip of my tongue as he left. As soon as his footfalls disappeared down the hall, I threw the pillow across the room, falling onto my back and kicking my heels into the bed in rage.

I showered and dressed in a long-sleeved, black dress that clung to my body and fell to the middle of my thigh. I pulled my hair up in a high ponytail, fluffed my bangs, and slipped on a pair of black pumps. Then I left the room and went in search of Iris.

She stood in the front hallway holding a tablet, her finger poised over the screen. She wore a white sweater and jeans and her hair was pulled back from her face in a loose braid. Despite how good our honeymoon had been and how little I wanted to return, it was nice to see Iris again.

She hugged me and drew back. "How was the honeymoon? How were the Adirondacks?"

So that was the story Lucien had told everyone. I'd forgotten for a moment that only Duran knew where we had actually gone for our honeymoon. A twinge of guilt went through me at having to lie to Iris.

"Amazing," I said. "It was cold, so we didn't get out too much."

"Do you need to get out much on your honeymoon?" she said, her eyes glinting.

I smiled and headed down the hall toward the kitchen to get a cup of coffee. Iris followed at my heels, her excitement palpable. We'd both been dying to discuss our honeymoons with each other and now that the men were out of house, it was the perfect time.

In the kitchen, Iris pushed the door shut and I began making a French press. In minutes, the kitchen was full of the smell of coffee and chocolate croissants. Iris sat down, crossing her long legs, and setting her phone aside to give me her full attention. Other than the quick chat we had had while getting ready for the wedding, we hadn't been able to discuss anything in several weeks.

"So how was it?" she asked, her voice hushed and excited.

I thought about it for a moment as I stirred cream into my coffee. "The honeymoon really was good. Lucien isn't what I expected at all.

Honestly, I thought I knew him before the wedding, but I had no idea what he's actually like."

"What do you mean?"

"He's far more...kind than I thought," I said. "And I'm saying that even though we had a fight this morning, so it must be true."

Iris tore her croissant in half and laid it aside. Her eyes were brimming with mischief and I knew what she really wanted to talk about. I'd been wanting to talk about it too, although now that I had the opportunity to, I felt a little shy about discussing my sex life.

"So how was *it*?" she asked.

"How was it for you?" I asked, smiling over the edge of my coffee.

"I told you," she said, looking over her shoulder make sure we were alone. "We didn't wait until we were married, but honestly it was fine because that way I was relaxed enough I got to finish a few times on our wedding night."

"We waited," I said. "But we didn't really do anything sexual before the wedding, so that wasn't a big surprise. I think arranged marriages are just a lot different than people who get to marry for love. Neither of us were really champing at the bit to get to it."

"Well...was it any good?"

"It was good," I said slowly. "I thought Lucien was just going to have sex with me and go to sleep or something like that, but he spent a lot of time making me comfortable and doing things that felt good for me too. I had an orgasm."

I flushed a little at my admission, but Iris was eating my words up, basking in the gossip. She must have been lonely, rattling around the Esposito mansion for the last month with no one to talk to until Duran returned at night.

"Really? I didn't have an orgasm the first time," she said enviously. "Maybe I should tell Duran that Lucien managed to get you off the first time, just to antagonize him. Did it hurt for you?"

"A little, but not like I thought it would," I said.

We talked like this for a while and then Iris went to make another pot of coffee. I sat at the table in silence, my conversation with Lucien this morning still churning in my head. When Iris returned, she set our second cups of coffee out and pulled her planner from her bag as she settled across from me.

"We don't have all that much to do before the party tonight," she said, flipping the planner open. "But Lucien told me on his way out that he wanted more flowers, so I have to call the florist. He said he wanted it to remind guests of a garden. I don't know why he was so interested in the floral arrangements, but I wouldn't want to disappoint."

"He knows I like flowers," I said quietly. "I used to grow them in my garden back at my family's house."

A pang of guilt went through me. Perhaps I had been too hard on him this morning. Maybe I had no right to ask about his father, especially when I knew he was so hurt by the topic.

"Are you homesick?" Iris's brows drew together in confusion. She was aware of how I felt about my parents.

"No, no," I said. "Can I ask you something kind of...off-topic?"

She shrugged. "Of course."

I took a quick breath. "Do you know what happened to Lucien and Duran's father?"

"He was killed." Iris frowned slightly and lifted her cup to her lips. "Duran doesn't know all that much about what happened. He was still a teen and Lucien never really talks about it."

"Doesn't that make you...I don't know...wonder what went down?" I asked slowly.

"I was curious, so I looked it up online and there was a little information," she said. "Apparently Carlo Romano actually had one of the police on his payroll open up an investigation into it. It was strange...I read the report and all the doors and windows were locked when it happened. They thought it might have been a servant or the groundskeeper, but they weren't able pin down exactly who."

There was a faint sick sensation in my chest and my hands were clammy despite being wrapped around my warm cup. "Were there any other suspects?"

She shook her head. "Everything was wiped clean, no prints, nothing on the security cameras. He was just dead."

"How did it happen? Was he shot?"

"His...um, head was cut off with a wire," Iris said, looking a little pale. "There were pictures and I wish I hadn't seen them. Don't look it up, the whole thing gives me the creeps and makes me nervous sleeping in this house."

"I'm sure the person who did it isn't around anymore," I said quickly.

"Yeah, I'm sure," she said.

I took a breath and got to my feet, the room spinning as I fought to get my bearings. How could I entertain these thoughts about my husband? Iris stood, but I waved her away, making an excuse that I had a sudden migraine and needed to lie down. She watched me go, her hands twisted together, and I felt a pang of guilt for worrying her.

Up in my room, I sat on the edge of the bed with my shoes off, the floor cold against the bottom of my feet. Unbidden, my mind went back to that night at the opera. How soft Lucien's mouth had felt against the arch of my foot and how silky it had been against the skin of my calf and the sensitive underside of my knee. His hands had been so gentle as he slipped my shoes on and beneath those icy eyes I'd thought I saw a flicker of warmth.

I squeezed my eyes shut. No, he might be a man operating outside the law, but he had a moral code like anyone else. He would never commit something so heinous as his own father's murder.

But as soon as I thought those words, I knew I was lying to myself.

Yes, Lucien absolutely would kill anyone he felt he needed to. The world went still as I recalled everything he'd ever told me about his father. That he was an abuser, a rapist, a cruel and ruthless underboss. And, I acknowledged quietly, a barrier between Lucien and his birthright. It only made sense that Lucien would have retaliated against him.

That was the sort of man my husband was and I loved him anyway.

The tight fear thrumming in my chest subsided slowly, leaving me feeling drained. I had no right to judge my husband for anything when I wanted him to kill Romano for what he'd done to me. We were both cut from the same cloth.

My fears weren't assuaged, but they were resigned at least. Feeling exhausted by the emotional roller coaster of the morning, I lay down for a while and rested. I didn't want Iris to realize I'd been lying about having a migraine, so I pretended my headache was much better when she arrived to check on me.

She carried a black dress bag over her arm when she slipped through the door. "Can I get you anything? A glass of water?"

I lifted the one by the bed. "I just had a little water. I feel a lot better. What do you have there?"

"Oh, I was shopping while you were gone and I saw this dress," she said excitedly. Iris had a soft spot for fashion and she spent a lot of time and Duran's money at the shops downtown. "I picked it up for you to wear tonight. After all, it's your first public outing as a married couple so you want to look perfect."

I slipped from between the sheets and stood. "May I see it?"

Grinning with anticipation, Iris laid it over the bed and unzipped the bag and drew out a dress of silky blood red. "Alright, so Lucien is either going to love it or he's going to make you go change," she said. "Put it on to get the full effect."

I sidled out of the dress I was wearing and Iris helped me slip into the red one. The waist was structured with a short corset and the bodice was padded with strapless cups that molded to my breasts and pushed them up. As I pulled it on, I realized it had an undergarment similar to panties sewn into the skirt. It wasn't hard to imagine why. The gauzy skirt had two slits that ran up to my hipbones. I couldn't have worn real panties underneath and I certainly couldn't have forgone underwear unless I wanted to flash everyone when I walked.

"You look amazing," Iris breathed. She ducked behind me and zipped up the back and arranged my hair over my shoulders.

I looked across the room at the mirror hanging by the door. She was right. In this dress, I was a queen, the kind of woman Lucien had urged me to be that night in Russia. Someone fearless enough to face my parents, to face my fears and uncertainty. A woman who deserved to walk on Lucien Esposito's arm.

"Thank you, it's perfect," I said.

We spent the rest of the afternoon getting ready. Iris wore a silky, beige dress with a lace back, a long slit up the side, and towering heels. She was breathtaking, as always. I did her hair, brushing it back into a sleek ponytail, and she did mine, straightening it and pinning in a low bun at the nape of my neck. She put light waves in my feathery bangs and I added a careful layer of red lipstick and it was time to go downstairs.

Duran stood at the bottom of the stairs, his brow cocked in appreciation as he took in Iris. She spun in a circle, almost losing her balance, and leaned forward to kiss him.

"How do you like my dress?" she asked.

He slapped her across the ass. "I like it. Easy access for later."

"Duran!"

Iris pulled him away to the front hall, her face stern, but a smile playing around her mouth. A little hurt that my husband wasn't waiting for me, I wandered into the living room, which was already set up beautifully for the party. Lucien was nowhere to be found. Several minutes passed and he still didn't show, so I went to check the kitchen. It was deserted. I leaned on the counter, tapping the toe of my high heel idly against the floor. In the distance, the front door opened and the first guests began to arrive.

Feeling frustrated, I climbed up the stairs and headed toward our bedroom. Perhaps he was angrier than I'd thought he was and he didn't want to see me. I had barely got more than ten steps up the stairwell when I heard my husband call my name.

Lucien stood at the bottom in a fitted black suit. He was so handsome, so deliciously ice cold and controlled I almost forgot we'd fought just hours ago. I wanted to put aside my hurt feelings and press against his hard body and kiss his neck, just above the crisp collar of his shirt.

He held out his hand and I descended the stairs. His brows rose a little at the sight of my naked legs and the strip of chiffon draped between my thighs and trailing behind me as I walked. He didn't say anything as he took my hand and led me into the kitchen and shut the door with a soft click. For a moment, I just looked up at him, remembering what Iris had told me, wondering if he was the man I thought I married or if he was far more cold blooded than I had ever imagined.

This was a man who had killed his father, a man who even now planned to kill again. Perhaps it was Lucien's coldness rubbing off on me, but the thought no longer bothered me as it had earlier. I studied him and he met my gaze, those hazel eyes dragging over my body, as lazy as the flick of his wrist when he tapped the ash from a cigarette.

It aroused me, the heartlessness of him.

"We're not to arrive at dinner until Duran announces us," he said, breaking the silence.

"Who's going to be here?" I asked.

"Everyone."

We were quiet for a long time until Duran put his head in and told us to follow him out into the dining room. My heart thudded, knowing who was waiting for us, knowing my parents and Romano would be there. Lucien stretched out his hand, palm up, and I placed my fingers across it. Then we followed Duran out into the hall.

There was a round of applause as we entered the room. Heart pumping, I skimmed the room, meeting my mother's gaze for a second. An overwhelming desire to look away filled me, but I remembered Lucien's words and kept my eyes on hers, staring her down. There was a long, intense moment as we passed her and then she lowered her eyes and a surge of heady triumph washed over me.

Coward. Manipulative, abusive coward.

Lucien paused before Romano, keeping me a step behind him. They shook hands and then Romano reached past him and took my hand, sending a shiver through me. The memory of his hand between my thighs was fresh and painful in my mind. I took a deep breath and lifted my eyes to him as he brushed his lips across my hand.

"Olivia Esposito," he said. "You are stunning."

"I know."

The words slipped from my mouth before I could stop them and there was an audible gasp from the room. Romano's face froze and we stood, gazes locked, and then he laughed.

"You are a feisty one," he said. "You have your hands full, Lucien."

Lucien's mouth twitched. "I do."

We sat down, Lucien at the head with me at his left and Romano in the next seat over. When Lucien leaned forward to fill his glass, I caught Romano's eye, determined that my slip wouldn't reflect badly on my husband. Even if it meant swallowing my disgust and apologizing to the man who had assaulted me.

"I'm sorry, I meant no disrespect," I said quietly.

Romano's eyes lingered on my breasts, unashamed. "I know," he said softly. "But I'll only accept your apology if you dance once with me tonight, Mrs. Esposito."

Stomach roiling, I inclined my head and turned back to my plate. The servants brought out the food and I took a deep breath and picked up my fork. I could feel my mother's eyes on me, already judging the new curves to my body. I found her gaze across the table and put a forkful of mashed potatoes into my mouth, not caring for the first time that they were drenched in butter.

Lucien was right about wanting power. It was a high I could get addicted to.

CHAPTER FIFTEEN

LUCIEN

I was rock hard beneath the table. Even having the entire outfit seated in the same room wasn't enough to deter the blood pounding in my groin. Something about the red dress she wore was sexier even than the black one that had shown an obscene amount of her breasts. Knowing I was done for, I glanced down at her lap, unable to drag my eyes away.

Her legs were fully visible through the slits in her skirt that ran all the way up to her hipbones. If it weren't for the lower portion of the dress that covered her pussy, she would have exposed herself with every step. She shifted in her seat and I caught her eye and she lifted a leg and crossed it over the other. Fuck, she knew exactly what she was doing. I ran my eyes down the curve of her calf to the red sandals that showed her manicured toes.

I needed to fuck her before the night was over. There was a bathroom just off the front room where the dance floor was located. If only I had the time now, I would pull her into it and lay her down on the sink, draw her silky legs over my shoulders, and sink deep into her tight pussy. She would moan and writhe and make that gasping cry that drove me wild as she came around my cock.

This wasn't helping. I glanced over at Romano and felt significantly less hot under the collar. He was looking down as well and I knew his eyes were on my wife's body, dragging over her legs. He was probably fantasizing about fucking her too. The thought sent a rush of rage through me, killing my erection.

After dinner, everyone gathered to the other side of the house. The front room opposite the living area had been cleared and the black and white patterned floor shone in the candlelight. On the far side was a bar where a few of the younger men had already congregated. I noticed Cosimo Barone leaning on the counter at the end, his arm around the waist of Lorenza Russo, a young woman who'd been widowed a few years ago, just shy of her thirtieth birthday.

I frowned, making a mental note to ask Olivia about it later. Lorenza was a good seven years older than Cosimo and if I was going to make him an underboss soon, I needed him to agree to a more useful match. Not that I begrudged his current choice. I'd fucked my share of women older than I when I was a young man and I understood the appeal.

After everyone was thoroughly lubricated with wine and liquor, the band in the corner struck up a slow waltz. I set aside my glass and looked for Olivia, but Romano was already leading her out to the dance floor, his hand on her lower back. Heat and anger rose in my chest, but I forced myself to keep my rage concealed and contained. It was a bold move for him to claim her first dance and I knew it wasn't lost on anyone in the room.

I felt their eyes on me as I stood on the edge of the floor. Duran and Iris began dancing on the far side and a few other couples followed suit. I paced along the edge of the room, my blood pumping beneath the surface. My face was a smooth mask, but beneath it all, I was seething, longing to tear my wife from Romano's arms.

He was taunting me, trying to draw my anger out into the open. It felt eerily like something my father would do. Humiliate me with his words, hurt me with his fists, strip away my dignity and my control. He'd deserved what had happened to him and Romano would too.

Another song started and Romano led a nervous Iris out to the floor. I kept back and allowed Duran to take Olivia's hand and join the other couples. The room was growing hazier as time went on, full of the scent of wine and whiskey, the thrumming of music, and the whirl of colorful dresses. In the center of it was Olivia, passed back and forth between the prominent men of the outfit as the orchestra played on. I'd known it would happen, we were the guests of honor after all, but seeing hands that weren't mine on my wife's body made me see red.

Then I saw her father cross the room in her direction and I sprang into action, striding toward them. She turned as we both approached and I put my hand around her waist and pulled her against my side. Her father's eyes narrowed for a moment and then he backed off, inclining his head. We were technically of the same rank, but I was Romano's favorite and the other underbosses conceded to me. Always.

"Duran," I said, catching his arm as he passed by. "Tell the orchestra to play a tango. And take my coat." I shrugged out of my jacket and took hold of Olivia's elbow, ushering her toward the center of the floor.

"What are you doing?" she whispered.

"You said you could tango," I said. "So just follow my lead."

The music started and her body lengthened, her shoulders going back. It had been a long time since I'd danced other than the waltz at our wedding, but I wasn't worried about embarrassing either of us. Thanks to my mother, I knew this dance inside and out.

We moved on beat, our bodies melding together as if we'd choreographed this dance a hundred times together. Her eyes burned dark and her red mouth parted as I spun her, catching her in my arms and dipping her back over my knee. For a second, suspended in time, I saw her laid out, her elegant body arching back over my leg, and my blood pumped faster. Then we were moving again, spinning across the floor, our bodies weaving together.

I was dimly aware everyone had stopped dancing around us and were now hanging back to watch. I flipped her to face out and she slid down against me, her head level with my groin for a moment. Her leg slid out to the side in a slow, sensual movement. My eyes fell on the arch of her pretty foot and I caught my breath at the sight.

Without thinking, I stepped back, spun her once on her heel, and pulled her close. She was a pure fire, her gorgeous body dressed in red with those long, long legs keeping perfect time with mine. Jesus Christ, as soon as I got her alone, I was going to remind her exactly who she belonged to.

I picked her up in one arm and her legs bent as I passed her over my knee, catching her wrists at the last moment and spinning her around my body. She was trusting me completely not to let her fall. I pulled her against me, her leg sliding out in tandem with mine. Her shoulders and head bent back in a graceful curve, exposing her throat to me.

The music thrumming in my ears, in my body, and I forgot myself completely as I dragged my mouth from her throat to the full swell of her breasts above her neckline. Her breathing hitched as my tongue flicked out and then I lifted her upright and we spun back into motion.

I could sense the music was coming to an end. Riding the final swell, I guided her toward the edge of the floor, our bodies moving in lightning fast movements. Then I spun her around my body and bent her until she was laid back across my knee once more. I dragged my hand across her throat, reminding her who she belonged to, claiming her in front of every man who had had his hands on her tonight. For a moment, her dark eyes cut through the sound and motion, cut right to me, and then I pulled her back into my arms just as the music ended.

There was a short silence and then scattered applause. No one knew how to react, but I didn't give a shit. I had made my point. Beside me, Olivia was flushed with embarrassment, her body now small and pressed against my side.

Duran ducked out of the crowd. "Jesus Christ, I think I need a cigarette after watching that," he said. "What the hell, Lucien?"

"Look at Romano," I said under my breath.

We both looked over at our boss, standing by the bar. His fingers were tight around his glass and his eyes were narrowed. There was a tightness in his body that hadn't been there before and when I met his gaze, it was glacially cold. He was livid, angry that despite his best efforts to undermine me, he was inferior. Olivia was mine.

Duran frowned. "So was that little performance about your wife or about your boss?"

Olivia stared up at him, her throat bobbing as she swallowed.

"I needed to send a message," I said shortly.

"Next time just piss on her. It'd be a lot easier," Duran said, turning away and taking Iris's hand to lead her back into the crowd.

Shaking off my annoyance at my brother's tone, I turned back to my wife, but she was gone. I scanned the room and caught a flash of red disappear around the corner as she fled into the hall. What the hell was wrong with her? She knew how I felt, knew that I hated the thought of anyone putting their hands on her body. If I'd had the freedom to do it, I would have snapped Romano's neck the moment he laid eyes on her.

I stepped into the hall just in time to see the door at the far end swing shut. Shoes clipping against the floor, I pursued her soft footfalls through the kitchen and into the back of the house. She was probably headed to the servant's staircase and from there, our bedroom, where she would inevitably cry or rage at me.

The back hallway was empty and cold from being shut off from the rest of the house. At the far end, Olivia was struggling with the back door, but it was locked. We always kept it locked in the winter. As I drew near, she gave a frustrated cry and kicked the door hard with her heeled foot.

"Where the fuck are you going, Olivia?" I snapped.

"Anywhere that isn't with you," she said, spinning around and pushing her back against the door.

"Why?"

"Because I thought that dance was for me, but it turns out you're just performing for Romano, the man who assaulted me. Why does everything have to be for fucking Romano?" she seethed.

"Because it does, because he put his hands all over you and I can't do a goddamn thing about it," I snapped, struggling to keep my face blank.

"Maybe I was angry enough to just give up and let him!"

"Why the fuck would you do that?"

"Because you lied when I asked you about your father," she cried. "You force me to go along with all of your plans, you lie to me, you shut me out. I'm your wife, Lucien, and I deserve to know what happened to your father."

My blood pumped cold and slow in my ears. I advanced on her slowly and she shrank back, her perfect, red mouth shaking with fear. Dear God, I wanted to fuck her even now. I needed to press her up against the door, rip away the fabric between us, and thrust into her hot, little cunt until she screamed. Until every man in this house heard what I did to her and knew who she belonged to.

"Do you really want to know?" I asked quietly. Her face was inches from mine. I felt the cold air seeping through the door against our bodies. "I turned off all the monitors, I drugged my mother and my brother, and then I went to my father's room. He was sleeping, but when I wrapped a razor-sharp wire around his throat, he woke. His eyes were open, looking up at me. I killed him and every day since I have lived without an ounce of regret for putting that motherfucker six feet underground."

CHAPTER SIXTEEN

OLIVIA

My heart beat impossibly fast and my mouth was so dry it felt like cotton. Lucien hovered close, his beautiful, cold face just inches away. An achingly long moment passed and then he leaned forward and his mouth brushed over my throat, his hot tongue flicking against the sensitive spot where my neck met my shoulder.

"Lucien," I breathed, my hands struggling up.

"What, baby, you want to run from me now?" he murmured. "Because I had the balls to do what needed to be done? I'll bet you won't complain after I slit Romano's throat and make you a queen. You want power as much as I do and you know it."

He was right. As much as it had angered me, my pussy had throbbed with need with every touch of his hand. I bit hard on my lip, the pain a welcome distraction, and raised my eyes to his endlessly cold gaze. Our gazes locked for a long moment and then he pushed off, striding to the center of the hall, his hands behind his back. He cut an austere figure, surrounded by opulence, stained with desire and sin.

He was consuming me, eating me alive, drawing me into a world where there was nothing but power and the constant need to spill blood.

Who had I become?

The backdrop of the chilly hallway glittered behind him, blue and silver, like midnight. The lines of his body were a work of art in the pale light from the windows. He took a single step, the sound reverberating through the empty mansion.

"I want you to run." Those icy eyes were as distant as ever, but now there was a glitter behind them. A fevered hunger that roused a shiver down my spine.

"You want me to run?" I repeated.

"Run, run until I catch you. Run to my study upstairs."

He'd allowed me only glimpses of this side of him, but nothing could have prepared me for the primal desire in his burning gaze.

"What happens when you catch me?" My mouth was dry.

He stepped close and his scent washed over me as he lifted my chin with the side of his finger. "You know what happens when I catch you," he whispered.

"Why do you want to chase me?" I breathed.

"Because I want to see those little feet try to get away from me before I pin you down and fuck you until you're crying for me to stop."

I gasped, a shiver going through my body, setting every nerve ablaze. My pussy throbbed and I squeezed my thighs together, slickness coating my folds. If it hadn't been for the thick fabric over my sex, I was sure I would have felt it slip down my thighs.

"So I'm going to give you a head start," he said, stepping aside to clear a path down the hallway. "You know where the study is. If you get there first, what we do is up to you. If I catch you, you're mine for the night. Understood?"

I nodded, my mouth dry. "What if you hurt me?"

A flash of darkness crossed his face. "I won't, but if you need me to back off, just say red and I'll stop."

I gazed up at him, his icy gaze boring down into me. Then I reached down and slipped off my heels, placing my feet on the cold ground. Lucien watched my every move, his body tensed beneath his dark vest and white shirtsleeves. I ducked my head and bolted, running past him toward the stairwell at the end of the hall.

I heard his footfalls as I reached the top of the stairs. He was gaining on me rapidly. When I reached the top, I whirled and saw him below me, his long legs eating up the distance between us. My heart fluttered against my ribs and I turned back, surveying the hallways on either side. His study was in the middle, accessible from both sides, but I wasn't sure which hall brought me there sooner.

Lucien was seconds from me when I darted from his grasp, choosing the hall on the left that led away from our room. I was sure I felt his hand graze my skirt as I fled from him, but there was no time to turn and look.

I turned the corner, the hall stretching long and dark before me. Behind me, Lucien's wingtips clipped against the carpet, drawing closer. So close. What would he do? What was there left to do that we hadn't already done? I was vaguely aware of the pulsing between my thighs and the desperate desire that coated my pussy. Whatever it was, no matter how much this terrified me, I wanted him to catch me just as much as I wanted to get away. Perhaps more.

There were two doors at the end of the hall and I paused for a half second. Which one? If I entered the wrong room, he could block me in, but if I entered the right room, I won.

A hand closed on the back of my neck and I was spun around and pressed against the wall. A hot mouth slid up my throat and a hard hand squeezed my breast until a shot of pain went through me. My hips bucked involuntarily, pressing up against the thick length of him. He bit down on the base of my neck and ground himself into me so hard I felt his cock twitch.

"You lose," he breathed.

"Lucien, please," I begged.

He picked me up and threw me unceremoniously over his shoulder. All the air went out of my lungs as his big hand wrapped around my upper thigh to keep me still. Then we were moving and a door shut behind us and he lifted me down, laying me on my back on his desk.

He bent over me, shoving his thigh between my knees, and pressed his palms to the desk on either side of my head. His eyes were glittering ice and his mouth was a hard line. His throat was flushed, glinting with perspiration, his collar was wet where it met his skin.

"What are you going to do to me?" I whispered.

He slipped his fingers around my neck, his thumb grazing my throat. His touch was tender, as it always was when we were intimate, and for the first time, I saw it reflected in his gaze. Yes, it was just a flicker, a single flame in a wasteland, but it melted me. Whatever he wanted, whatever he intended to do with me, I was his to use as he pleased.

"I want to fuck your ass," he said softly.

A ripple of shock went through me. "My...what?"

"I've had you every other way, now I want you like that," he said, his chest rising and falling rapidly.

My body quivered and he ran his fingertip lightly down between my breasts, to my waist, and then flipped me onto my stomach. A gasp burst from me, my legs going weak at the mere thought that he wanted such a thing and that if I didn't use my safeword, he would do it.

And suddenly, I didn't want to stop him.

His fingers worked at the clasp of my dress and then the zipper hissed and cold air hit my back. His touch was firm, dominating, but incredibly gentle as he worked the garment from my body. Underneath, I wore only a black lace thong. His breath caught and I heard my dress hit the floor somewhere behind us. Then his hands were on me again, the fabric of his suit pressed against my naked body.

"You want your ass fucked, don't you?" he murmured in my ear. "Because you know you'll take it like a good girl and thank me for it when I'm done with you."

I whimpered, every rational thought driven from my mind.

"Tell me you'll take it like a good girl," he said.

I hesitated, delicious shame flooding me.

"Olivia, when I ask you a question, you answer it. Understood? Now, tell me you'll take it like a good girl?"

My mouth was dry. "I'll...I'll take it like a good girl," I whispered.

"Where are you going to take it?" His voice was smooth as silk. "Where are you going to take my cock, baby?"

My God, my body was on fire. He slid his hand, his lean fingers spread wide, over my hip and under my lace thong. His fingertips dug into the soft flesh of my ass, kneading it hard enough to make me wince.

"Where am I going to fuck you?" he pressed.

"My ass," I whispered, mortified.

He brushed a kiss between my shoulder blades, trailing his mouth down to my lower back. Every nerve in my body trembled at his touch and my knees shook like they were about to give out. He lifted my panties from my hips and slid them slowly down my legs, his fingers brushing against my sensitive flesh with every inch. I whimpered and he gave a soft growl of satisfaction.

I heard his chair pull closer and I looked up. It was then that I noticed the mirror directly across from the desk, my reflection gazing back at me with with glittering eyes and a flushed face. He sank down behind me and his eyes fixed on my body, naked and bent over his desk before him.

I closed my eyes as his fingers slid up my thighs and parted me. Yes, I knew he had seen that part of me during sex, but this was the first time he had directed all of his attention to it. I was ashamed to admit it, but it filled me with such an intense pleasure to know he was looking at me there. He did nothing for a long moment and then his wet fingertip circled my asshole and I gasped, my eyes widening.

"You're so tight," he said, teasing the sensitive skin. "But we'll loosen you up, make it feel good for you. Make you come around me."

He bent his head and then his hot tongue slid over my tight hole. My fingers dug into the desk so hard they turned white and stars blinked in my vision as blood rushed through my body, pooling between my thighs.

"Oh my God," I whispered.

He flicked his tongue, teasing the sensitive skin, sending bolts of pleasure down my thighs. With one hand, he cupped my pussy, his middle fingers finding my clit and working it gently. His tongue lapped over me in short, soft strokes, caressing me the way he always did with my clit. Deep within my hips, an orgasm began building.

I moaned, tension rising hard and fast. This was extraordinary, every touch like fireworks across my sensitive skin, every pass of his hot tongue sending more wet arousal down my thigh. The hot coil between my legs was building, tightening, drawing so close that my body shook.

Then he pulled back and stood abruptly. An audible gasp burst from my mouth and I turned, but he kept me still with a firm hand to my upper back.

"Eyes ahead," he said.

Frustrated, soaking wet, and still shaking, I turned back to the mirror. He took something from the drawer and I heard a bottle cap snap off and then cold liquid slid over my ass and pussy. His fingers swiped over me, gathering it, and circled my asshole. Biting my lip, I arced my spine, the sensation like fireworks through my body.

"I'm going to put my fingers into you first," he breathed. "You know how to tell me to stop if you need it. Do you understand?"

"Yes," I whispered, nodding almost frantically.

"Relax," he said, his voice low and soothing. "Think about coming on my cock, think about my tongue on your little pussy, think about whatever made you so wet when you sat on my face and dripped into my mouth."

A dozen images flashed through my mind and I moaned again, arching my spine as the tip of his finger breached my ass. Fuck, that felt better than it had any right to. He slid a hand beneath me and cupped my breast, playing with my nipple, and slid his finger the rest of the way in. I whimpered, my pussy aching, my clit swollen and throbbing with need. I was full and empty all at once and it was driving me wild.

He waited, lingering over me with his gaze locked in mine in the mirror, his finger inside the most private part of me. Then he began moving it, touching me with slow, even strokes. I rolled my head back, digging my fingernails into the polished wood of his desk. Oh my God, that was amazing. His other hand found my clit and he swirled the pad of his finger over the sensitive nub, teasing me with the lightest touches.

Then his touch was gone, just as soft pulses of pleasure began rising deep inside. I gave a short cry of frustration and he hushed me, stroking down my back as the tip of his cock traced over my asshole. He was incredibly hard. I bit back a whimper as he braced against the desk and pushed slowly against the tight muscle until the tip slipped inside me.

"Oh, fuck," I breathed, pain and pleasure splicing through me.

My legs shook as he pressed his cock into me with slow, even pressure. The sensation was like nothing I'd ever felt, a frustrating mix of fullness and emptiness all at once. God, it was painful and perfect having him in my ass, filling me until I couldn't take another inch, his thick length stretching me just wide enough to send bolts of pleasure through my body.

He slipped his hand up to my throat and lifted my chin to force me to meet his eyes in the mirror. He was almost panting, his chest rising and falling feverishly as he pulled back, drawing himself halfway from my body. There was a glitter in his stoic gaze, a deadly glint that betrayed his lust as he pushed back in. His cock moved deeper and deeper, the silky skin of his length rubbing against the tight ring of muscle.

I gripped the desk, my mouth falling open. His lips twitched and he reached around and dipped his fingers into the dripping wetness and swirled it over my clit. Yes, my God, yes. He swiped his fingers over the sensitive nub, his hips moving in a steady rhythm as he fucked my asshole. The combination had my orgasm rising so fast I saw stars in the corner of my vision and I lost control of my body as I came.

Pleasure moved through me in waves and I clung to the desk and rode it out helplessly, my ears ringing and my body trembling beneath him. He swore, weaving his fingers into my hair and bending my throat back.

"Take it, baby," he purred, his breath hot on my neck. "Goddamn, take it in your ass like a good, little fucktoy, like my good, little pet. Who do you belong to, baby?"

I whimpered, broken beneath him. "You, I belong to you."

"Who's fucking your perfect, tight asshole?"

"Y—you."

"Say my name, baby," he urged between heavy breaths. "Tell me who owns you."

Never had I felt so completely surrendered to anyone in my life. He commanded every brush of pleasure and ounce of pain that rippled through me. And I took it, weak and bent over before him, hanging from his strings like a puppet.

"You own me, Lucien," I whimpered.

"Fuck yes, baby, fuck yes." He released my hair, his hands going to the desk on either side of my head as he braced himself. His hips pumped in long, slow, sensual strokes. When I managed to look up and saw him in the mirror, bent over me with his eyes dark and his throat glittering with sweat, a flood of wet arousal gushed down my thigh. I had never seen him so undone, balanced on the brink of losing control.

I wanted him to tip off the edge. I needed to see the rawness beneath his cold, polished exterior, needed to have him fully with no barriers between us. He was my husband; we kissed, fucked, and slept beside each other, but I still didn't truly know him the way I longed to.

I bent my head to the side, exposing the soft flesh where my neck met my shoulder. There was sharp intake of breath and he swore through his teeth.

"I need to fuck you hard, baby. Can you take it?"

Could I? I wasn't sure, but I wanted it badly so I nodded. He groaned, his gaze meeting mine in the mirror, his lids heavy and his chest heaving. His length pulled from me slowly and his hand dug into my hips hard enough to spark pain. I winced, and while I was distracted by the sensation, he slammed into me until he was buried to the hilt.

My God, if I didn't give myself up to him fully, he would tear me apart. My body turned to water, limp beneath him, my head bent back to expose my throat. He fucked into me, his collar soaked in sweat, his lip curled back to expose his teeth, and his lids heavy over his darkened eyes.

Out of nowhere, an orgasm hit me like a storm, tearing through my body and sending a gush of wetness down my thighs. He fucked harder, riding me through the pleasure as my vision flashed and sweat broke out over my body. His mouth dragged over my upper back, licking up my perspiration, a feral growl rumbling in his throat as he tasted me.

Then his movements became abruptly erratic and he pressed his face against my upper back. His cock fucked up into the deepest parts of me and his hips spasmed as he let a moan of utter relief that came from the bottom of his soul. I felt the orgasm pump through his body as he released himself deep inside, filling me.

"I love you," he breathed, barely loud enough to hear.

I froze, my vision flashing and my breath catching in my lungs. Had he just said that? We stayed locked in place, his mouth hot against my skin and his large body draped over mine as if he wanted to keep me here beneath him forever.

"What did you say?" I whispered.

He lifted his head and licked up the side of my neck. "I said I love you."

"You do?"

"I wouldn't lie about that, baby."

I swallowed through the dryness in my throat. "I love you too."

He kissed my shoulder, his tongue flicking out again. Then he lifted himself slowly onto his elbows, his cock softening a little, and pulled from my body. A little moan escaped my mouth as he did. There was something deeply satisfying about him finishing in my ass. When we returned downstairs, his cum would still be inside me.

He turned me around, supporting my body with his forearm. My bangs were sweaty and sticking to my forehead and my nipples were raw from chafing against the desk. He brushed my hair back and cradled my face in his big, rough hands.

"Are you alright?"

I nodded. "It was intense. I think I'll probably be sore tomorrow."

"Good sore or bad sore?"

"Good sore."

He kissed my forehead and pulled me against his chest. "You're such a good girl, so well behaved, so obedient. I'm so proud of how well you took my cock in your ass, baby."

My God, he knew exactly what he was doing when he talked like that. My body flooded with warmth again and I squeezed my thighs together, pressing my face against the front of his vest. I wanted to stay like this forever, wrapped in his strong arms with my body still tender and marked from his touch.

"We need to go back downstairs," he murmured into my hair.

"I don't want to."

He pushed me back gently and took me by the chin. "Behave yourself, Olivia. You're already on thin ice, even after being such a good girl for me."

I frowned, unsure what he was talking about. "Why am I on thin ice?"

His eyes narrowed as they skimmed over my naked body. "Wearing that dress, letting every underboss in this room put his hands on you. Letting your first dance go to Romano."

"You expect me to say no to the boss?" Indignation flared in my chest.

He didn't answer. Instead, he ran his wide hand up my side and over my breast, squeezing it and twisting my nipple until I winced. I bit my lip hard. Jealous Lucien was a different man and he both aroused and frightened me.

"Every goddamn time we go out together, you wear some shred of clothing that barely covers your cunt. What am I supposed to think, Olivia?"

How dare he even hint at suggesting I was trying to entice Romano?

"I—"

He took my jaw in his hand. "I changed my mind, they can wait down there. Go to our bedroom, baby, I'm not finished with you."

Not wanting to taunt him further, I slipped on my dress and zipped it up the back, taking my shoes in my hand. He grasped my wrist and led me down the hall, his shoes clicking against the floor. They could probably hear our footfalls downstairs. A rush of shame flooded me as I realized what this must look like. They all had to know Lucien had disappeared with me and why else would he do that except to fuck me?

In our bedroom, Lucien locked the door and went to the bathroom. I followed, hanging back as he turned on the shower and began stripping his suit off. The front of his pants were stained dark with lube and my arousal.

We washed quickly, our bodies just touching beneath the water. Then I toweled dry and went to sit down on the edge of the bed. Lucien remained in the bathroom for a moment longer and then he stepped out, fully naked and already hard. His skin was still a little wet, water droplets glittering across his tattoos.

"I love you, baby, but I don't think you understand that you belong to me," he said quietly. "I think you say it, but you don't mean it."

"I do mean it," I whispered, my mouth dry.

He crouched before me, his eyes cutting deep. "No, you keep your pretty, little mouth shut unless I open it to put my cock in. The only sound you can make, the only thing you can say is your safeword. What is it, baby? You're allowed one more word, so tell me what your safeword is."

"Red," I whispered. My heart thudded in my chest and my mouth was dry, but between my legs, I was already soaked.

"Smart girl," he purred, rising and towering over me. "Now, I'm going to tell you exactly what to do and you show me you're mine by being obedient."

I nodded.

He flipped me onto my back, lifting me easily and tossing me against the pillows. A gasp tore from my lips and his face darkened as he moved atop me, his hands planted on either side of my body.

"I told you to keep your mouth shut," he said, his voice cutting like a knife. "That means sounds, not just words. Can you be a good girl and do that? Or do I need to fuck your throat to make you understand?"

I shook my head and then nodded, unsure which question I was supposed to be answering. He seemed satisfied by my response and the darkness left his face, replaced by glittering lust in his cold gaze. I shivered, so incredibly aroused and enticed by this man, by this side of him I never could have imagined existed when I had first met him. He was always so guarded, so meticulous, so aloof, in public, but in private...my God, in private he ruined me.

He pushed his fingers between my thighs, shoving them fully into my pussy. Before I had a chance to adjust, he hammered his fingers up into me, his gaze locked on mine.

"If you want to walk around dressed like a whore, fine," he breathed. "I'm going to cover you with my cum and don't you fucking dare clean it off."

The image of him finishing across my breasts flashed into my mind and a bolt of pleasure arced through me, lifting my hips off the bed. Before I could orgasm, he pulled his fingers out and pushed my legs open and thrust his cock into me. I bit down hard, barely able to keep quiet at the sudden intrusion.

"Good girl, you keep that mouth shut," he breathed, pistoning his hips into me. "I'm going to ride this tight, little cunt the way I want to because you fucking belong to me."

He gathered my wrists in one hand, pinning them above my head. With his other hand, he spread my thighs as far as they could go. There was a flash of fever in his gaze, a glitter of lust, when his eyes raked over my body, open and spread out for him. His chest rose and fell and a trickle of sweat slid down into the ridges of his stomach as he pushed in with heavy strokes.

"You feel that, baby? You feel how hard your tight, little body makes me? Oh God, put your feet up on my shoulders—just like that."

He released my wrists and seized my ankles, pulling me close as he sat back into a kneeling position. His lean fingers dug into my calves and he pushed his mouth against the arch of my right foot as he hammered into me. His tongue snaked out and then he bit my ankle, his teeth sinking into the sensitive flesh.

I cried out and he paused, his barren eyes fixing on my face. My heart thudded and, for a brief second, I entertained the possibility of fleeing from him. But it was no use, he would always catch me.

He leaned forward, my ankles still up on his shoulders. His hand snaked around my throat, his fingers pressing into the sides of my neck.

"I thought I told you to be quiet," he whispered. "Were you quiet? Answer me now."

I shook my head quickly.

"You want to know what happens to bad girls?" he asked, cocking his head.

I shook my head again.

"They don't get fucked gently," he said hoarsely. "They get fucked like little whores, on their knees with their face in the bed."

He flipped me over and took me by the back of the neck, pinning me down. His heavy cock breached my pussy again, thrusting all the way home until a twinge of pain went through my hips. He put his hand on the headboard to steady himself and his hips began driving into me in a relentless rhythm.

My life flashed before my eyes. This was another level. He'd never even come close to fucking me like this, even the night of the opera. His cock hammered into me, hitting my innermost point and dragging across my G-spot with every stroke. I dug my fingers into the bed, turning my head just enough to let me breathe, and gave everything up to him. He wanted to use me, to mark me, to claim my body, and if this was how he did it, so be it.

He wasn't a good man. His desire for power, for control, consumed him and turned him into something terrifying. But despite knowing he was the villain in this story, I still wanted him. I needed him to own my body like this, to exert his will over me. He was dangerous like fire, but

I wanted to ride that edge and feel him burn my flesh, to make me feel alive.

"Take it," he said through gritted teeth. He spat onto my back and slapped me hard across the ass, the crack reverberating through the room. "You're already on your knees, so go on, beg for me, baby."

I tried to obey, but the only thing that came from my mouth was a desperate whimper. Everything in me screamed for release. His body was relentless, driving into mine without mercy. Pain spiked through my hips as he slapped me twice and I bit my lip so hard I tasted blood. My God, if he didn't stop I was going to break into a thousand pieces.

His cock grew even harder, filling me until I was whimpering silently, teeth gritted and breasts heaving against the strain. The unrelenting thrusts sped up even faster and he released a groan from somewhere deep within.

"You can talk now," he panted. "Beg me for it, baby. Beg for my cum inside your sweet, little cunt."

"Please, please, I want your cum in me," I panted, barely able to get the words out.

He growled, slamming into me hard enough to make the bed crash against the wall. "Fuck, I'm going to cum in your tight pussy. Fill you up, get you pregnant, baby."

He collapsed, his body almost crushing mine as he emptied himself inside me. Every nerve in my body tingled, shocked by what had just happened, but even more shocked by his words. Did he have some kind of kink or had he made a Freudian slip? Did he actually want to get me pregnant?

I kept still, suddenly embarrassed by what he had said and done. He pulled himself slowly to his feet and went to the bathroom without looking at me. My body tingled and soreness throbbed through my pussy as I lay on the bed, my eyes fixed on the ceiling overhead. I didn't move even when I heard the bathroom door open and he went into the closet to dress.

Then he stepped up to the side of the bed, his face so bleak it sent a shiver through me. He pressed my legs apart and pushed his fingers into me, gathering his cum and spreading it across my breasts and stomach.

"Wear that, baby," he said, his tone light and distant. As if he hadn't just fucked me hard and threatened to get me pregnant. "Put your dress back on, fix your hair, but don't clean my cum off your body."

Then he was gone, disappearing through the door. I closed my eyes, my mind a confusing mess. I was torn between wanting to be angry with him or cry because he'd left me without a word of comfort. It was so unlike him. From the very beginning, he'd been gentle and attentive to me. But now that he admitted his feelings, he was more distant that ever. He'd walked out without giving me an orgasm. I always came before him and sometimes during, but he'd never walked out without bothering to pleasure me.

I squeezed my eyes shut and put my hand between my thighs. My clit was hot and pulsing and it took less than a minute for an orgasm to ripple through my body. The immediate frustration faded, but the pain in my chest remained.

He had hurt me with his insinuation that I had put myself on display for Romano and the other men of the outfit. Did he really think that? Or was he just horny and jealous and it was making him say things he didn't mean? I rubbed my eyes, wiping away the tears, and sat up slowly. Everyone downstairs had to know what we were doing and the prospect of facing them again sent a wave of shame through me.

But it had to be done. I stood and put the red dress back and went to the bathroom to fix my hair and makeup.

CHAPTER SEVENTEEN

LUCIEN

Guilt churned in my stomach as I watched Olivia play the part of the gracious hostess for the rest of the night. She chatted, sipped champagne, and made sure to personally bid each guest goodbye as they left. Then she helped the servants clean up the front room before going upstairs to get ready for bed.

Trying to tamp down my guilty conscience, I stepped out onto the front porch and lit a cigarette. The air was icy, cutting through my suit, but it was a welcome relief after being inside with dozens of guests for the last few hours. It had snowed heavily during the party and the trees glistened in the dim light.

I wanted to ask myself why I had said I wanted to get her pregnant, but deep down I already knew. After almost a decade of paranoia, I finally had the freedom to get my wife pregnant and the idea was tantalizing. Never would I have imagined that would get me hard, but I had throbbed almost painfully when I'd said that to her while buried in her pussy.

The door behind me opened and Duran stepped out. He was quiet, his black eyes glittering in the light cast from the snow. I could sense his disapproval of my behavior and a ripple of annoyance went through me. He held out his hand and I passed him my pack of cigarettes and lighter. The silence drove on as he put a cigarette to his lips and flicked the lighter, illuminating his face for a moment.

"Thanks," he said, passing the pack back to me.

"If you want to say something, just say it," I said wearily.

"Okay," Duran said, his eyes fixed off the porch somewhere in the dark. "I think you're wound pretty tight about what's coming up on New Year's Eve. And I would hate to see you take it out on your wife."

I drew in a long breath of smoke and released it out into the icy air. "I didn't hurt Olivia," I said shortly.

"There are a lot of definitions of hurting someone."

"Just spit it out, Duran," I said wearily.

"Alright, she's clearly in love with you. She hangs on your every word, she waits around for you to get home every day. If you don't see the look on her face when you come in at night, you have to be stupid. She and Iris talk and I know her background. She's fucking sensitive and it would break her to see this...side of you."

Anger rose in my, sharp and fast. "What side exactly?"

"The side of you that can't get enough power, that's obsessed with it," he said. "The side of you that just fucking steps over the line. Don't drag that shit home and take it out on her. Don't use her as a tool against Romano."

"I—"

"Just listen to me for once, Lucien." Duran squared his shoulders, planting his feet apart. "I know you're in a tough position where you need to look a certain way to the rest of the outfit. I realize the stress you're under. But your wife has to be protected from all of this...from you."

I wanted to snap at him, to put him in his place. After all, he was a soldier and I was his underboss and he had no right to speak to me like that. But he was right and I knew it. I put my cigarette to my lips and breathed in, holding it in my lungs for a while as I allowed myself to calm.

"Just this once, I'll admit you're right," I said finally. "And I should probably go speak with Olivia."

"Damn right, you should," Duran said.

I sighed and flicked the cigarette into the empty pot on the front stairs. I wasn't sure what to say to Duran, so I just put my hand on his shoulder briefly as I walked past him to go back inside.

But it wasn't just that I had used her against Romano, or that I had embarrassed her in front of our guests by dragging her upstairs and fucking her. The worst thing I'd done, Duran wasn't even aware of. The worst thing I'd done tonight was unintentionally insinuate that she'd worn that dress to entice Romano, the man who had assaulted her. Never had I meant to do that and I was willing to get on my knees if that was what it took to apologize.

When I went upstairs, our room was quiet. Olivia was already in bed, her body a tight knot beneath the heavy comforter, just the top of her dark head visible. The guilt was so acute it was almost painful as I stripped off my suit and slipped into bed in my boxers. My side of the bed was cold, but I felt the faint traces of heat coming off her body.

"Are you awake, baby?" I asked.

There was no answer. I rolled her onto her back, but she was fast asleep, her lovely face relaxed. I tugged up the front of her silk nightgown and despite everything, I felt a glimmer of triumph that she was still marked with my cum across her breasts and upper stomach.

Maybe I was an evil bastard. Duran was right—she did need me to protect her from myself.

When I woke the next morning, it was still dark. I rolled over and reached for Olivia out of habit, gathering her against me. Her body was limp and warm nestled beside mine, her ass fitting perfectly against my groin. She would be too sore from what I'd done to her last night to take me now, nor did I think it was a good idea until I'd apologized to her. But it still felt like heaven to rub up against her soft curves.

God, she was perfect and she didn't deserve the way I'd treated her.

I pressed my mouth to the side of her throat and she stirred a little, but remained asleep. Downstairs, I heard the grandfather clock strike six. I needed to get up and face the dozens of task and obligations I had waiting for me. It was getting difficult to handle planning this coup and my duties to the outfit at the same time.

I dragged my body from the bed and stumbled into the shower. Beneath the hot flow of water, I leaned my head back against the tiles. I needed to do something to make this up to her, but I had no idea what kinds of things women liked. I'd never had to apologize to anyone and I certainly had never bought anyone a gift before.

I dressed in a crisp, gray suit and went downstairs for an espresso before I left for the office. The servants had put the house to rights after the party and everything was clean and orderly as I liked it. In the kitchen, I found Iris sitting at the counter typing on her laptop. She'd had to give up her job on social media, but she still managed to keep up with her anonymous fashion blog and even made a small income from it. Not that she needed to anymore.

"Good morning," she said, her voice stiff.

Iris had never liked me, but I could tell she was colder than usual today. I nodded and poured my espresso and leaned on the counter across from where she sat. She shifted uncomfortably and pulled her oversized sweater around her lanky frame.

"What?" she asked.

"I know I was an ass last night," I said, forcing the words from my mouth. "And I need to make up for it. So, give me your advice on how."

Her mouth parted in surprise. "You want my advice?"

"What do I do? Olivia is sleeping and I don't want to wake her. But I need to do something before I come back tonight."

Iris frowned and rested her chin on her palm. "Well, I don't know exactly what you did, but as long as you didn't do anything...really bad, I would say flowers and jewelry might help."

"Really bad?"

"Duran made it seem like maybe you...hurt her," Iris said hesitantly. "I don't think I believe that. You're in love with her. And I don't think you would do that to any woman anyway."

Had she thought I had forced myself on my wife? The thought turned my stomach and a sick sensation rose. It took me a moment to compose myself, ensuring my face remained completely blank.

"I would never do anything to Olivia against her will or hurt her," I said. "I behaved...badly, said some things I didn't mean, but I didn't harm her."

"Well, send her flowers, write her a note. If you really mean it, make it expensive," Iris said, turning back to her laptop. "And say you're sorry in person too. That means a lot."

An hour later, I sat down at my desk in my office with my phone to my ear. I called my assistant, a slender, graying woman who had worked as my secretary for the last ten years. She handled any small, personal tasks and ran errands for my legitimate businesses. She answered on the first ring, her voice prompt and formal.

"Can I help you, sir?" she asked.

"Can you have some flowers sent to my wife?"

If she was surprised by my unusual request, she didn't show it. "How many flowers, sir? And what kind?"

I squeezed my eyes shut, pinching the bridge of my nose. "I don't know. Maybe three hundred white roses? Or maybe that's not enough.... Just have them make up some bouquets until they have about a thousand stems total. And I want to send something else...maybe a necklace."

"I'll pick something out," she said. In the background I could hear her pen scratching. "What does she like?"

"I...well, her engagement ring is a diamond on white gold, so something to match."

"Alright, sir, when would you like this delivered?"

"As soon as possible."

"Would you like a card with a message?"

I paused, considering it for a moment. Every part of me wanted to just ignore this whole thing and sweep it under the rug as I usually did when I offended someone close. After all, she was my wife and she answered to me, not the other way around. Any man in the outfit would have backed me up on that. But, I fucking loved this woman, despite my best attempts not to, and the fact that I had hurt her pained me.

"Just tell her I'm sorry."

"Of course, sir," she said, completely professional. "I'll have it sent to Mrs. Esposito right away. Also, I was just about to call you this morning. Mr. Salah is in town and he requested to meet you and the other Mr. Esposito for lunch."

I checked my watch. "Alright, thank you."

Ahmed Salah was a close family friend of both Duran and I. He was a talented made man, originally from England, but he now made his home across the globe. My father had often taken us on trips to Cairo and we'd met Ahmed there when we were young. At the age of nineteen, Ahmed had saved Romano's life during a shootout and in return, Romano had made him the first non-Italian made man. Despite this, Ahmed's loyalty remained to Duran and I and he'd agreed to aid in our coup.

He hadn't left Egypt for several months, but during his honeymoon in Cairo, Duran had made plans for Ahmed to join us for New Year's Eve. We needed him if we were going to take down the boss. Ahmed was an excellent marksman from his time in the British army and he knew the weapons he worked with better than any soldier under my or Viktor's command.

I took the Tesla out to join Ahmed and Duran at one of our clubs. I knew we were meeting there for security purposes, but it felt strange to be in a place I so strongly associated with my bachelor days. When I stepped through the doors, a slender, blonde woman greeted me and took my coat. She wore a short, black leather skirt and a lace brassiere that showed faint traces of her nipples. Before, the sight would have gotten me hard, but now it did nothing. Olivia had ruined me for all other women.

Ahmed sat with Duran in the far corner of the room. There was already a bottle of wine at the table and a platter of fresh espresso. As I approached, Ahmed stood, unfurling his tall body, and shook my hand warmly. He looked good, windswept and healthy, his dark eyes alight.

"Ahmed went and got married," Duran said. "Didn't bother to tell us."

"It wasn't planned," said Ahmed. "She's pregnant and she didn't want to have the baby out of wedlock. Adriana's oddly traditional about certain things."

"Congratulations," I said. "Was this...part of the plan?"

"Yes and no," said Ahmed, shrugging. "But we were in Cairo drinking a lot and fucking most of the night. She can't take birth control for health reasons and she just looked too good to pull out, so here we are. It wasn't planned exactly, but it wasn't a surprise."

"Well, congratulations," I said, inclining my head.

"You better make sure I get out of this alive," Ahmed said, shaking his head. "Each time I stop and think about what we're about to do...I just hope we can pull it off."

"We'll pull it off better than you pulled it out at least," said Duran, smirking.

"Ha, very funny," said Ahmed in stilted French. "But in all seriousness, what is your plan, Lucien?"

I poured an espresso and lit a cigarette and shifted back in my seat, "Viktor will be here in a few days," I said, also switching to French. "I have a meeting set up with the four of us at my residence. We'll all go over the details together then and iron things out."

"Let me guess," said Ahmed. "I'm the sniper who takes out the guards."

"Close. You're the one who makes sure no on leaves through the front door. If Romano or Aurelio attempt to, you'll shoot them on the spot. Duran's job is to pretend that he's cheating on his wife so he can use the entrance through the kitchen to access the control room. From there, we can cut the cameras and dispose of the guards."

"How many guards are there normally during parties?" Ahmed asked.

"On average, over the last three years, Romano has sixteen guards patrolling the property and house during social events. But we only have to worry about five of them in the control room and on the upper level of the house. The others will be downstairs and shouldn't notice anything if all goes according to plan," I said.

"And if it doesn't?"

"We have two out of the six underbosses on our side, although they don't know it yet," I said. "But they will back me when it gets down to it, I have no doubt. Romano's worn out his welcome in their territories and I've built strong relationships with them. Then we have you Ahmed, Duran, and ten of Viktor's men. Even if this goes to shit, as long as we keep our heads, we'll come out on top."

"And if it doesn't, what happens to our women?" Ahmed crossed his arms over his chest.

"Adriana is still in Cairo, so she should be safe," I said. "Olivia and Iris will go to Russia to live under Viktor's care, along with Sienna. Whether we're successful or not, she belongs to him."

"You're a cold fucker, trading your cousin like that," Ahmed said.

"It's how things are done. And Viktor isn't a cruel man. On the contrary, I think she'll get a better life with him than she would marrying Aurelio Romano."

"I have heard things about the Romano son," Ahmed said, nodding slowly. "Not good things."

"He's rough with some of the women at the clubs and he forced a waitress at one of Romano's parties a few years ago," Duran said. "But apparently roughing up women is something Lucien does now too."

"What?" Ahmed's forehead creased.

"Shut the fuck up," I snarled, leaning forward. "If you must know what I did with my wife in the privacy of my bedroom, I fucked her consensually and, yes, it was rough, but she had a safeword. The only thing I'm guilty of is embarrassing her, for which I've apologized."

Duran lifted his palms and sat back in his seat. Beside him, Ahmed watched us both, his eyes flicking back and forth over his espresso. There was a long, tense moment and Ahmed let out a low whistle.

"If you two are going to pull this off, you need to get over whatever this is and get on the same page. I don't care if you have to fight it out in the parking lot, but I won't go into a combat zone led by two men at each other's throats."

I released a tense sigh. "We don't have any issues."

Duran pressed his lips together in a thin line. "We do not."

"Clearly," said Ahmed, raising his brows.

We talked for another half hour, discussing the finer details for a while. The conversation moved in a more casual direction as it wore on into the afternoon. I knew I needed to get back to the office, but it was good to take a moment to breathe for the first time since long before my wedding.

I left a little before five, heading back to the office to finish up a few contracts for my less legitimate businesses. Then I pulled on my overcoat and went to the revolving door in the front of the building to wait for the valet to bring my car around. It was snowing lightly outside and I leaned my head against the wall, gazing out into the dark.

For the first time, I dreaded the thought that I might die. I had something to live for, something to look forward to at the end of the day. In the quiet months between when I'd brought Olivia to the mansion and our wedding day, I had grown sensitive to the sound of her feet and the soft lull of her voice. And, if I was truly honest with myself, I had began to love her on our wedding night. How could I have helped myself? She was a bright spot in an otherwise dark world, a piece of captured light, a flame to melt the deepest parts of myself.

The door opened and the valet appeared, cutting short my reverie. The drive home felt ten times longer than usual, and when I finally pulled into the snowy driveway, the house was dark except for a light on upstairs in Duran's room.

I put the car in the garage and went inside and headed to the kitchen for a drink. The light over the stove was on and Duran stood at the counter, shirtless, with a glass of bourbon in his hand. When I entered, he froze, looking up with his dark eyes wary like an animal.

"You're back late," he said.

"I needed to catch up on a few things," I said, taking the bottle from him.

He swirled the liquid in his glass for a long moment, his gaze still fixed on me. "Look, I know you've always looked out for me. Protected me," he said slowly. "I just had some intense flashbacks last night, because of how rough our father was with mom. But I shouldn't have assumed you would hurt Olivia."

It hadn't crossed my mind that was reason and a pang of guilt went through me. Of course, it made sense now. Even as an adult, Duran still bore the marks of someone who'd grown up around abuse and violence. And despite the tough front he put on, I knew he was by far the more sensitive son. I had taken the brunt of it, but I'd dealt with it far better than Duran had. I had managed to make some sense of it and found a way to turn it into something I could control. But Duran hadn't.

"I'm sorry," I said quietly.

His brows rose. It was one of the few times in our lives I'd apologized to him.

"Thanks," he said, clearing his throat.

I set the bottle aside. "I should go to bed."

He nodded and I left him standing there, his face half darkened by shadow. I went upstairs to my bedroom and pushed open the door slowly, the scent of roses hitting my nose. The bedside lamp was on and Olivia was curled up in a cloud of white sheets and blankets. She wore a silky, green nightgown that just brushed the top of her thigh and her dark hair was braided over her shoulder.

When I stepped inside, she looked up and closed her book. I stood for a moment, looking around the room in surprise. For some reason, when I'd ordered the flowers, I'd imagined very small roses, like the kind that grew in our garden. No, these were large white roses and there were dozens of bouquets filling every space in the room. Set up on the dresser, along the windowsill, even on the floor.

"Thank you for the flowers," she said.

I felt a muscle twitch in my face. "I might have gone a little overboard."

"You might have."

I slipped my coat and vest off and rolled up my sleeves. "I'm sorry, baby."

She sat up, her slender legs hanging off the bed. "I wasn't angry, Lucien, just hurt."

I went to her, kneeling in front of her and running my fingertips over her thighs. "I never meant to insinuate that you were trying to dress for Romano or anything like that. He's a monster and I know it's painful for you to even be around him. And I'm sorry that you have to be."

She bit her lip, her fingers fidgeting.

"I'm sorry I lost control, that I embarrassed you. I'm sorry for all of it. But most of all, I need you to understand that it will never happen again. And I mean that."

Her eyes were wet and soft as they fixed on me. Her fingers ran down the side of my face and she kissed me, her mouth impossibly gentle. "Thank you, of course I forgive you."

"Good." I kissed the side of her neck.

"Did you mean it when you said you loved me?"

"More than anything," I murmured, my mouth still pressed against the soft skin of her throat.

She drew back to look in my eyes. "You're a frightening man. You're still so...bitterly cold inside sometimes. And you're power hungry and willing to do anything to get what you want."

"That's true." What was the point in denying it?

"But I love you," she whispered. "I don't care if you scare me sometimes, I know you would never hurt me."

"Never."

She traced my face with her soft fingertips, touching down the bridge of my nose, circling my mouth. "Did you pick out the jewelry or did your secretary?"

"I had my assistant do it. She's got better taste than I do," I said.

She went to the dresser, taking out a large, flat box covered in black velvet. I rose and crossed to her as she turned it around and lifted the lid. Inside was a thick, diamond necklace with glittering stones hanging like dewdrops. She slipped it from the box and I took it from her, turning her to face the mirror over the dresser. Her body tensed a little as the cold metal touched her skin and I clasped it at the nape of her neck.

She was beautiful, but more than that, she was my queen, my beautiful *principessa*. The necklace covered from the base of her throat all the way to where her cleavage started. The lowest stone settled in the silky dip of her cleavage, just between her perfect breasts.

"This is expensive," she breathed.

"Very," I said.

"I don't know if I can keep this."

"I have a lot of money," I said, amused. "If I thought I couldn't afford it, I would have put a price limit on my assistant's purchase. No, you deserve this, and much more."

I picked her up in my arms and took her back to bed, laying her down. She kept still, allowing me to slip her nightgown from her, leaving her clad only in the diamond necklace. God, she was devastating. I bent my head and took her nipple in my mouth, the firm flesh heavenly beneath my lips. She gasped and closed her eyes as I flicked my tongue gently against her breast.

"Why did you say what you said last night?" she whispered.

I raised my head. "About what?"

"About getting me pregnant."

I sighed, resting my chin on her sternum. Part of that outburst had been purely driven by my need to have her, to exert my ownership over her. But another part was that same small desire I'd felt in Russia to see her pregnant, to know she was carrying my child. She was my wife after all.

"Do you want to have a baby?" she asked, her dark eyes fixed on mine.

I hesitated. The concept of wanting a child, of that even being an option, after so many years, felt so foreign.

"I would," I said finally.

Her breath caught. "When?"

I considered it for a moment, although I already knew the answer. "Not until after I'm settled in as boss. Maybe, if everything goes well, you can stop taking your birth control in February. Is that what you want?"

She bit her lip, chewing on the sensitive flesh as her dark eyes searched my face. "I would like to have a baby. Maybe if things were different, I would want to wait. But I think it's better we do it soon."

"You're talking about our age gap," I observed. "You have a point. When our first child is ten, I'll be forty-seven."

"First child? How many do you want?" Her brows drew together.

I traced my fingers over her bare stomach, imagining her pregnant. She would be gorgeous, round with my child, her breasts swollen. "I don't know. As many as it takes to have a son."

She rolled her eyes a little. "You made men are all the same."

"I can't help the way things are."

I laid my head on her lower belly, my arms slipping up to cradle her body. She was warm and perfect beneath me. Her skin smelled faintly of flowers and when I turned my head and ran my nose over the apex between her thighs, I caught the faint scent of her sex. Sweet and tangy. My cock hardened against the bed.

She sighed, a sound that came from deep inside. I parted her thighs just enough for me to slip my tongue between her folds. She tasted like coming home after a long time wandering in a dark and lonely place. We lay together, warm and tangled up in the sheets together, surrounded by the scent of roses. I ate her slowly, whispering praise to her lovely body under my breath until she came in a quiet rush. Then I gathered her against me and we slept.

CHAPTER EIGHTEEN

OLIVIA

Lucien was tense the next few days. Outwardly, he was as calm and collected as ever, I felt the edge in everything he said and did. When I woke in the morning and went to join him in the shower, his shoulders were tight. He would keep still as I rubbed the hard muscles at the base of his neck and down his back, tracing the scars and tattoos that covered his skin. At night, he took me gently with a quiet kind of desperation. Almost as if he were trying to memorize the feeling of my body beneath his and the taste of our mouths together.

He spent three nights leading up to New Year's Eve in his office with Viktor, Leonid, Duran, and Ahmed. I chose to ignore it, keeping to myself. I loved my husband, but I had no desire to see the bloody details of his plan. I didn't want to be involved any more than I already was.

Instead, Iris and I spent the day before shopping. Despite my husband's reaction to my clothing before, I decided to pick out something even riskier than the red dress. On our way home, we stopped by a high-end lingerie store and I chose a few pieces that I was embarrassed to even let Iris see. When Lucien pulled this off, when he became the most powerful man in the outfit, I was going to fuck him in the closest available room. It gave me such a rush to think of him on his knees in front of me, all that power at my feet, his perfect mouth working between my legs.

The next day, Lucien was gone at the office with Duran for most of the afternoon. Viktor had come in the early morning hours and left with five of his men and Ahmed, all armed to the teeth. Now the house was silent and empty.

I went to the bathroom and soaked in the tub, scrubbing every inch of my body, and shaving until my skin was silky. I'd gone the day before to get my pussy waxed and it was so smooth it felt almost slippery. That was the way Lucien liked it and it made my sex throb when he slipped his hands over the sensitive skin and locked eyes with me, giving me that look that made my knees weak.

I spent a while curling my hair and smoothing my bangs back discreetly until they were invisible. Then I tied my hair at the nape of my neck and shook out the ponytail, the loose curls tickling my naked back. I rubbed expensive, musky lotion over my body and went to the box with the lingerie and pulled aside the lid.

I lifted the delicate, silver lace bustier, as fine and soft as spiderweb in my fingers. It fit beautifully, lifting my breasts to give me the perfect amount of cleavage. Then I took the panties, made of the same barely-there lace, and slid them up my thighs. Instead of fabric over my pussy, there was a single thread of real pearls that nestled against my skin. I shifted, pressing my thighs together, and the pearls rubbed deliciously against my clit.

I reached across and took my phone out of my purse. I rarely used it except to text Lucien while he was at work, but an idea had been forming in my head all day and I finally felt brave enough to try it.

Positioning the camera on the sink, I tapped the timer and turned around, bending over to expose myself. Then I spread my pussy, sliding my fingers through the wet folds, and began rubbing my clit. I was already soaked, and the thought of Lucien seeing me touch myself on video had my heart thumping. Pleasure surged within a minute and I came hard, gasping as my pussy clenched around my fingers.

I sent the video right away, afraid if I waited too long I would lose my nerve. Then I set aside the phone and applied my makeup, trying to ignore my racing heart. For some reason, sending my stoic husband a dirty video scared me more than the night that awaited us at the Romano mansion.

My phone remained silent as I got my dress from the closet. I went to stand before the mirror and slipped the sheer fabric over my hips and up my torso. It was almost transparent everywhere except for a portion over my ass and pussy. The structured bodice clung to my breasts and had crystals sewn into the lace that glittering like starlight. The draping skirt was silvery gauze edged with white velvet so that it dragged behind me when I walked, the fabric parting to reveal my entire left leg. The sleeveless top left my shoulders and throat bare and I settled the necklace from Lucien around my neck.

I was standing up from putting on my heels when I heard the click of Lucien's wingtips. My heart caught in my throat and I turned just as my husband came through the door, stopping short as his eyes fell on me. He had his phone in one hand, his knuckles white around it.

"Olivia," he said quietly.

For a moment, I thought about shrinking back, but then I squared my shoulders and met his gaze. That endlessly cold gaze I loved so well.

"Do you like it?" I asked.

He moved toward me, setting his phone aside. "You look fucking incredible," he breathed. "How am I supposed to get anything done with you sending me videos of your cunt? Or dressing like that in front of me?"

He took me by the back of the neck and pulled me near to kiss my mouth.

"I thought it might give you something to look forward to at the end of the night," I whispered.

"I'm going to need you to suck me off before that."

I shook my head. "Not yet. You make it through this and I'll do anything you want," I said. "You keep talking as if you doubt yourself, but I know you'll succeed. You will make it through this because that's the kind of man you are, Lucien. And when it's done, all you have to do is say the word and I'll be your whore."

"Jesus," he breathed.

"I love you."

His face softened a minute amount. He bent forward and kissed my mouth long and deep. "I love you, baby."

For the first time, Lucien had a driver take us in a sleek, black SUV. We sat with our hands clasped together, the silence between us heavy with anticipation. It was bitterly cold outside and fine snowflakes fell in sparse flurries outside the window. The drive to the Romano mansion felt like it took an age and with every passing second, my anxiety grew.

We pulled up before the doors. Everything was decorated for the holiday, but knowing what we were about to do, the glittering lights were almost grim. Lucien helped me out of the car and guided me up the stairs, one hand clasped around mine and the other on my lower back. For a moment as we ascended the stairs, his arms around me, I felt safe.

Then we entered the front hallway, packed with people, and I tensed, almost stumbling. Lucien leaned forward to removed my coat and pressed his mouth to my ear.

"This is it, baby. Stand up straight, shoulders back," he said. "Good girl."

A rush of warmth surged through me and I straightened my spine. He held out his arm and I looked up at him, curling my hand beneath his elbow. He wore a dark blue, Italian wool suit with a faint checked pattern and a dark silky tie. It made a striking picture against his dark hair and hazel eyes. And beneath it all, under the guns and knives hidden on his figure, was his hard body, already tensed for action.

We entered the living room packed with people. Iris stood on the right side of the room by the large window with Sienna by her side. I frowned as I released Lucien and made my way over, wondering if she knew her fate. When I approached, Iris swept aside her sleek, black dress that pooled around her feet and hugged me.

"You look amazing," she said. "Gorgeous enough to be a queen."

As she said it, her eyes widened slightly and I knew at once that Duran had finally told her. Now that I looked at her, she was a little bit pale and she kept chewing on her lower lip. Sienna approached behind her in a draping gold dress with a plunging neckline.

"Hi," she said quietly. "It's been a while."

I leaned in and hugged her. "It's good to see you. Have you talked to Lucien?"

She frowned, glaring across the room to where Lucien stood with Romano and Duran. "Yeah."

"What did he say?" Iris asked, leaning closer.

"He told me that the man I thought would be my fiancé is not my fiancé any longer," she whispered. "And, as usual, I don't have a say in it."

"I didn't have a say in who I married," I said. "And neither did Lucien."

"It's barbaric," she said, shaking back her long, dark hair. "Have you met V?"

"Yes, he's kinder than I thought," I said. "Very traditional, conservative even. His house is absolutely magnificent. If it were up to me, I would have stayed longer...but Lucien has duties elsewhere."

She bit her lip. When she raised her champagne glass to her lips, there was a large, gold ring glittering on her finger.

"Is that Aurelio's?" I asked.

She nodded. "Lucien told me to wear it."

"Probably for the best."

Iris pressed the back of her hand to her cheek. "I need a drink. Does anyone want to go to the bar?"

I nodded. "I'll have a little champagne. We need to make sure to stay sober though."

We gathered by the bar and I ordered a glass of chilled champagne. Everywhere I went, I felt eyes on me. Once or twice I caught the glances of some of the made men from other territories and I felt their gazes undress me as I walked by. When I met their eyes, they looked away, although it knew it was only out of respect for Lucien.

"Sienna."

We turned and Aurelio Romano stood there, one hand in his pocket and the other cradling a glass. He was handsome enough, but there was a sharp cruelty behind his eyes that he'd inherited from his father. Sienna was lucky to be marrying Viktor instead.

I gathered my courage and held out my hand. "It's nice to see you again, Aurelio," I said smoothly.

He accepted my hand, brushing his lips across my fingers. His eyes trailed over my breasts without shame and I fought the urge to look away. He clearly felt he had some claim to my body, the way his father had when he'd touched me in the garden, and it roused red hot anger in my chest.

"Does your husband allow you out in that?" Aurelio said coolly, raising a brow. "Or is he just being cuckolded? I know what you did the first time you came here with Lucien so it wouldn't surprise me."

Iris gasped and Sienna's mouth fell open in shock. They both looked at me, unsure of how to react. My heart pounded in my chest and, for a moment, tears blurred my vision. I blinked rapidly, forcing myself to remain calm. He would be dead before the end of the night and there was no need to make him pay for his words.

"My husband is secure enough to allow me to wear what I please," I said coldly. "He has nothing to overcompensate for."

Aurelio's jaw twitched. "You know, if you hadn't been sold off to Lucien first, I would have gotten you."

I took a slow sip from my glass. "I doubt it. Arranged marriages are only useful if both of the people involved are actually important."

"You fucking bitch!"

"I didn't come here to start a fight, you did," I shot back.

"What the hell is going on here?"

I jumped as a firm hand slid down my back and rested just above my ass. Lucien stood behind me, his broad body squared up to Aurelio. He was as relaxed as ever, but there was a barely perceptible tenseness to his jaw the sent off warning bells in my head. Whenever Aurelio was killed, Lucien would see to it that he died painfully.

"You should keep your woman in line better," Aurelio snapped.

Romano appeared behind him, putting his hands on his son's shoulders. "Now, now, let's diffuse the situation. We don't want our New Year's Eve party turning into a bloodbath."

"No, we don't. Thank you, Carlo," said Lucien, his tone almost warm. Sometimes it chilled me how well he was able to conceal his true feelings.

Romano pulled his son back into the crowd and Lucien turned to face the three of us. Iris and Sienna stood perfectly still, both too shocked to speak. A twinge of guilt went through me for causing a scene, but it wasn't enough to make me back down. Angry blood still surged through my veins. I turned on my heel and headed toward the bathroom in the hall, but Lucien caught my arm as I left the living room.

"You are jeopardizing this," he said softly.

"He was rude to me," I protested.

"I know he was, but you know it doesn't matter at this point. I should fuck your mouth to make you think twice about using it."

I gaped at him and he cocked his head, his cold eyes raking over my body. Sometimes I forgot that he hadn't changed, he hadn't become less monstrous now that I was in love with him.

"Can you be good?" he pressed.

I nodded stiffly. Lucien ran the backs of his fingers over my cheek and then he was gone, his dark figure wending its way back into the crowd.

CHAPTER NINETEEN

LUCIEN

Now that we were here and our plan was underway, all of the nerves I'd kept under wraps had disappeared completely. The familiar sensation of the hunt settled over me. My senses perked and time seemed to slow a little the evening wore on. Every brush of contact against my body or ringing voice sent me on high alert.

As we wrapped up dinner, I sat by Romano with my wife on the other side. Olivia hadn't spoken to me since our disagreement in the hall. She didn't seem angry though, just distracted and a little anxious.

We rose and I saw from the corner of my eye, Duran leave the room. He had his hand wrapped around the wrist of one of the serving girls and he was feigning slight drunkenness. I excused myself for a moment and ducked into the living room and strode down the hall to the bathroom. Once inside, I locked the door and took a tiny earpiece from my pocket. It fit deep inside my ear, making it almost impossible to see.

I tapped it lightly and there was a light rushing sound and then I heard Duran on the other end.

"...want to fuck. Just go on, no one will notice us," he said, slurring a little.

I left the bathroom, heading back down the hall. On Duran's end I heard a faint scuffle and then a girl moaned loudly.

"Easy there, you are married," I said lightly.

Duran ignored me and I heard a door creak shut and then there was a light thud, like a body hitting the ground. I heard his footsteps climbing the stairs and then another door shut and he paused, panting for breath.

"I'm in," he said. "And there's no guards. What the hell?"

I stilled. "No guards?"

"No one," Duran said. I heard his footfalls and then the sound of a door locking. "Where the hell are the guard—oh, shit."

There was a clattering of falling bodies and Duran swore. For a second I could only hear his quick breaths and then the sound of something heavy dragging across the floor. Then there was a sickening thud and a whimper that almost sounded like a woman. There was a long silence and then another body hit the ground.

"Duran?" I said, resuming my slow walk down the hall.

"There were two guards actually, both having a go at one of the serving girls," he said. "Strangled one, snapped the other's neck. The girl's tied up with her mouth gagged."

"Again," I said, "you do have a wife."

"Fuck you," Duran said. "Do you have Viktor?"

"I'm here," came Viktor's lightly accented voice. "We're waiting."

"Alright, Lucien, it's on you."

I ran a hand over my hair and stepped back into the living area. Everyone had congregated from the dining hall and were getting their after dinner drinks from the bar. Olivia stood on the far side of the room with Iris and Sienna and I made a beeline for them.

I cradled Olivia's bare arm in my palm and I led her a few steps away. Her dark eyes searched mine, a hint of fear in them. Other than that, she was holding it together remarkably well. When this was over, I was sure I could find some way of rewarding her good behavior.

"It's time," I whispered. "Stay with Sienna and Iris until I disappear upstairs with Romano. Then if things go wrong, all three of you will go outside where V will be in a car waiting outside the gates."

"What?" she asked, her eyes wide.

We hadn't discussed this part of the plan before. I knew she would protest against leaving me, so I'd deliberately withheld it.

"V will keep you all safe," I said. "Trust him and no one else. Understood?"

She looked like she wanted to say more, but I bent down and kissed her mouth quickly. I wished I could kiss her deeply, revel in her taste one last time, but I didn't want to draw attention. She let her fingers trail down my arm as I stepped back from her and went in search of Romano.

I'd suppressed the memories of what Romano had done to me for so long I barely remembered anything save the driving need for revenge. But now as I walked toward him, they began bubbling up to the surface. The smell of the cell he'd kept me in, the freezing cold stone floor against my bare skin. The hours of starvation and sleep deprivation. Being held down as he flayed the skin from my body, little bit by little bit. Death was too good for this man, but it was all I had.

I leaned in as I approached him. "I need to speak with you privately."

He turned, his brows drawing together. "Why?"

"Aurelio and Sienna...I have some...concerns," I said. "But I want to handle it between the two of us. There's no need to drag them into it."

Romano narrowed his eyes as they fixed on his son across the room. "Of course. Let's go and get it done."

"Thank you, sir," I said, falling into step with him.

We headed toward the back of the house, but instead of taking the stairs, Romano turned and opened the door to his little used back office.

We hadn't planned for this because most of the time, it sat empty. I hesitated and then stepped through, keeping my body relaxed.

"You don't use this office much," I remarked. I heard Duran swear quietly in my earpiece.

"My other office is being renovated. I'm having the fireplace removed," said Romano, taking a seat across the dark oak desk. "Old houses have their charm, but they're damn hard to take care of. I sometimes think I should get a penthouse in the city and be done with the mansion."

"Tradition is important," I said, removing my coat and taking a seat in one of the velvet armchairs. "This office isn't so bad. It's got a nice view of the north corner."

I heard a series of unintelligible instructions as the men adjusted their positions. The only thing it really affected was the men assigned to cover me. They would have to adjust their equipment so, if need be, they could enter a level lower than anticipated.

And the back door wouldn't be covered. A twinge of worry went through me, but I ignored it. I was trained for this, I could handle whatever happened.

"Drink?"

I nodded and Romano leaned forward to fill two crystal glasses with bourbon. Taking one, I settled back and rested my chin on my fingers.

"I hate to even bring this up," I said carefully. "But I heard something the other day and it bothered me."

Romano's sharp face tightened for a moment and he cocked his head. "Well, out with it."

"I can't hand Sienna over to Aurelio now that I know he forced a girl at one of your parties," I said, keeping my tone cool and unemotional. "I can't be assured he won't treat her the same."

Romano leaned back and crossed an ankle over his knee. His dark eyes narrowed and his mouth thinned, anger surging through his body.

"How dare you speak like that," he snapped. "You agreed to give her to my son. What he does with her is non of anyone's business."

"She was placed under my care by her parents. I'm doing my duty."

"She is a *woman* under your care. Are you going soft, Lucien?"

"I don't think there's anything left in me to go soft. Not after what you did."

The silence was deafening. I had never before brought up what Romano had done to me because doing so meant bringing down his wrath. His shoulders tensed and he leaned forward, his lean body unfurling as he got to his feet.

"Do we have a problem, Lucien?" he asked quietly.

I rose and looked him in the eye. "Yes, we have a problem. Did you honestly think you would get away with what you did to me? And are you stupid enough to think I wouldn't retaliate when you touched my wife?"

Romano's hand moved across his chest and began sliding beneath his coat, but I moved faster. My pistol was in my hand and trained on my boss. Every trace of unease drained from me and I swore I felt an icy draft flood through my body, freezing everything inside me. All that was left was a dark, pure drive to kill, to end the man standing before me.

"You would kill your boss?" Romano said, his body tense.

"I killed my father," I said. "I know you suspected it for years. I killed him because he was a goddamn abusive asshole. Because he beat and raped my mother and terrorized his family and he deserved it. Because he was as cruel as you are."

"I admired your father," said Romano. "He did what needed done. Unlike his son."

"I'm doing what needs done right now," I said. "I'm going to put you down like an animal."

"Then what? Do you think you have the balls to be boss?"

"Whether or not I'm successful as boss means nothing to you. You're going to be six feet underground."

I took a single step back to put some distance between them, but before I could pull the trigger, something flew at my face. Instinctively I ducked, pulling my gun back to protect it from being seized. The object barely missed my face, smashing against the wall behind me and spraying my back with shards of glass and bourbon. I spun on my heel and discharged the gun twice, the silencer muffling the sound.

Both shots missed. Romano fell to the ground, kicking the chair to the side. I vaulted over the desk, landing with my feet on either side of his body and dropping to my knees to protect my groin. His heels scrabbled against the floor as he reached for his gun.

I had a single moment to decided if I should toss aside my gun in favor of my blade. I wanted him dead, but I also wanted to feel it, to have his blood on my hands. Without hesitating a second longer, I threw my gun aside and removed my knife, cutting through his shoulder holster and tearing his guns away. I flung them aside and they skittered beneath the bookshelf and out of reach. In a heartbeat, I had my knife pressed to his throat.

"You going to fucking kill me without a weapon?" Romano snarled, baring his teeth.

"I don't give a fuck if I give you an honorable death or if I execute you like a dog," I hissed.

Romano bucked his hips with slightly more force than I was prepared for and it threw my weight off just enough. He vaulted his body, throwing me onto my side, and scrambled to his feet. I'd expected him to go for my gun or attempt to kick me while I was down, but instead he headed for the door.

Swearing under my breath, I followed him, bursting through the doorway less than a second after him. I darted around him, rolling to cover ground faster, and lifted my knife to the level of my chest. He paused, knowing his way into the front of the house where the guests congregated was blocked. The only way to escape was through the back door.

He ran like a fucking coward. I surged after him as he pounded down the hall and fumbled with the lock, throwing the door ajar. For a moment, suspended in time, he looked over his shoulder and then he ducked into the whirling snow and darkness outside.

No, he wasn't getting away with this. I hadn't waited for this day for years just to have him get away with what he'd done to me. I burst out into the cold, the wind biting my shirtsleeves. I barely felt anything other than the faint sting of snow against my face and it felt good, it felt like rage and the taste of blood on my tongue.

Up in the distance, I saw Romano's figure enveloped by swirling snow. The lights along the driveway cast just enough of a glow to see the outline of his body. He was headed for the river, for the bridge that led to the guardhouse. I spurred myself to run harder, my shoes slipping in the deep snow as I pursued him out into the icy void.

If I died tonight, I would die with honor. I would lay my life on the line to kill this man. My only regret would be leaving Olivia, beautiful, impossibly sweet Olivia. All around me the world was ice and darkness and impending blood, but inside I carried her in my veins, imprinted beneath my skin from her touch.

Romano approached the bridge and turned, heaving for breath. He was already soaked in sweat and his face burned pale beneath the lamplight. Knife out, blade glinting in the dark, I advanced on him with a slow tread. A flash of fear surged through his body like a shiver and his dark eyes widened as he backed up, eating up the distance to the railing at the apex of the bridge.

"Don't kill me," he heaved. "I'll give it to you, everything I have. You can be boss...just don't kill me."

"I don't remember you taking pity on me when I begged you," I snarled.

He shook from cold and fear, but my body was sure and steady. I was born for this, born for this cruel winter that never melted into spring. The cold I had fostered for so long, holding it in my hands like a life-giving spark, rose now to protect me. Nothing would stop me, I had killed my apathy cleanly long ago and replaced it with nothing but the need for power and blood.

Romano saw it in my eyes and his jaw shook. Then he took hold of the railing and vaulted cleanly over the side, his dark body falling...falling into the endless mist. I scrambled to the edge of the bridge, leaping over the railing and balancing on the very edge. The ends of my wingtips hovered over the abyss.

No, he wasn't going to cheat me out of this death, this kill that was rightfully mine. The drop was too short and the river too deep to kill him—he was somewhere below me, still alive. Up above, snow swirled out of the dark and down below it fell into nothingness. Without hesitating, I stepped off the edge and everything blurred into mist and snow lashing against my skin.

The cold consumed me as I hit the water, my body colliding with Romano's. He made gurgling sound and began swimming hard for the shore and I followed him. As soon as I could stand, I lunged at him, catching him this time and pushing him down beneath the water. He was exhausted, the fight slowly draining from his body, but I'd never felt more alive.

I dragged him to the shore and pulled the knife from my belt. He made a faint sound, a plea for mercy, and I slashed the blade across his throat. Blood sprayed and euphoria burst in my chest, stronger than any drug. I wanted to fucking bathe in it. He sputtered, his hand raised for a second, grasping weakly at my shoulder. And then he was gone, his eyes dead and his mouth slack.

I remained crouched over him, panting. I had done it. It was over. The cold was a reality now and my skin burned with it. I needed to get the body back to the mansion and get out of the cold as soon as possible. Putting my weight on one knee, I lifted his limp body and slung it over my shoulder. He was lighter than I'd thought, but it was still a struggle to get up the side of the embankment to the bridge.

The front door of the house glowed in the distance, blurring as my lashes froze in the wind. My exposed skin was slowly going numb. The only heat came from the dripping blood seeping down my back. The world spun and my body shook, almost convulsing with each step. The snow clung to my shoes, freezing around the bottom of my pants, dragging me down.

I made it to the front steps. As I climbed them, I heard music and I felt warmth radiating from the walls. I shifted Romano and jerked open the door, kicking it open and stepped inside. Then I moved across the hall, ice falling from my body with each step, and entered the living room and threw his body down onto the floor.

The room went completely quiet and then someone shrieked and started sobbing. There was a clattering of feet and Duran and Ahmed appeared behind me, pressing a gun into each of my hands. On the other side of the room, Olivia stood in the corner with her face white and her eyes wide. I didn't blame her. I must have looked terrifying, covered in blood and soaked to the skin.

"What the fuck?"

Federico, one of the underbosses stepped forward and knelt beside Romano's body. "What happened?"

I lifted one of the guns. "Romano is dead. I am your boss now."

There was an audible gasp and then everyone began speaking at once, their voices a whirlwind around me. I shot once into the floor and there was another shriek and then heavy silence. The men pressed back, using their bodies to cover their women. Beneath all the confusion stirred a strong current of fear.

"Romano was unfit to serve as your boss," I continued. "I am taking his place."

Footsteps sounded and Aurelio pushed his way through the crowd. When he saw his father, he gave a hoarse cry and fumbled at his belt for his weapon. I lifted my gun, but Ahmed was faster. He discharged two shots into Aurelio's head, sending him down in a heap over his father's bloody body.

Several of the women began sobbing and whimpering in the corner. I glanced at Olivia, but her face was set, her red mouth pressed together. When I met her dark eyes, they burned. My God, I wanted to drag her into the hall and take her against the wall, to fuck all the adrenaline out of my body while she filled the mansion with her gasping cries. But that would have to wait.

"Does anyone else have any concerns about the transfer of power?" I asked, cocking my head.

Federico stepped forward. He had a calculating expression his face. "I had no great love for Romano. He violated my—someone close to me and he lost my trust then. I'll publicly accept you as my boss."

"You'll be rewarded for that, you have my word," I said.

"How can we trust you after this?" said another underboss called Amadeo, a young man who had already showed remarkable talent.

"Because I intend to lay down rules. Protections against the abuse of power from your boss. You will not have to fear imprisonment or torture or the rape of your women. What happened to me at Romano's hand will never happen to you or your sons. I might not be a...good man, but I am reasonable. I'll ensure you're treated fairly."

"You're going to take over now, in the middle of the war with the Russians, and pull all that off?" Amadeo said, frowning.

Duran ducked his head, speaking softly into his shoulder. I knew he was calling Viktor to join us. Less than ten seconds later, the front doors creaked and I heard the heavy flurry of footfalls. Viktor turned the corner, dressed in a gray suit, with Leonid at his heels. There was another gasp and several of the underbosses and soldiers drew their weapons. I glanced at Viktor, but he kept still, his hands behind his back and his heavy eyes unreadable.

"We're not fighting a war with Russia," I said, raising my hands. "I've made peace with the Bratva. You will not send your sons to war and you don't need to fear the kidnapping of your daughters any longer. Viktor has agreed to a truce, an alliance, between us."

Quiet murmurs spread through the space, rising to argumentative voices. Finally Federico moved forward, his face dark and his hand tensed over his gun.

"How do we know he'll keep his word?" he growled.

I turned, skimming my gaze over the crowd until it fell on Sienna. She stood against the far wall, her arms clasped around her body. I beckoned to her and every eye in the room pivoted, falling on her trembling body. She hesitated and then began walking toward us, her steps a little unsteady, but her shoulders back and her chin high. A rush of pride flooded me. She was an Esposito through and through.

She stopped before me and I reached out to take her hand, turning to Viktor. He studied her face for a long time. It was the first time he'd seen her up close and in person. The entire room was silent, faces creased in confusion or dismay as they realized Sienna's fate. The men approved, I could tell, but the women were horrified.

"Sienna Esposito, it's lovely to meet you," Viktor said, offering her his palm.

She slipped her cold fingers in his, but kept quiet as he drew her aside. He placed his hand on her lower back protectively and she flushed at his touch, dropping her head.

"From now on, there will be a bond between Italy and Russia in our city. Their godfather will wed my cousin, marrying into the boss's family. It'll ensure our alliance."

There was a long moment of silence and then Ahmed stepped out from behind me.

"I pledge myself to the new boss," he said.

"As do I," Amadeo said.

A ripple of surprise moved through the room and I dipped my head to Amadeo in gratitude. He studied me, his eyes boring into me, and then he nodded in response and stepped back.

"Fuck it, I do as well," said Federico. "It can't be any worse than it was."

One by one, the underbosses paused before me, taking off their guns and placing them at my feet. A symbol of their allegiance. It wasn't as if they had a choice when it came down to it. I'd killed the boss and his son and, according to our tradition, I was next in line to lead. There was no contingency for how the situation had come about.

In the far corner, I caught my father-in-law's eye. He stood with his arms crossed, blatantly refusing to come forward and lay his gun before me. His face was red with anger and his eyes glittered as they fixed on me. I cocked my head at him, daring him to speak or make a move, but he remained still. It didn't matter that he refused to give his allegiance because I was going to replace him with his son. He and his wife could live on the lowest social rung for what they'd done to Olivia. They were lucky I wasn't executing them in the street.

I felt something bump up against my side and I turned to find Olivia slipping her hand beneath my elbow. Her brows scrunched together as she studied the bloodstains on my wet shirt. I bent and pressed my lips to the top of her head.

"Are you hurt?" she whispered.

"No, it's all Romano's blood," I said.

I straightened and cleared my throat and the room fell silent. "Each underboss will meet with me in the coming weeks. I want to know more about your territories, what you're dealing with, and what resources you may have been denied that you need. As of right now, go home."

As the crowd dispersed, leaving the house empty, I pulled Duran aside. He was almost giddy that we'd pulled it off and it took me several attempts to get him to focus on my words.

"Tomorrow morning, have our coroner clean up the body. We'll go with murder-suicide," I said, looking down at Romano and his son's still forms. "I need to go speak with my wife in the office."

"Okay, have fun speaking with your wife," said Duran, stepping backwards into the hall where Iris stood. "I'm going to speak with mine somewhere upstairs. I have a shit ton of adrenaline I need to work off. Meet you back at the mansion."

He snatched Iris's hand and pulled her out of sight, their footfalls echoing. I turned, skimming my gaze over the empty room. The grand piano sat silent, the Christmas decor a lopsided mockery beside the bodies on the floor. Even the lights glittering around the windows and doorway felt uncanny. I took my wife's hand and led her through the silent room, through the dining area where the empty plates still littered the table, and toward Romano's study.

"Where are we going?" she asked, her voice a little hoarse.

"I'm going to fuck you on Romano's desk."

If she was shocked, she didn't show it. I stepped into the office and guided her after me, closing the door firmly behind us. The chair was overturned where I'd left it when I'd pursued Romano from the room and my gun was still on the floor. I picked it up and slid it into my shoulder holster and turned to face my wife. Adrenaline surged through my body, pooling blood in my groin until I was painfully hard.

"Come here," I said, beckoning her with my middle and index finger.

She obeyed, coming to stand between me and the desk. I ran one bloody finger down the side of her face, tilting it up and kissing her mouth slowly. Her body warmed, her lips parting to give way to me. The familiar taste of her covered my tongue and my dick throbbed against the wet front of my pants.

I knelt before her, shifting her to sit on the edge of the desk. All night, the image of her pussy and that string of pearls had teased the back of my mind. Now that Romano was dead, now that we were free, I finally had the chance to eat her the way I wanted.

She gave a little gasp as I tore the slit of her dress wider, the gauzy material giving way easily beneath my fingers. I nudged her thigh up, parting her legs further. Dear God, that sweet, little cunt had been just inches from the opening of her skirt all night. She probably still had the wetness coating her thighs from earlier when she'd sent me that video.

She gasped and her fingers wove into my wet hair. For the first time, she pushed my head down, guiding my mouth onto her pussy. Fuck, that sent a shock of arousal straight to my cock. Maybe I should let her take charge more often.

I barely had time to entertain the thought because her sweet folds were on my mouth, her taste filling my senses. I curled my tongue around the string of pearls, moving it aside, and dragged my tongue over her swollen clit. Her body tensed and she moaned, pushing back so that she sat fully on the desk, one arm propping her body up. She spread her thighs, her slender fingers tangling further into my hair, holding my head steady. Then she began moving her hips, the pearls and her clit grinding against my tongue.

My cock twitched, hot and on the edge. I dug my fingers into her thighs and let her ride my face until her legs tensed and clamped around my head. Her pussy throbbed under my mouth and she cried out as she came, a rush of wetness slipping down my chin.

Fuck, I needed her right now. I pushed her back, getting to my feet and unfastening the front of my pants. I grabbed her around the waist, yanking her off the desk and turning her around, bending her over it. The string of pearls across her cunt was in my way and I broke it with a quick jerk, pearls flying across the floor. With one hand on her lower back, I released my cock and thrust into her in a single stroke.

A shock went through her and she seized the edge of the desk, wordless sounds coming from her mouth. I fucked her hard, releasing all of the adrenaline surging through me. The desk rattled loud enough I knew they could hear it through the house, but I didn't care. After all, the only person I would ever have to answer to again was pinned under my body, her pussy wrapped around my cock.

CHAPTER TWENTY

OLIVIA

Lucien's first few weeks as boss were tumultuous. He'd predicted that the first night as we lay in bed, but I hadn't realized just how difficult it would be. The underbosses, although all of them had declared their loyalty to him with the exception of my father, pressed their limits. Lucien had several hours of tense exchange with each of them in his office in the city and came back exhausted, but triumphant. I wasn't sure if he'd talked to my father yet, but I didn't want to know. I'd purposefully avoided any contact with my family since the wedding.

In late January, I came back from lunch with Iris to find Lucien striding down the hall with his phone to his ear. When he saw me, he hung up and beckoned to me with his pointer and middle fingers. Iris excused herself and ducked upstairs, the sharp sound of her heels clattering through the house.

"Olivia, I was just calling you," Lucien said, kissing me briefly. "Your brother is here."

"My brother?"

"Here, come to the study with me," Lucien said, slipping his hand around my waist.

Confused, I allowed him to whisk me to his downstairs office. Inside, the fire was burning and the room smelled faintly of cigars and wood smoke. Cosimo sat on the edge of the desk, his arms crossed and a dazed expression on his face. When he saw me, he rose and moved to me swiftly, gathering me in his arms. I hugged him back as a wave of relief washed through me. It was good to finally be able to see him in person.

"I've removed your father as underboss," said Lucien, sitting down behind the desk. He began rifling through papers briskly as though he hadn't said something of real significance.

"You did what?" I gasped.

"Your father is retired," Lucien said. "I forced him to retire and Cosimo will take his place."

I gaped at him. "Cosimo isn't old enough to legally rent a car, he can't be underboss."

"Yes, I can, Olivia," said Cosimo firmly.

I turned to him and it hit me then that at some point, during all of this turmoil, my brother had grown up. He was a man now, not a boy playing with drink and women as he'd been just a short year ago. What had happened to bring about such a change?

"Twenty-three is old enough," Lucien said.

I laid aside my purse and sank into the chair by my husband's desk. "What about our parents?"

"They will live the rest of their lives out comfortably, they have the money. But I won't have them in my home, and I expect the other underbosses not to accept them socially either. After what they did to you, they're lucky they're getting to live."

Being a social pariah was a fate worse than death for my mother. I stared at the ground, pretending to frown, but inside, I was deeply satisfied. All the abuse my parents had heaped on me was done with one goal in mine—to further their social status. And now because of that abuse, they had lost the thing they craved the most.

It was a fitting punishment. I looked up at my husband and his mouth twitched with the ghost of a smile. Warmth welled in my chest and I resisted the urge to get up and kiss him.

"I...I need to ask you something," Cosimo said, turning to Lucien.

"Ask away, I've been granting favors all week. What's one more?"

Comiso shifted and crossed his arms. "I want your permission to ask Lorenza to marry me."

Lucien's eyes narrowed. "Lorenza Russo?"

Cosimo nodded.

"She's a widow and she's a good seven years older than you. But the main problem is that her family isn't particularly important.

There's no advantage to that match. You're an underboss now and you need to start thinking like one."

"I love her," said Cosimo quietly.

"Your sister did her duty and married me, now you do yours and marry the woman I choose for you," said Lucien coldly. "I won't argue about it any longer."

Cosimo seemed to withdraw, his body going tense. When it was time for him to go, I hugged him close, away from Lucien. "Let me talk to him," I whispered.

He kissed my cheek. "Thanks, sis, but I don't think it'll help."

The sadness in his eyes pained me. That night, I stood by the sink in the bathroom, brushing my teeth slowly as I waited for the right moment to speak with my husband. From the bedroom I heard Lucien end a phone call and then he walked up behind me, stripping his shirt and pants off and tossing them in the hamper.

"Amadeo is fucking idealist and I need a little less of that right now," he said wearily. He bent over the sink and splashed cold water over his face.

I laid aside my toothbrush. "Can we talk?"

He straightened, toweling off his face and neck. "What is it, baby?"

"I think you should let Cosimo marry Lorenza," I said carefully. "What if you had fallen in love with me and we couldn't be together? It would feel terrible?"

"I got lucky and fell for the right woman," Lucien said. "Cosimo is being foolish. He doesn't know what he wants, he's too young."

"He's older than I am."

"You're more mature."

"That's true, but at least think about it."

He came up behind me, sliding one bare arm around my waist and rested his chin on my head. "If he can give me one good reason as to why it benefits the outfit, I'll reconsider."

"I'll think of something," I said, smiling. From Lucien, that kind of leniency was a gift.

He went back into the bedroom and I heard him get into bed as I braided my hair and rubbed cream into my face. Then I turned out the light and stepped into the bedroom to find him already lying on his back with the covers over his legs.

"Come here, baby," he ordered.

I went to him, kneeling on the bed by his side. His eyes, those eyes that were as glacial as ever, roamed over my body. His lips parted as he ran his fingers over my bare leg, slipping them beneath my short nightgown to caress my inner thigh. Then in a fluid movement, his broad body as graceful as a panther, he flipped me onto my back and pinned me to the bed.

His mouth skimmed over my collarbones and he kissed between my breasts. My nipples hardened and heat curled in my pussy, wetness teasing at my folds.

"Lucien, I—" The words faltered in my throat.

He raised his head. "What is it?"

"I didn't take my birth control this morning."

There was a long moment of silence. His mouth parted and his eyes met mine, drawing me into their endless depths. There was something on his face, a glimmer of something that I'd never seen there before. It looked almost like excitement.

"Well," he said. "Would you like to fuck then?"

CHAPTER TWENTY-ONE

LUCIEN

FIVE YEARS LATER

I entered the door of the new Esposito mansion—formerly the home of the late Carlo Romano—and removed my coat and hat. The housekeeper, a pleasant middle-aged woman who ruled the house with a firm, but gentle touch, appeared at my elbow. I thanked her as she took my things and went to hang them up.

"Where's Olivia?" I called, as she turned the corner into the kitchen.

"Oh," the housekeeper said, putting her head back out into the hall. "She's upstairs with your son."

My son. The words were still unfamiliar, even after almost three years. Every time I heard them, they filled me with a sense of pride, a sense of security. My son, my future and my legacy, secured as the next boss through bloodshed by my hand. It was a fitting beginning to the Esposito dynasty.

I climbed the great staircase leading to the second floor. I'd had the house cleaned from top to bottom, every trace of Romano scrubbed from every inch before I moved my wife in. Duran and Iris had taken over the original Esposito mansion and were renovating it, much to Olivia's dismay. She enjoyed the excess of it all, but Iris's tastes were a little more tame.

Stepping as quietly as I could, I made my way to the nursery. I pushed the door open and there was my wife, nestled up in the rocking chair by the window. She was sleeping, her face relaxed and her body curled. I leaned over the toddler bed and brushed my fingers over my son's back. Marco slept, blissfully oblivious to the world, his chubby face turned to the side. His little shock of dark hair hung over his forehead and his lids were tightly shut over a pair of hazel eyes.

I bent and turned on the nightlight and unplugged the Christmas tree in the corner. Olivia stirred, a quiet sound escaping her lips, and looked up at me. Gathering her in my arms, I carried her limp, warm body out into the hall and shut the door.

"You're home early," she murmured.

"It's six. Exactly when I said I'd be back," I said. "Iris and Duran should be here any moment and then we can get on the road."

It was our wedding anniversary and, with Iris's help, I had planned a night at one of the most expensive hotels in the city. We would have dinner, which, thanks to four years of having a therapist come to the house every week, Olivia actually enjoyed now. Then we would have drinks sent up to our suite and as the night wore on, I would get enjoy my wife uninterrupted. Without a toddler knocking on our door while we were in the middle of sex to ask for a glass of milk and a midnight snack.

My wife descended the stairs thirty minutes later dressed in a sleek, black dress. My pulse thudded in my ears and my cock hardened at the sight. It was the same dress she'd worn that night at the opera in Russia. She was beautiful, her hips wider beneath her trim waist and her breasts fuller after having Marco. I pulled her against me and kissed the side of her neck.

"I thought I tore that dress," I murmured.

"I bought another one," she said, stepping back to spin so I could look at her from all angles.

"Well, I suppose I'll have to tear this one off you later as well," I said.

As we ate in our private room at the restaurant, surrounded by candlelight and the soft smell of freshly cut flowers, it struck me how things had changed. Just a few years ago, I was still under Romano's thumb, about to be married to a woman I scarcely knew, much less loved. And she had been a scared, abused girl, too afraid to even eat the food on her plate.

Now I commanded hundreds of men, and although every day was a new fight, I was glad to be boss. Olivia had settled into her role as my wife and she no longer shrank back in fear when we went out in public. No, now she commanded the room with those burning, dark eyes that could consume a person whole. And together we had a legacy, a son who would one day grow up to be as ruthless and powerful as his father.

That night, surrounded by huge glass windows that offered a prime view of the city, I lay with my wife on the enormous bed in the center of the room. She was on her back, her skin crisscrossed with the straps of her black lingerie, gazing up at the crystal chandelier overhead. The light caught her eyes, glittering in the darkness.

"What are you thinking?" she whispered as I kissed up her bare stomach.

"I'm thinking I'm going to keep you up most of the night," I said.

I slipped between her silky thighs and pulled her panties to the side, dipping my head for a taste of her. She moaned softly and her lashes fluttered.

"God, you do that so well," she breathed.

I raised my head and she made a sound of disappointment. "I know I said that all I wanted was one son, but I've been thinking lately that maybe we should try for another baby."

Her brows rose and she took her time before she answered. "I haven't taken my birth control yet."

We looked at one another for a long time and then her face broke into a smile and I climbed over her body. Her legs fell open, exposing the strip of black lace over her pussy. My cock throbbed against my underwear and I reached down, wrapping my fingers around her panties, and tore them open. She gasped, her back arching, and dug her fingers into my sides.

I buried myself in my wife, losing track of time as the night wore on. Things wouldn't always be this perfect—there would be days ahead filled with blood and violence. That was my burden as the boss. But at the end of each day, I would shed those ugly things from me and return to my wife and children. And for a warm, glittering night, the world would be good.

THE END

Did you enjoy Captured Light? Please consider leaving a review or rating.
Continue Lucien & Olivia's story! The second and third books in the King of Ice & Steel Trilogy can be found on Amazon KU.

OTHER BOOKS BY RAYA MORRIS EDWARDS

All on Amazon KU

KING OF ICE & STEEL TRILOGY READING ORDER

Captured Light

Devil I Need, the sequel to Captured Light

Ice & Steel, the Conclusion to Captured Light & Devil I Need

(August 25th 2023)

CAPTURED STANDALONES READING ORDER

Captured Desire - Iris & Duran - out September 5th 2023

Captured Light - Lucien & Olivia

Captured Solace - Viktor & Sienna

Captured Fantasy - Cosimo & Lorenza

Captured Ecstasy - Peregrine & Rosalia

THE WELSH KINGS TRILOGY

Paradise Descent, Book 1 in The Welsh Kings Trilogy

Prince of Ink & Scars, Book 2 in The Welsh Kings Trilogy (out

April 2024)

Made in United States
Troutdale, OR
06/09/2024

20437631R00179